THE WATCHMAKER

Christine Morris Campbell

CHRISTINE MORRIS CAMPBELL

ISBN-13: 978-1508942566
ISBN-10: 1508942560

This book is a work of fiction loosely based on facts and events which occurred in Victorian Edinburgh.

DEDICATION

To my ancestors whose colorful lives inspired me to research and discover life in Victorian Scotland.

THE
WATCHMAKER

CHAPTER 1

1851

Edwin Turner looked at the waves as they lapped against the harbor wall. Fairly calm for this time of year, he noted. He had never sailed in a ship before; well, there was a first time for everything and this was that time. He could only wish his first time did not have to be this voyage. Edwin thought over the events of the last few months and he could only wish his life had gone differently.

Lydia, his youngest daughter, less than a year old, would never know her father. "I suppose that isn't a surprise to the family. I was in prison when she was born," he thought. 'A petty thief', the judge had called him.

It seemed that when he became a watchmaker he had earned a respectable job, something that required skill, knowledge, and an eye for detail. Certainly his father-in-law, William Berridge, had been the epitome of respectability. Yet things had not turned out so well for Edwin. He loved the work; he enjoyed the solitude it required. He also enjoyed concentrating on the inner workings of watches. He had heard of but only once seen a wristwatch. That seemed like that would be a fad that would never catch on. A rather feminine way of wearing a watch, although he did not see why a lady would need to monitor the time in the same way as a gentleman. There was something rather noble about a gentleman as he removed his watch from his waistcoat, pondered its face and then deposited it securely back in its pocket.

The last couple of years had been hard for Edwin. Too many babies too fast. Too many mouths to feed and not enough work or money. Edwin had not meant to steal those six watches. He had just borrowed some money against them for a short time. He had not expected the owners would want them back so fast. He knew that they were all rich enough that they had other watches. Yet that had been his undoing; that is why he was now shackled to the man in front of him, a Scot by the name of Jim Alexander, arrested in Glasgow, both of them bound for Van Diemen's Land, on the other side of the world, an island off the coast of Australia.

Silently the men waited, all 280 of them. It was going to be a crowded ship. As they had gathered together Edwin had heard the accents of the others and recognized Geordie, Glaswegian, London and a host of North Country dialects. Now, cowed by the brutality of their wardens, and silenced by their truncheons, they waited to board the *Aboukir.*

It was Christmas Eve 1851. Edwin thought of his wife Ann back home in Edinburgh. He wondered what she would be cooking, whether her mother would take care of her, how she would manage with the children. Punishing the father for thievery was one thing; but the whole family was affected by it. Who was now to put bread on the table? It would be hard for Ann. She knew how to sew and could work as a seamstress yet her hands were already full taking care of the bairns.

Edwin felt a keen sense of shame when he thought of Ann. He had fallen in love with her so easily, bewitched by her innocence, beauty and modest smile. He had promised to protect her in front of God and everyone in the Church of Scotland kirk in Edinburgh. He had been raised Church of England and found the Church of Scotland rather austere but Ann wanted to be married in her local kirk and Edwin did not want to deny her wishes. She asked for so little.

Edwin turned his attention to what was happening around him. He surveyed the small town of Plymouth, made famous amongst the English for Sir Francis Drake's expeditions. English schoolchildren were all taught that Sir Francis had continued his bowling game until its completion despite seeing the Spanish Armada. You could actually see the famous green, the Hoe, from Edwin's viewpoint at the harbor. Now however it was filled with an angry mob jeering and laughing at the convicts as they waited on the quayside to board the vessel. There were guards at the end of the jetty to block the people from approaching the convicts, most of whom stood sullenly, looking at their feet, trying to ignore their surroundings.

Edwin shifted his gaze to his fellow travelers. Many of them were clearly farm laborers, poorly dressed, their clothes grimy and malodorous. You could still smell the farm animals on them. They looked better nourished than others though and looked muscular and strong. They might survive this journey better than some of the others. While on the prison hulk Edwin had heard dreadful tales of this voyage and the deaths that sometimes occurred on the way to Australia.

By contrast, Jim Alexander was dressed as a tradesman but his jacket was well-made and looked designed for him. A tailor perhaps, Edwin guessed. The shoulders fitted him so well that Edwin knew it was not second-hand. Other than exchanging names Jim had not said a word. He stood stoically, a typical Scot, you might say.

Jim looked to be about 35, the same age as Edwin. There was a small group of youths, some of whom looked to be only about ten years old, set to one side. Some were clearly unable to control their anxiety and tears rolled down the cheeks of more than one. Edwin remembered then his first-born, Alfred, only eight, and was glad he would be safe at home and not having to face this voyage. Alfred had cried pitifully when Edwin said goodbye to him at the Edinburgh High Court. Edwin had to look away from the youths and turn his mind to something else.

The *Aboukir* rocked gently in the water. "Strange name for a ship," Edwin mused and then he remembered that it was the site of a battle between the British and the French off the coast of Egypt. The British had won, thanks to Lord Nelson's leadership. The *Aboukir* would be home for him for the next two months, such as it was. Food and water were being loaded onto the ship right now under the supervision of the master of the ship, John Robertson. There were to be 280 prisoners, twenty-seven soldiers and their commander, a surgeon, and twenty-five crew members.

Loading the supplies was a slow process and it was hard for Edwin to see the food sitting on the dock not ten feet away from him and not try to steal something. He had grown used to having little food while in the jail in Edinburgh and in Millbank but he had never had to look at the food either as he did now. It was easy to do without food when you couldn't see it or smell it. You could smell those Cox's Orange Pippins a mile away! Not that he would get one to eat on the ship. Those apples would be destined for the ship's master and officers. This was going to be a long trip.

CHAPTER 2

1842

William Berridge sighed, pushed back his chair and rubbed his eyes. He had been working on this particular watch for far too long. He knew it was partly his own doing - it was such a delight to work on a Longine. The Swiss certainly knew how to make watches. Founded only 10 years earlier in 1832, the Longine company had fast established a fine reputation for the precision, beauty and design of their watches. This watch, belonging to Sir Charles Mortimer, was no exception.

Everyone knew Sir Charles to be a fellow who delighted in gourmet food, silk clothing and the latest styles in furnishing. He was moneyed, powerful, and given to some excess, although in only the finest aristocratic way, of course. Sir Charles wanted only the best for himself and his daughter, Mary Elizabeth Mortimer. Sir Charles came from humble beginnings, the son of a cabinetmaker. His rise to prominence in political and court circles could only be attributed to his years of service during the Napoleonic Wars. At a time when the British were struggling on all sides - war against America and war against France - the economy and resources were stretched exponentially. Sir Charles found he had a remarkable skill for procuring whatever the British Army needed, and he was able to line his pockets rather handsomely too.

For his effort, Sir Charles was knighted, to his great pride. There was a wonderful satisfaction in being called "Sir Charles" wherever he went. His ears certainly never seemed to tire of it. True it was not a hereditary title, which would have been nice, but he had no male heir to inherit the title so Sir Charles was only mildly chagrined that his title would die with him.

More impressive to Sir Charles was his access to court circles. It was too bad that Lord Nelson had died so suddenly at the Battle of Trafalgar as he had been a fine bridge partner and a fair poker player. Yet these days Sir Charles could still find a group of gentlemen at his club on Piccadilly, whenever he was able to visit London. That didn't happen too much these days. His job as equerry to the court in Holyrood Palace in Edinburgh demanded that he stay in Scotland most of the time.

William Berridge had served in the Napoleonic Wars too, although he had been significantly closer to the frontline than had Sir Charles. William was a quartermaster and had been in charge of the weapons and accoutrements that Sir Charles had procured. It was a good job for William.

He saw some fighting - goodness, everyone did. Sometimes there were just not enough men to fight. In sheer numbers, Britain's population of thirty million was only half that of France. Yet France had struggled too because of fighting on so many fronts. In an attempt to cut off British supply lines from Russia, Napoleon had invaded Russia in 1812. The

French had been astonished that the Russians would burn their own villages rather than succumb to the French. Even worse, when winter came, the French were ravaged by hypothermia, shortage of food for the soldiers and the horses, and they still had to defend themselves against persistent attacks from Russian peasants. There was no doubt that the fight with Russia had been particularly devastating for France. It marked the beginning of the end for Napoleon.

William was definitely one of the lucky ones. He was proud to have served in the battle at Waterloo where Napoleon was finally conquered. Yes, sir, when William's right arm ached where he had been lanced during that battle, he could at least remember that he had fought in a just battle. Tempers had flared between the British and the French for centuries, and it certainly felt good to put those French in their place.

How life had changed for William! He had enjoyed military life; he enjoyed the camaraderie with the men and the discipline. His job required organization and routine; attention to detail was one of his strong points, that's for sure. It certainly served him well in his current profession. He missed the military when the war with France was over, yet it was good to be in one's own business, following a profession he had always loved. Luckily for William, his father had been a watchmaker too. William Berridge Sr. had taught young William all he knew about watchmaking and watch repair. When it came time for William Sr. to retire, then he had a son who was eager to take over the business, and who loved the profession as much as he did. It was true he had to wait a few years while William Jr. was fighting for his country, but that was fine. It gave young William a taste of life and excitement before he settled down to what was for William Sr. a very serious business.

William Sr. died five years after young William's return from Waterloo. The business had done well. At first the older Berridges settled in the Old Town in Edinburgh. It was convenient to the Castle and to Holyrood Palace and that of itself brought a good share of business. After a number of years though, Margaret, William Sr.'s wife, grew restless. She was increasingly disenchanted by the overcrowded conditions of the tenements in Old Town; she noticed too that many of the wealthier Scots were moving to the New Town. The new houses were more spacious, the streets wider. Margaret had heard that New Town's new crescents and wide boulevards resembled the new housing in Bath. She had never been to Bath but was sufficiently worldly to know that Bath was the cultural epitome of elegance.

William Sr. concurred; he adored his wife. She was a petite, dark-haired woman who had maintained her fine figure despite having five children. William's first wife had died but Margaret had warmly accepted her two stepchildren. She was a shrewd business-woman too; if she thought it advisable to move to

New Town then William Sr. would deliver what she wanted.

15 Jamaica Street was a good place for their business. Only a few blocks from the main street, Princes Street, Jamaica Street had four story homes, with commercial space on the first floor. This meant that the two Williams, who now worked together, could ply their trade below and sleep above the business. After William Sr. died, William Jr. sat at his father's workbench and continued the trade.

William Jr. sighed again. His back was hurting and the light was going. At this time of year the days seemed very short to him. Seven and a quarter hours of daylight did not provide him much effective work-time. He could always use gaslight but that was expensive and it did not provide him with the natural light he really needed to be able to work the intricate parts of the watches.

William took pride in his work. He was meticulous - his wife Lillias said, to a fault. Yet he felt there was no need to repair a watch unless it was absolutely perfectly done. Perfection was a must. Time had no value to him if it were not accurate. It had no value to anyone. Why repair a watch if you didn't do it right?

Sometimes it seemed there was almost too much work, but he wouldn't complain. Better to be able to have good food on the table. William didn't need much. Some of those fancy people in Morningside were showy; they had pianos in the drawing room yet only kippers for tea. That kind of life wasn't for William. A warm hearth and a tender wife to come home to were what mattered to William. And he had that for sure. He thanked God every day for Lillias, his dear wife. She reminded him of Margaret, his mother, and that wasn't such a bad thing.

The two had three children; they had been lucky. Some of their friends had stillborns but Lillias was a strong woman and she had no problem delivering her babies. Her sister used to laugh at her and tell her she had babies like some women shelled peas. William thought over his family now; he enjoyed his evenings best, when he could sit in front of his little coal fire and be with his children.

These days though he saw less of his two sons, Henry and Hugh. They had both become stocking makers and that seemed to take up much of their waking lives. William was not even sure they would remain in Edinburgh. That industry was developing rapidly in the border towns. As the conflict with America diminished, trade with the New World had substantially increased, and the cotton and woolen mills in northern England and the border towns had been running at full throttle, until recently. Henry and Hugh thought they could find better paying work in Dumfries. The thought of them moving away distressed him for several reasons. He knew Lillias would be disappointed to lose them, for their companionship, and for the money they brought into the household. Seeing them in Dumfries would be impossible; it was almost as difficult to get there as to London.

To add to his anxiety, he had heard of the strikes in August that year at the cotton and woolen mills in Stalybridge and Ashton, and several other towns around Manchester. In Halifax, six men had died during strike action. The movement had started in the coalmines and spread quickly to the mills. Working in a mill did not seem as reliable a source of work as watchmaking. The strikes had originated because the mill owners wanted to lower wages. William never had to face that; he never would go on strike. He was his own man and there would always be a demand for his kind of work among the wealthier classes.

William had always hoped that he would have a son to follow in the business. He really could not understand why his boys would prefer to work in a factory. He knew they enjoyed being around other boys their own age; he knew too that they valued their independence. Yet why would anyone make stockings when you could make watches? It made no sense. Nothing could compare to the feeling of making a watch, sometimes using parts from other watches, to come up with a masterpiece, a timekeeper like no other. To know that you have created a unique machine which accurately marks time. Now that was perfection.

CHAPTER 3

1842

Edwin Turner leaned back against a tree and waited for the Observatory to open. He liked to arrive early. It gave him time to look over the city which he had learned to call home. English-born but already Scottish in his heart, Edwin thrilled once again at the magnificent view set before him. True there was the constant smoke plumes from coal fires (Edinburgh was not called Auld Reekie for nothing), but the view from Calton Hill was spectacular. To the west he could see the stark outline of the Castle, majestic and somewhat forbidding. From this side it looked impenetrable.

Edwin let his eyes wander east and took in the tall granite tenements of Castle Hill and the High Street. He knew they were teeming with people who jostled for space, light and food. For many it was a constant struggle against poverty. He lived in Borthwick's Close just off the High Street, and he himself had to contend with the smells, the noise, the squalor. Yet from a distance the houses looked just an extension of the castle, strong and built to last for centuries.

At the very end of the High Street he could pick out Holyrood Palace. Queen Victoria would visit here for a week in July on her way to Balmoral; rather a large house for one woman for one week a year, Edwin thought. Yet he loved the traditions and when the Queen arrived earlier in the year Edwin had been glad that it had been on a Sunday so he could go and see her arrive at Holyrood.

The people of Edinburgh had hoped that she would arrive at Haymarket Station which marked the opening of the Edinburgh-Glasgow line. However, the Queen had demurred this time as it was still too complicated to get from London to Scotland by train. Edwin knew it would not be long before London and Edinburgh would be connected directly by train. He had heard tell that America had already built 3,000 miles of railway track. When George Stephenson invented the Rocket public railway transportation and ran it on the line from Stockton to Darlington, it was clear that life would never be the same for anyone. The possibilities were endless for this faster mode of transportation.

Edwin had arrived here by stagecoach from Nottingham in the spring. His parents had both died in the typhoid epidemic of 1842 and there seemed no reason to stay in Nottingham although he did have work there as a stocking maker. Edwin felt restless and when he heard that work was available in Edinburgh he headed north.

At first he was unsure whether he would stay. He had expected to find work as a stocking maker but manufacturing in Edinburgh was very much second to finance and government. There was one mill but they were not hiring.

Edwin was able to find work at the Scottish and Newcastle Brewery in Horse Wynd in Old Town.

It was convenient to his room, it was employment and gave him access to some strong beer, although Edwin was never much for drinking. It also enabled him to pay his rent, but Edwin did not expect to work there long. As soon as he could find something better Edwin planned to move on.

As a Sassenach or Englishman, the Scots viewed him with suspicion but Edwin's charm and cheerfulness soon won over the most dour of Scots. Edwin was a hard worker and did not shirk. No one could fault him for that!

Edwin looked around as he heard the door to the Observatory open. For two hours he would have opportunity to look at the telescopes, read about the planets and stars and, for a time, his life would stand still as he dreamed of a world beyond space and time. He loved the world of trains with their belching smoke, noise, and speed yet Edwin loved even more the tranquility, distance, and vastness of the planet world.

For a moment though he stopped and gazed at the fine building in which the Observatory was located. It was certainly built to last, made of granite and styled after a Greek temple. In a place where time and distance were linked, it seemed as though the architect wanted to make time stand still by building an edifice which actually mirrored a former culture. It was for this and other classical buildings around the city that Edinburgh had earned its title of "Athens of the North".

As he walked up to the stout wooden door held open by a porter, he noticed a neatly dressed, middle-aged man approaching. The man wore a simple black frock coat and Edwin noticed he also had a grey waistcoat from which was suspended a silver watch chain. His bearing was erect, and his greying sideburns and rather long hair all contributed to the appearance of a successful tradesman.

In deference to him and in recognition of his own rather shabby appearance, Edwin stood back and let the older man enter the Observatory first. Edwin was always neat and clean, at least when he wasn't working, but his clothes had seen better times. Thankfully his mother had taught him to repair his jacket as needed and he was glad of that. He could not afford a new jacket and trousers until he had worked another month or two. He was glad there was no charge to enter the Observatory.

The older man nodded to Edwin, recognizing that Edwin had stood aside for him. He passed and then turned to him and said, "I believe I have seen you here before several times?"

Surprised that the other man would speak, Edwin nevertheless answered, "Yes, I come every chance I can get."

"I believe you are interested in the new refracting telescope?"

Edwin was surprised at this comment because he was unaware that he had been observed. Once inside the Observatory he was lost in another world, a world which escaped the squalor, noise and hardship of his life. In the Observatory he could dream of another place and time. He wondered if there was life on other planets. It seemed impossible to find out. Perhaps the birds would find out but man could only speculate.

"Yes, sir. It's the first one I've seen. My uncle told me about them. He worked in the service of Mr. Thomas Henderson and learned a lot about astronomy from him. He taught me about it too."

Edwin was referring to the Scottish Astronomer Royal, a man distinguished in astronomy circles by being the first man to accurately measure the distance to a star. Henderson worked at the Observatory daily but was rarely seen when the public visited on Sundays.

William Berridge Jr., for that was who the middle-aged, neatly dressed stranger was, raised his eyebrows and smiled. He enjoyed the enthusiasm of the younger man.

"Excuse me," he said, "I should introduce myself. I am William Berridge."

"Edwin Turner, sir."

"How long have you been visiting here?" William enquired.

"I only arrived in Edinburgh in March but I try to visit each Sunday when I don't work."

William noted Edwin's accent. An Englishman. Well, that was all right. He had served with many in the Napoleonic Wars and they fought as well as the Scots. He owed his own life to an

Englishman who took the brunt of cannon fire which would otherwise have killed William.

William took the watch out of his waistcoat and looked at the time. The Observatory had been opened precisely at 2 o'clock, which he would have expected. If the Observatory could not get the time right, then no one could. Although William was fascinated by the telescopes in the Observatory, his primary reason for coming on a Sunday afternoon was to synchronize his watches. The one he had with him today was particularly important. It was the Longine belonging to Sir Charles Mortimer.

He went to the cabinet where the Observatory clock was encased. He flipped open the silver engraved cover of the Longine and checked the watch's elegant black pointers. It really was a beautiful watch, with its clear white face, fine black hands and Roman numerals. He could easily read it even though his eyes were not as strong as they used to be.

Well, that was another problem. William worried about his eyes. He knew he was at the age when many men seemed to not see as well as previously, and he needed his eyes for the fine detailed work that he did every day. He blamed his failing eyesight on having to work in poor lighting but he knew that aging was affecting his vision too.

The Longine was engraved inside the cover. 'To Sir Charles Mortimer from Queen Victoria.' It was really rather surprising that the Queen would give Swiss watches when there were so many other items from her Empire that she could give. William was well aware, as were all British subjects, that the British Empire was expanding globally and he was proud that the British were leading the way in industry, science and commerce. True, the British could no longer claim dominion over America and that was a sad loss, but trade with America was still good. The American demand for British products seemed insatiable. Certainly it was keeping William's two sons busy in the stocking factory. He had heard that the mills in Lancashire and Yorkshire were running at all hours to keep up with the demand.

"Four minutes past two," noted William as he looked at the Observatory clock. He checked the Longine. Yes, it was perfect. William was not surprised; he knew he was a good craftsman but there was always a special delight in recognizing that once again he had repaired a watch and it was running perfectly. Sir Charles would be sending his valet to the shop tomorrow to pick up the watch.

William placed the watch back in his waistcoat pocket and looked around. He had some time to look at the telescopes before he needed to go home. This was his Sunday afternoon treat. As a little boy William had spent many evenings lying in a field behind his grandparents' house outside of Dunoon, gazing up at the sky and dreaming. They lived near Loch Eck, and the stars were particularly brilliant over the loch. He wondered how far the stars were away from Earth and what the moon really looked like close-up. He loved to look at it when it was like yellow cheese; rather like Double Gloucester, he always thought.

He knew from the published works of Thomas Henderson, whom he had met one afternoon while he was visiting the Observatory, that the closest star was Alpha Centauri, some 3.25 light years away from Earth. Thomas Henderson, when he did appear in public, was a quiet, unassuming man with gentlemanly demeanor. He had talked to William at some length about his findings from his work at the Cape of Good Hope in South Africa, and William remembered how Henderson's eyes had brightened and how his face became very animated as he discussed his computations. William had left school at fourteen but not before he realized a deep interest in physics and mathematics.

William had been fascinated with the Observatory since he first visited it. There had been an Observatory on this spot since 1776. From time to time it had been closed to the public; or an admission had been charged, but now it was free again and William relished the opportunity to look at the telescopes.

There was a great Transit Circle; it had been made in Germany. Mounted on a horizontal axis, it was used to measure the position of the heavenly bodies. In the next room he would see the three-foot Altazimuth Telescope which, along with the six-foot Mural Circle, had been made in London by Troughton and Simms. The Altazimuth telescope was actually named for its mount which allowed rotation of the telescope through two perpendicular axes, one vertical and one horizontal. It had proven to be an easy mount to use mechanically, and was therefore very popular, but William was aware of its limitations for tracking astronomical objects in the night sky as the Earth spun on its axis. Along with a Sidereal Clock by Bryson and a Mean Time Clock by Reid and Auld, Edinburgh was in synch with the rest of the world.

CHAPTER 4

Edwin watched as the older man deposited the watch into his waistcoat pocket. He commented, "That's a beautiful watch."

"Yes, I've been repairing it and now it is working perfectly again," commented William Berridge, a note of pride in his voice.

"May I see it, sir?" inquired Edwin, rather surprised by his own boldness but suspecting that he would be very interested in the mechanism.

William Berridge was surprised too by the young man's impudence but Berridge was proud of his work and it really was a beautiful timepiece. He withdrew the watch from his waistcoat pocket and carefully held it out, still attached to its chain, towards Edwin.

"Did you make it yourself, sir?" asked Edwin, noticing the other man's pride.

"No, but I wish I had. I do make watches but I have never made one as fine as this. This is a Longine, made in Switzerland. I've repaired this one. There really wasn't a lot wrong with it. Its owner had just neglected to clean it. It was fully wound but dirty."

"You mean that he overwound it?" enquired Edwin.

"No, that's just a myth. You can't overwind a watch. Watches require regular cleaning and lubrication. As it works, the watch collects dirt and the oil dries up. Then the mainspring doesn't have the force to turn the watch and it stops. The owner then winds it again and again as it keeps stopping. Eventually the mainspring does not have the force to turn, even at full wind and it eventually stops, still at full wind. The problem is not that it was overwound, the problem is that it was not cleaned and there's a dirty part. If you cleaned a watch regularly it would never stop at full wind. But it keeps me in business!"

Edwin looked at the case of the watch. It was beautifully engraved with a design of a soldier holding a musket on the front. The silver shone; the watch looked almost brand-new. William flicked open the cover and inside Edwin looked at the gleaming pearl face with its black Roman numerals and its sharp pointers. In very small letters below the number six he could read the words, "Longine, Swiss Made". The watch had a very quiet tick, almost imperceptible.

"It really is a beauty. You're lucky to be able to work with such beautiful things," said Edwin somewhat wistfully.

"Where do you work?" asked Berridge, not particularly interested but wishing to be polite as he had engaged the young man in conversation in the first place.

"Scottish and Newcastle Brewery, sir. I just started work there in March when I arrived from Nottingham. I'm actually a stocking maker but there's only one mill here and they're not hiring. I took what I could find but I am looking for other work. Working in a brewery is not for me. I don't care for the noise nor the smell of the place."

Berridge could certainly understand as, on a windy day, he could smell the brewery from his front doorstep. If the wind was in the wrong direction, that is. Berridge enjoyed the end product from the brewery as much as the next man but he had to admit, he really did not care for the pungent odor as the beer was being made.

"A stocking maker! That's what my sons do. They have been thinking of going west to Dumfries or Glasgow for work as this mill has been slowing down production."

"I really don't want to leave Edinburgh. I like it here. The pay's good and I have a decent place to live. I love coming to the Observatory on Sundays and like walking on Arthur's Seat if I have spare time."

William could understand that. He had spent many hours up Arthur's Seat too. He loved the view from there. You could see the castle so clearly and on a good day you could see the Firth of Forth, the whole port of Leith, and sometimes the ferries crossing the river. You could see Holyrood Palace too. When the Queen had arrived earlier in the year he had watched her procession enter the gates of Holyrood from the summit of Arthur's Seat. He loved the fresh air in his lungs and the solitude, for there were few who ventured there. He always felt like a new man after he had hiked to Arthur's Seat.

William liked the openness of the younger man. He was self-assured and confident, and appeared to have an intelligent interest in his surroundings. Encouraged by Edwin's openness, William reached in his pocket for an instrument to open the back of the watch as he was confident that Edwin had never seen the inside of one. He was correct, Edwin had not but was clearly interested.

"The watch is driven by a mainspring. That's what needs to be wound periodically. The force of it works through a series of gears which power this part here. That's called the balance wheel and its job is to oscillate back and forth. Its rate must be constant to keep the watch in time. Now this part here, can you see it, is called an escapement. It allows the wheels to move forward a tiny amount each time the balance wheel swings. That moves the watch's hands. Everything has to be constant and regular. It's this last part that makes the ticking sound you can hear," explained William as Edwin looked at the watch intently.

Edwin marveled at the compactness of the watch. It seemed almost impossible that so many tiny parts could work together so precisely and rhythmically. He was surprised to see the gold parts, he had expected it to be silver like the casing. He commented on that and William explained that gold really was the preferred metal for the internal parts of a watch. It was really a personal preference though as the gold was soft enough that over many years the parts would wear and need to be replaced. William enjoyed the watch's gold insides; it looked more expensive and superior, he always thought. Interesting though that the Longine watch was actually handcrafted by peasants in their homes and then the final assembly was actually completed by one man, Auguste Agassiz. Hard not to be impressed!

William enjoyed the young man's enthusiasm. He noticed how carefully Edwin handled the watch with his long fingers. Edwin's hands were large but they handled the watch with delicacy. His nails were trimmed and clean. Edwin had understood everything Willliam had explained to him about how the watch worked and he seemed genuinely interested.

On an impulse, which was actually somewhat extraordinary for William, he asked Edwin, "Do you have any interest in learning more about watchmaking?"

Edwin paused for he had never considered it until that moment and then he said, "Yes, it would interest me very much. I enjoy details and like things to be perfect. A watch has to be perfect or it has no value, does it?"

William thought, "A man after my own heart."

Spending hours working on watches gave him plenty of time to consider the value and importance of measuring time. Sometimes he wished he could buy some time. If he had more time he would love to spend more hours with his family, more hours studying physics, and more time hiking. The older he became the more he realized how short his life really was and there were plenty of things he would like to do.

Of course he was not much of a dreamer. No point really. You were given your measure of life and you were born into a family in a certain social class and that was pretty well where you stayed. William would never be rich but he had a comfortable living and he could at least take off Sundays. Just as well really as Lillias, his wife, would have had a few sharp words to say if he worked on a Sunday too. On Sundays when he tramped on Arthur's Seat or visited the Observatory, Lillias could be found at the kirk. She was a devout woman and she wanted to be in church every Sunday. Fortunately she did not require that of William. Working on a Sunday would have stretched her temper though.

William replied, "That's exactly what I think too. The Observatory is going to close in half an hour. I would like to look around until it closes but then I am going home for tea. Would you care to join me for a spot of tea? My wife is expecting me right after it closes. You might be interested in seeing my workshop. I live on Jamaica Street just above my shop."

Edwin answered, "I'd enjoy that very much unless it's a lot of trouble for your wife. I don't want to impose but I am free and never turn down a cup of tea."

"My wife will be delighted to have someone to experiment on with her latest cake. She makes a wonderful Dundee cake. I love her baking and she only bakes for Sundays. It's our treat for the week."

Edwin and William spent the next few minutes wandering through the rooms admiring the telescopes and reading the notes made by the astronomers who worked in the Observatory. All too soon it was time for the Observatory to close to the public for another week. It was amazing how popular the Observatory had become. True, it was free to enter yet there was more than that which appealed to the people. Reaching out to the moon and stars was even more attractive by its sheer impossibility. It was like seeing something which was truly beautiful that you could never afford or perhaps like a woman you would like to get to know but she was out of your class. Yet the moon looked so remote, cool, and perfect, particularly in its fullness. William loved the summers best as you could enjoy that big Double Gloucester moon and it would shine so brightly that it was safe to walk out at night, even through the docks at Leith, because it was almost daylight until after eleven o'clock.

Edwin and William stepped out into the autumn sunshine. The sun would be going down soon and already there was a crispness in the air. They were a striking pair; William, with his greying sideburns, still walked with a military bearing and looked the distinguished, retired soldier that he was. By his side strode Edwin who was six inches shorter but who could match William's stride with his energy. His hair was a dark mop framing a freckled face with ruddy cheeks. His eyes were bright blue, the eyelids slightly hooded. His nose was straight and looked well with his rather high cheekbones. It was easy to see that he spent time outdoors whenever he could.

They descended Calton Hill, and as they did, they passed a finely castellated and turreted building which resembled a city wall or an entrance to a castle. Casually Edwin asked William what it was and he learned that it was the Edinburgh Gaol.

"Definitely not a place to visit," remarked William Berridge, with a wry smile. He had never been inside but the tales of torture, starvation and deprivation were infamous. The worst criminals, the ones awaiting execution, were manacled to a wall, unable to move. It had been built some twenty or thirty years previously to replace the Old Tollbooth which had been demolished. It was an even worse place to be imprisoned than the Old Tollbooth, recounted William. The Old Tolbooth had stood for centuries in the High Street in Old Town. This new prison was cold and desolate; when food was given to the prisoners it was inadequate and infested.

"Even if it is horrid on the inside, it is certainly quite a magnificent building on the outside," remarked Edwin.

"Aye, I heard tell that Lord Cockburn, he used to be our Solicitor General, said that 'It had been a piece of undoubted bad taste to give so glorious an eminence to a prison,'" remarked William.

Not sure of how to respond to that lofty sentiment, Edwin decided to say nothing. In any event neither man had any expectation of being held there, but they both unconsciously hurried past it and gladly entered St Andrew Square; they then opted to walk through the park instead of skirting its perimeter. The trees were decked in their autumn colors and Edwin felt rather like a small boy as he kicked the large horse chestnut leaves. Some of them were as big as his hands. Because the weather was so pleasant on this autumn day many people were out strolling or sitting underneath the trees. The parks were just one of the reasons Edwin loved Edinburgh. The New Town was designed so that there were parks and trees and places to relax.

They exited the square on the north side and then walked past St Andrew's Church. Once they started along George Street both men picked up speed, perhaps thinking ahead of the Dundee cake and tea. Edwin rarely ate cake, he could not afford it, but he was looking forward to a slab of Mrs. Berridge's cake. This was an unexpected treat. Sundays were usually a rather lonely time for him. He enjoyed solitude and quiet but he found Sundays rather long sometimes. This was the time when he missed his family and longed for his deceased parents. To find someone with similar interests as he, was a find indeed.

Swiftly they walked along George Street, both admiring the Georgian architecture and stepping carefully to avoid other passersby and gawkers. For on Sunday afternoons people would wander from the Old Town through the Gardens on Princes Street and then along George Street for their constitutionals. This particular afternoon was no different. The weather had been warmer than usual for October and Edinburgh citizens were keen to take advantage of the heat before the long, chilly winters set in. Edinburgh was no place to be in winter. Standing on Princes Street on a blustery bone-chilling day is an experience that most people would not forget. Edwin had not experienced this yet but had certainly heard about it. William had lived in Edinburgh for so many years that he was accustomed to bundling up with extra mufflers and gloves before he ever ventured along Princes Street. He was not about to complain about a "fresh" wind.

But today though the weather was balmy, for Edinburgh. As Edwin and William walked along George Street neither stopped to look in the shop windows. There was a fine wine shop and an equally fine jewelers on the north side of the street.

Mappin and Webb was an old English company which had grown rapidly and had expanded its business into Edinburgh. Specializing in silver but also selling other items, Mappin and Webb had a lovely bay window display which beckoned to William. He hesitated for just a moment and then stopped to admire the jewelry and watches in the window.

They certainly had an attractive assortment of necklaces, rings and timepieces. He felt a slight pang of envy when he looked at the collection. These were his competitors, yet he realized that he could not really challenge their skills. He was one man and Mappin and Webb was an already well-known company. He realized too that he could give up his own business and join a business such as this one. With the quality of his craftsmanship he could easily find work with a major jeweler. Yet he did not want that either. There was a lot to be said for controlling one's own time, being one's own boss, even if it meant that some weeks the pay was not good and food was therefore scant at the Berridge family table.

William straightened his shoulders and glanced ruefully over at Edwin who was watching him.

"I love the kind of work they do but I just can't compete with their prices. I just hope they don't put me out of business. I think there's a need for the independent craftsman. I know all my customers personally and know their watches better than I know the back of my hand. After all, I made some of them!"

"I am looking forward to seeing your shop," Edwin said quickly. "I wouldn't feel comfortable going into such a fancy shop and I dare say others feel the same way. Oh, I didn't mean that in an unkind way. I've not even seen your shop yet but you implied that it was smaller than this one."

"It is, indeed. But, we are almost there. We need to turn right here." The two turned onto Frederick Street and headed north until Frederick Street turned into Jamaica Street. Although it was hilly neither man paused in their stride until they reached the stoop of 15 Jamaica Street.

CHAPTER 5

There was nothing remarkable about the stoop of 15 Jamaica Street. It had clearly been scrubbed recently, even perhaps yesterday, but that was not unusual. A mark of a good housewife was how well she cleaned her stoop and no one wanted to be criticized for being less than tidy. Life in Edinburgh had its standards and the cleanliness of the stoop was just one of them.

However Edwin was unable to completely see the stoop because there, blocking his entrance, was a large ginger tomcat. It had a large head with a rather long pointed nose, two well-defined ears, a white spot on his chest, and four white socks on his feet. His body was muscular and he looked rather well-fed. Clearly he was a good rat-catcher. At this moment his ears were on high alert and his coffee-colored eyes looked questioningly at Edwin.

"Don't worry, old man," said William. "This is my new friend, Edwin. Edwin, meet Toby."

Edwin was unsure whether he should shake the cat's paw but decided against it. Toby seemed mellow and so Edwin merely stroked his head which elicited a rather strange mewing sound from Toby. Toby certainly did not have the voice to go with his body.

"Toby is my daughter Ann's cat. He survives quite well by hunting and the odd scraps we give him. He's become quite the defender of the family and guards our house well - when he's not sleeping."

"I didn't realize you had a daughter. How old is she?"

"Nineteen. She works with her mother and takes in sewing jobs. You will meet her today, I think. I know she had some sewing to deliver earlier today but I think she will have returned by now."

Toby was not about to budge from his step but he allowed Edwin and William to climb over him. As William entered his apartment he called out to Lillias, his wife, "I'm home and I've brought a visitor."

Lillias appeared in a doorway and seemed totally unsurprised by Edwin's presence. Edwin suspected that this was certainly not the first time that William had brought home new acquaintances to meet his family.

William introduced Edwin to Lillias and she greeted him with a ready smile and said in what he recognized as a Glaswegian brogue, "Come right in and make yourself at home by the fire. It's starting to get chilly outside. From where do you know my man?"

Lillias was short and she wore her dark hair in a braid on the top of her head. Her hair was graying but the braid suited her and she did not look severe as some women do who wear such a hairstyle. Her brown eyes were lively and from the creases on her face Edwin believed she was probably a woman who laughed a great deal. She helped William off with his coat and indicated to Edwin where he could place his jacket and his cloth cap, the latter of which he had removed as soon as he saw Lillias.

They all entered the modest living room in which a tiny coal fire burned. It added cheer to the room although it was still smoking a little. At the small square table there were three places set for tea but Lillias quickly took another mug and plate from a cupboard on the wall opposite the fireplace. She set it on the table and invited Edwin to sit there. The kettle was being heated over the coal fire and she took it off the rod and poured the hot water into a brown betty teapot which she kept on a small table to the left of the fire. Edwin remembered how his mother had a similar teapot. It was said that the best tea in all Britain came from brown betty teapots. He did not know if it were true or not but liked the idea as his mother had believed it. He suspected that the clay with which it was made might have had something to do with it, or perhaps it was the shape of the pot. It looked fat and warm and comforting like a teapot should.

Mrs. Berridge then brought a plate of jam sandwiches to the table where Edwin was seated and an oblong fruitcake which Edwin took to be the Dundee cake. He had only been in Edinburgh since March, and cake was a luxury, so this would be his first bite of Dundee cake.

Just then the door opened and in walked a young girl wearing a black wool coat. She looked momentarily surprised to see Edwin sitting at the table and waited until her father introduced him.

"Ann, I would like you to meet Edwin Turner. He spends his Sundays at the Observatory too. I've been there today and invited him to join us for some tea. Then I want to show him my workshop."

Ann responded, "Pleased to meet you, Mr. Turner." Edwin noticed immediately that her accent was different from her mother's, who was pure Glaswegian. Ann had the slower, more refined and gentle Edinburgh accent, similar to William's. On the other hand, Lillias moved quickly and spoke quickly too. She seemed to be in perpetual motion.

"Miss Berridge, how nice to meet you too. I hope I am not interrupting a family tea. I've enjoyed talking to your father this afternoon. We share the same interest in telescopes and astronomy. I'm looking forward very much to seeing his workshop too."

Ann said, "Not at all, Mr. Turner. I'm happy you share the same interest. I frankly don't understand much of what he talks about so I'm pleased he can find someone who does."

As Ann spoke Edwin was able to take a good look at her. Ann was dark like her mother but had a slender frame. She was quite tall, almost as tall as he, he noted. She smiled politely which highlighted a dimple on the right side of her face. Not beautiful, he decided, but she was attractive and was surprisingly poised, a trait she may have learned from her father.

Edwin felt at rather a loss for words which resulted in him speaking far more than he intended in his effort to overcome what he perceived as a shortcoming. He explained that he had learned about telescopes from his uncle, that his parents had died and he had moved up from England as he wanted to see the world a bit and he had nothing to tie him any longer to Nottingham. He had hoped for work as a stocking maker but had not been able to find it and so had work at the Scottish and Newcastle Brewery but he really wanted to find something a little different.

Edwin stopped, somewhat aghast at himself for speaking too long and revealing so much about himself. He was normally fairly reserved and was not inclined to talk much about himself. His mother had always taught him it was best to listen. So much to that. In one ear and out the other, he thought.

William was watching and listening carefully as Edwin spoke. He did not seem to disapprove of what Edwin had said and clearly Ann was also interested. To stop himself from speaking even further Edwin decided to sample one of the jam sandwiches. He then sipped his tea to which he had added milk and a spoonful of sugar.

He felt strangely at home here. It had not been as easy as he had expected to move from England. He knew that some Scots did not like the English and he had heard more than once that he was taking a job which should belong to a Scotsman. Nevertheless, he was persevering and he enjoyed the simplicity of life here. He realized that the dourness which some Scots affected masked only a warmth and friendliness which struggled to remain hidden.

Dourness in people did not distress him. He noticed Toby walk through the room and realized that even the cat had a dour attitude. Toby took his family responsibilities seriously and he was not about to crack a smile, even if he could.

At this point Toby wrapped himself around Ann's feet and she struggled to keep her ankles hidden by her dress as Toby tried to cuddle her feet. Clearly Toby was an admirer of Ann and Edwin had no problem understanding that. She was certainly charming.

His attention was taken though when, upon finishing a slice of Dundee cake, William stood up and suggested that they go downstairs to his workshop. Edwin fortunately had just finished his cake too, declared it the best he had ever tasted (truthful as it was the first) and he stood up too. He bade farewell and thanked Mrs. Berridge, and he bowed to both ladies.

Climbing over Toby who had already deposited himself at the door again, William and Edwin descended the stone staircase and entered the workshop and business premises of William Berridge, Jr.

On both sides of the door were two grandfather clocks, both showing exactly the same time, which by now was something that Edwin would have expected of William. It was two minutes to the hour. Edwin turned to the workbench and noticed a couple of small timepieces there. He also saw several watch parts, and on a side bench he believed he saw the beginnings of a watch, perhaps one which William was making.

William saw him looking at it and explained what he was making. He was usually able to make watches and sell them to wealthy people who had more than one timepiece. He could custom-make them. Most people did not care about the inner workings but they cared very much about the clarity of the face and the design on the casing. Frequently the design would reflect the work or the interest of the customer.

At that moment the grandfather clocks chimed and from a couple of work table drawers Edwin heard the sound of ringing. William did not seem to notice but, to Edwin's ears, the hour was marked as an event for he could hear several timepieces recording it.

A moment later he heard the sound of a cuckoo. It was coming from a clock hanging from a wall above the workbench. The clock had a painted square, flat, wooden face above which there was a wooden semi-circle decorated with flowers. The cuckoo popped out from a door in the middle of the roses. It was a pendulum clock, noted Edwin. William explained it belonged to a customer who had recently taken a Grand European tour. He had bought this clock in the Black Forest area of Germany. According to the customer, these clocks were all the rage now in Germany. Having seen one previously William knew that although cuckoo clocks were the rage now they had a long history, the earliest ones dating back to the second century in Greece. Their style had changed over the years but the basic mechanism of the bird and the cuckoo call remained unchanged. This particular clock's bird would not always emerge from the trapdoor. It was possible to turn off that mechanism so it did not sound during the night but this bird wanted to sleep more than it was supposed to.

Edwin was captivated by it and by the two longcase clocks both of which had sounded the identical chime, the Whittington chimes. William explained this chime was particularly popular as were the Cambridge Quarters which was a chime modeled on bells in St Mary's near Cambridge. He explained that being a watchmaker was normally a job in itself and the training for it was different from that of a clockmaker; but on occasion he liked to work on the longcase clocks, particularly when the repairs were often simple. Customers did not always treat their clocks well, and the job of winding them was turned over to the staff who also did not know how to treat them well. More than once William had found that a clock which was not working had its hands either touching each other or the glass front casing, either of which would cause the clock not to work. William was paid for the repair but it was sometimes difficult to transport the clocks and not always worth the effort. He definitely preferred working on watches and would only take in a clock as a favor. One of the clocks he had now belonged to Sir Charles Mortimer, whose Longine he had just repaired. Because he had the watch to repair he decided it would be good business to repair Mortimer's clock too. He wryly noted to Edwin that Mortimer's clock was a thirty-hour clock but it had a false keyhole on it so a visitor might view the clock and assume it was an eight-day clock, which was more expensive.

He continued, "I was wondering if you might be interested in learning how to repair watches. The apprenticeship is for seven years which is a long commitment. Some of the time you would just have ordinary jobs such as being a porter. I've not used a porter before but could see that it could be of value and it would be a good service to provide my customers. You would have to pick up and return watches to the customers and when I have free time I could show you how to repair watches. My business is expanding and my sons have no interest in the work. They'd rather work in a factory. I've had one apprentice previously but he started his own business when he joined the Guild and I've been managing on my own since."

Edwin was surprised by the offer but only took a couple of seconds to think about it. He liked William; the two men had similar interests, and he thought William would be good to work for. He thought too that he would enjoy the detailed work as he was good with his hands and he liked precision. He would also welcome the opportunity to hopefully see more of Ann. She was worth pursuing, he thought. This would be life-changing for him though because, if he were to devote seven years to learning a trade, he would be set up for life. There would be no going back and pursuing something else.

The two men talked for a while about what William would expect of Edwin and what hours he would work. William was willing to match Edwin's pay at Scottish and Newcastle, which made the decision far easier. Edwin did not want to get into debt by taking a lesser paying job. He would not however see any significant increase in his pay until he had finished his apprenticeship. After another fifteen minutes of conversation, Edwin had agreed to give his notice at the brewery and he would begin work on Monday a week later.

At this point William stood up and held out his hand. The two men shook on their deal and Edwin walked out of the shop, William locking the door behind him. Edwin would have liked to see Ann again and see how she reacted to the news that he was going to work for her father. Only a week or so though and he would be working there six days a week anyway and hopefully he would see more of her then. Seven years would offer a lot of opportunity to see Ann, he mused.

CHAPTER 6

Christmas Day 1842 was a bright crisp day in Edinburgh. It had snowed early the day before and there was still some snow on the ground in places but the pavement was clean, and Edwin turned smartly out of Borthwick Close where he shared a room with a brewery worker. He enjoyed the sunshine and it reflected his happy attitude as he strode along the High Street.

His feet knew the way well by now. He had started his apprenticeship with William Berridge and not infrequently he had been invited for tea with the Berridges. Even though he now saw William Berridge sometimes seven days a week this did not seem to bother either of them. He saw little of the Berridge sons who worked in the stocking factory; and by now he was already glad that he was not working there or at the brewery either. Yes, life was shaping well for Edwin. He enjoyed the freedom to be able to go around town picking up and delivering watches. More than that though, he enjoyed working with delicate instruments, controlling time, as it were. William Berridge had proved to be an able teacher and Edwin applied himself well to his newfound trade.

Edwin decided to cross the Princes Street Gardens via the Mound. This small strip of land divided the Gardens into two sections. Right now the Gardens were privately owned but there was a movement in the Edinburgh City Council to make these Gardens open to all the public. The current owners had all manner of restrictions on who could enter the park. If you needed a bath chair to get around then you had to declare that your illness was not contagious. This seemed rather extreme when there were so many illnesses which could take away one's ambulation.

The Gardens despite their restrictions were attractive to look at from the Mound. In the distance Edwin could see the ongoing construction of a train station. It would bring the railway line from Glasgow right into downtown Edinburgh. Current visitors to Edinburgh had to get a charabanc or carriage from the Haymarket Station at this point. The new Waverly station was slated to open in three years time.

Edwin knew that the Gardens used to have a loch. It had been man-made but had been drained many years ago. Originally designed as an added defense for the Castle, it had been unsuccessful in keeping out sewage from the Old Town. It did not help that some of the residents used it as a garbage dump and the smell had been frequently putrid. No stranger to squalor, Edwin was glad that these days he spent most of his time in the New Town. Edwin was fastidious, a quality which was particularly appropriate for a watchmaker.

At the end of the Mound, Edwin turned left onto Princes Street. As it was Christmas Day it was rather quiet and the usual tradesmen were not plying their wares on the side of the street. He noticed several fine carriages moving at a dignified clop along the street but his passage was largely unimpeded by pedestrians and his pace quickened as he turned onto Frederick Street.

As he walked along, even though he was looking forward to the day ahead, Edwin could not help thinking of the previous Christmas when his family had still been together. What a happy time that had been! His mother had prepared a chicken for dinner. That had been a real luxury. She also made his favorite mince pies and he had been lucky enough to find the small sixpence in the pie. There was only ever one sixpence in a batch of mince pies; Edwin's mother had always made sure that when she offered him the plate of mince pies that the plate would be turned in such a way that he would get the pie with the sixpence. She had been a warm and loving mother and he missed both his parents terribly. It was hard on a day like Christmas not to be sad for whom one had lost. But at least he had a day today that he could look forward to.

Edwin enjoyed the Berridge family very much but his interest today was focused on Ann. Over the last couple of months she had been present at Sunday tea and they had engaged in casual conversation. Sometimes Edwin felt her looking at him when he was looking at his plate. He tried not to stare at her but she was lovely and not staring was becoming increasingly difficult. A few times a week she would pass through the shop on the way to deliver her sewing orders and she would stop and look at what the two men were working on. Edwin had seen some of Ann's sewing and embroidery and she was clearly talented. Like him, she had an attention to detail, presumably something she had acquired from her father.

Edwin continued up Frederick Street and on to Jamaica Street. The neighborhood was not quite so fine as he stepped farther away from Princes and George Streets. Nevertheless it was very respectable and well-kept. Finally he arrived at 15 Jamaica Street, on the right side of the street. He climbed the stairs and there was Toby waiting to greet him. By now they had struck up a friendship of sorts and Toby stretched out his front paws, lifted up his rear end, waved his unusually long tail and granted Edwin passage into the Berridge household.

As he entered the flat Edwin called out, "Merry Christmas!"

At once William and Lillias appeared and hugged him warmly. They had both grown fond of him in the short time they had been acquainted. William was pleased with the quality of Edwin's work and by his enthusiasm.

They were also secretly rather pleased that Edwin seemed to have an interest in their daughter. It wouldn't be a bad match for Ann, they thought. William still regretted that his sons had no interest in his business. Perhaps Edwin would be able to take it over. Now that was jumping ahead though, cautioned William to himself. Let the young people work these things out for themselves. That is what he and Lillias had done and it had worked out well. She had waited patiently for him as he went to war and as he spread a few wild oats. After their marriage she had worked alongside him and encouraged him to open up this business. Its success was due not least to her encouragement. They had a loving, caring marriage which he knew not many of his friends could claim to have. He could only hope that Ann would find the same with whomever she married.

He had already noticed that Edwin had a wild streak. He wanted to take chances and shortcuts sometimes in his work. William was a little bothered too that Edwin had come north so quickly after his parents died. That did seem rather impulsive, yet it also reflected his adventurous spirit.

"Come on in," urged Lillias, helping Edwin take off his coat. "Take a seat by the fire. Ann will be home presently. She has been visiting that old friend Margaret whom she told you about last week. Margaret is alone and bed-ridden. Ann wanted to see that she had some Christmas dinner."

Edwin was not surprised to hear this as he had already perceived that Ann was a generous and caring person. At that moment the door opened again and Ann entered, followed closely by Toby. This was no surprise again to Edwin either as he had noticed how the ginger tomcat was never far from Ann whenever she was in the house.

"Merry Christmas, Edwin," Ann said, her cheeks still rather rosy from the nippy Christmas air and the brisk walk home.

"Merry Christmas to you, Ann," Edwin replied, noticing that Ann was wearing the same black coat which she was wearing when they first met but she now sported a bright red scarf too. That came as no surprise to Edwin as he had seen Lillias knitting such a scarf several times recently. "What a pretty scarf."

"Thank you, it's from Ma and Father. Have you been here long?"

"No, just a minute or two before you. I heard you were visiting your friend, Margaret. How is she?"

"Not well. She has apoplexy and she is very weak. I took her some soup as I thought she would not be able to eat the chicken. She ate very little. I fear for her. I shall see her again tomorrow."

This only confirmed what Edwin already knew about Ann. She was a caring girl who fretted when others were in trouble. Her mother complained sometimes that Ann did not like to charge for her work and it was difficult at times as they needed the money. William and Lillias lived very simply but they were able to get the things they needed when everyone worked. Life was better for them than for many but it was still not easy.

The table was set today in the middle of the room and the fire provided the room with a nice warm glow. Lillias had just put the roast chicken on the table and she had some Brussels sprouts, carrots and potatoes too. What a feast! Edwin was particularly pleased to see the Yorkshire puddings, which reminded him of his mother as she could cook them so well.

Once again William's sons were absent; today they were visiting friends in Dumfries where they were now working at a stocking manufacturer. Edwin had met them only once, and then only briefly. He found them both rather surly and oafish, such a contrast to their sister.

On a little table in the tiny kitchen Edwin noticed his Christmas pudding. It was his contribution to the dinner. He had wanted to bring something for the meal and he also knew he really wanted to have a plum pudding. His family traditionally ate it every Christmas and he did not want to miss it this year. A friend had made it for him and it looked lovely. Lillias had steamed it and then turned it out on a metal platter to cool a little. Edwin did not know where she had found holly but there was a piece on the top making the pudding particularly festive. Edwin noticed that there was a bottle of grog alongside the pudding and he hoped William would flame the pudding. A waste of a good drink but it was just for Christmas. He had been told that Hogmanay was more important to the Scots than Christmas but as he looked at the feast on the table it looked as though Christmas was very important too.

They sat down and William said grace. He did not attend church but he was still thankful for all he received. William did things properly and that included taking care of his communication with his Provider. Lillias said a rather loud Amen as he finished and turned her attention to the chicken. It was a meager looking bird, for chicken was not cheap, and she handed the knife to William so he could carve. William began serving the chicken, giving Edwin the first piece as he was the guest, even though he ate at their table very regularly.

Ann was sitting across from Edwin and she smiled as he took his first bite of the chicken. It was the first he had tasted in many months and it melted in his mouth. Chicken was a luxury to be savored. Usually he ate it only at Easter and Christmas. He felt so lucky to have been accepted into this home. His mother always said that he seemed to be able to land on his feet. He certainly felt that now.

Not wanting to talk with food in his mouth and hating to swallow the tasty morsel of chicken he had there, he let his eyes wander around the small room. The walls were bare except for a sampler which Ann had made. It had the alphabet across the top and pictures of small houses in the lower portion of the picture. Its motto was not unusual - 'Home Sweet Home', and at the very bottom it said that it was made by Ann Berridge, aged 9. Certainly Ann had been accomplished at a young age. He could understand why there was a demand for her needlework now.

"This chicken is lovely, Mrs. Berridge," he commented. "I don't get to eat chicken very often. It's a rare treat."

"It is for us too, lad," rejoined Mr. Berridge. "That's what makes it even more special. I remember the first time I ate chicken", he continued. "It was at Hogmanay in 1799. We had a special celebration for the turn of the century. My mother prepared a chicken and we had a special meal to bring in the New Year. That was the first year I went out first-footing with my father."

Edwin was familiar with the Scottish custom of first-footing whereby people went out with whisky and sherry to celebrate the New Year. It was customary for people to invite strangers into their home and each toasted each other with the whisky. The invitees would carry their own bottles so they could offer drinks to those who invited them in. At midnight it was thought lucky if a tall, dark-haired man entered the house first. He was to carry a coin, a loaf of bread and a piece of coal for the occupants, bringing hopefully wealth, food and warmth to that household. The custom was carried out in England but certainly not with the almost religious fervor with which it occupied the Scottish mind. Not much would be talked about between now and Hogmanay, a week later.

"You are familiar with first-footing, Edwin?" Edwin was, partly because William had already talked about it several times in the last couple of months. "I hope you will join us this year to see in the bells," said William. "The first-footer is supposed to be dark-haired. I fear with my greying hair that I am no longer quite dark enough but you should do a champion job."

Edwin was surprised and delighted at the idea. He accepted quickly and then turned his attention to his food where Lillias was taking away his plate and carrying the Christmas pudding to the table.

William stood up and reached for the grog. Sure enough, he planned to flame the Christmas pudding. It only lasted a few seconds, less than a minute, but they all felt cheered by the tradition. For once it was nice to have a really full stomach and know that they had not finished yet. Lillias served the plum pudding and Edwin tasted it. He savored it as he remembered how much he had enjoyed doing this with his own family. He wished they could have been there today. He thought they would have approved of his apprenticeship. He hoped so.

Edwin was sure too that they would approve of Ann. After dinner he planned to ask William if he might formally court her. He was just waiting for the right opportunity. It came a few minutes later when Lillias and Ann started to clear away the dishes. William, who could not lay work aside for even a day, wanted to show Edwin a watch he was making in the workshop. The two men headed downstairs as the women cleared away the dishes.

"Glad you could be with us today, Edwin. I'm very glad that you have begun the apprenticeship. This line of work is not for everyone but you have the discipline and attention to detail which is required. I was pretty sure when I met you that you had the fortitude necessary to complete the apprenticeship. It's true you've a long way to go but you've made a good start. My daughter seems to have taken a shine to you I've noticed too."

Surprised by his good fortune that William had addressed the issue even before he had, Edwin hesitated for a fraction of a second. He was not used to William being blunt spoken. He then decided to head forward on what he wished to say.

"I have taken a shine to her too. I wanted to talk to you today to get your approval to court her. I hope it meets with your approval. I think Ann is a wonderful girl and I would like to get to know her better."

"She's a bit young yet and doesn't really know what she wants. However I feel sure that she'll be safe with you. You are seven years older than she is and that bothers me a little, but you're good and steady. My goodness, you are only talking courting anyway. An awful lot can happen before you get to the altar."

Edwin was rather hoping that the altar would come sooner rather than later with Ann but he did not want to startle Ann's father so he thanked him. He then spent as little time as possible looking at a new watch with William before heading back upstairs to see Ann and ask her to take a walk with him.

CHAPTER 7

Sir Charles Mortimer looked at his Longine watch for the tenth time in as many minutes and wondered, also for the tenth time, how much more time his daughter would need to get ready to go out to dinner with their friends. He had really coveted another friend's Longine when that man first purchased it but now Sir Charles rarely thought about how much he had wanted the watch. To have been given one by Queen Victoria was an unexpected joy and achievement for him. Acquiring things was Sir Charles' business and he was good at it. He had gained stature in court because of his ability to acquire for the British Army anything it needed. He had lined his own pockets with that work and now he was living with the fruits of it.

Sir Charles' drawing room overlooked Charlotte Square. He was proud of the exclusive address and enjoyed viewing the park outside and the fine Georgian buildings surrounding the square. It was relaxing and pleasing to him. One of his favorite things was the key to the Square. Entry was restricted only to residents of the Square, which made it particularly refined. Not that Sir Charles wanted to walk in the Square. No, that was fine for the children and their nannies. What pleased him was he had something that no one else could easily afford or acquire.

Working as an equerry to Queen Victoria at Holyrood Palace had many advantages. He was welcomed into Edinburgh society, even though he was an Englishman, because he was well acquainted with the Queen. It provided Sir Charles with a steady source of income and really not much work except when the Queen was at home in Scotland. Naturally he had an office in the Palace and he went there several days a week if only to be seen entering the Palace.

Sir Charles was very glad that the nature of his work had changed; previously an equerry would take care of the stables and Sir Charles was not fond of animals, save for his rather overweight King Charles spaniel named Louis. He recognized it was rather an unfortunate name for the dog. He would prefer to have called the dog anything else but that French name but it was what his daughter favored, so Louis he was. Louis was stretched out in his usual indolent way at Sir Charles' feet. Absent-mindedly Sir Charles stroked Louis' head and Louis turned his rather sad black eyes in Sir Charles' direction, wondering if he were going to receive a treat. Sir Charles was indulgent to the dog but at this time he was preoccupied.

He and his daughter Mary were to attend a dinner at the home of Sir James Forrest, Baronet of Comiston. Sir James had been the Lord Provost of Edinburgh since 1837 and Sir Charles knew him in that capacity.

Sir James only lived around the corner on George Street but the carriage was waiting for Sir Charles and Mary. It was unseemly to arrive at Sir

James' house on foot. Sir Charles had been a tradesman of sorts but that had been a long time ago; he was not now about to be seen waiting on the doorstep of Sir James.

Anxiously he rang the bell for his butler Edwards who appeared promptly as he was always available to Sir Charles when the latter was home.

"Please find out from Miss Mary's maid how much longer Miss Mary will be," requested Sir Charles in an exasperated way. "I don't want to be late. Miss Mary likes to arrive fashionably late but I see nothing to be admired in that. I do not want her to have that reputation."

At the back of Sir Charles' mind was the fact that his daughter still needed to find a husband. She had come out in London last season but had unsuccessfully found a husband. Rather a gaunt and plain looking woman, Mary had failed to captivate any man and Sir Charles was more than a little worried that she would wind up a spinster, lonely and unloved. He had hoped that she would find a pecuniary match with an heir to a fortune but that had not happened.

Edwards did not return as Miss Mary herself entered the drawing room. She smiled handsomely at her father who was always won over by her charm. As a father he was able to overlook her rather prominent teeth and somewhat large nose. He immediately forgot how long he had been waiting and complimented her on her new dress. It was a lilac muslin, off the shoulder, with a large collar and tapered waist which ended just below her natural waist. The skirt was full and the tapered waist made Miss Mary look more slender than she really was. Her dark, shiny hair, which was her best feature, was dressed in the style of the time - parted in the middle with ringlets over each ear. Miss Mary wore an amethyst and diamond pendant on a gold chain which she had been bequeathed by her mother.

Sir Charles straightened his brightly colored waistcoat, smoothed over his frock coat and picked up his top hat. With his tall collar and long sideburns he looked quite the dandy and younger than his sixty-eight years. He extended his right arm to his daughter and the two walked out of the drawing room, out through the double doors of their residence and down the three steps into the waiting carriage.

Sir Charles looked forward to the evening ahead with some satisfaction. He enjoyed the company of Sir James Forrest with whom he regularly played whist and poker. He knew that he had been particularly favored by being invited for Christmas dinner to the home of Sir James. He was anxious too to meet Sir James' son, Albert, who had recently returned from a Grand Tour of Europe and had found employment with the very respectable firm of solicitors, Russel and Aitken of Falkirk. Sir Charles had heard on good authority that Albert planned to settle down and marry. He hoped that Miss Mary and young Albert would find each other mutually agreeable for that would take a weight off his mind.

CHAPTER 8

Edwin walked into the Berridges' flat and found Ann sitting by the fire, sewing as usual. He told her that he had asked permission of her father to court her if that would be acceptable to her. Ann raised her head and nodded shyly. Edwin suggested they take a walk so they could work off the effects of the special Christmas dinner. Ann liked the idea so she picked up her black coat and Edwin helped her to put it on. She then wrapped the new red scarf around her neck, added a bonnet to her attire and she was ready to go walking.

They went downstairs, saying goodbye to William who was still pottering around his workshop and they walked up Frederick Street until they reached Princes Street. Edwin rarely had time to walk through the Gardens as, during daylight hours, he was always working. He relished the opportunity to walk there even though it was the wrong season for flowering plants.

A large clock had been set into the side of the hill descending into the Gardens. It only had the hour hand although Edwin had heard that there were plans to add a minute hand. The clock had been extremely colorful during the summer when the bed had been filled with petunias, alyssum and lobelias. Now there were green bedding plants to mark the hour hand and the times were defined by different greenery. William had told Edwin that the mechanism for the clock had been placed in the nearby plinth of Allan Ramsay, the famous Scottish poet. He said that similar clocks developed later just had their mechanisms buried under the flower bed.

The hour hand at this time marked two o'clock which meant that the pair had a couple of hours before dark to wander through the park. Ann wrapped her arm through Edwin's extended arm and they walked down the steps until they reached the deepest portion of the Gardens. From here Princes Street looked to be a steep climb up on their right. On their left the Castle stood impenetrable and dark. Its sheer elevation and rugged cliffs would make it almost impossible to besiege, yet attempts had been made successfully and unsuccessfully to lay siege to it. It had figured prominently in the War of Scottish Independence and it still housed a formidable garrison. Edwin was not an expert on castles as he had not traveled extensively but he could recognize this Castle as being majestic and striking. Ann had grown up with it on her doorstep, so to speak, but she was still proud of it. She never tired of seeing this symbol of Scottish power. A Scot by choice and by birth, Ann was proud of her culture and she enjoyed sharing it with Edwin, a Sassenach.

Ann had been surprised when her father had taken on a Sassenach apprentice yet she knew him to be a fair man, and doing a job right and well was more important to him than one's nationality. At some point William's family had some English blood for Berridge was an English moniker, yet William's mother had been a McBride.

Ann would enjoy showing Edwin her Edinburgh. She had lived here all her life and could not imagine living anywhere else. She was as much a part of Edinburgh as Edinburgh was a part of her. Ann could not imagine that she could ever feel any happier than she did in this city. A proud Scot, Ann loved the sophistication of this city. True, she could only view the sophistication and the aristocracy from a distance but she was still proud that England viewed it as a serious and formidable partner in the United Kingdom.

The two walked slowly through the Gardens trying to prolong this moment of privacy. So many people lived in the same building as the Berridges and the noises carried through the walls so much that it seemed it was difficult to find a quiet space.

Edwin learned from Ann that she had visited the Observatory with her father but she had not found it very interesting. She talked a little about her sewing work. Many of William's customers had become her and Lillias' customers too so Edwin and Ann were able to share stories and opinions of their customers. Both enjoyed the opportunity to 'see how the other half lived'. Neither could imagine living with so much wealth. It certainly made one want to work harder to try and achieve the things that these aristocrats had. Edwin had heard of people getting rich in America, that they were not bound by the class system as the British were. Edwin had even considered moving to America. He liked the idea of being able to move up socially based on his own hard work. In the back of his mind he cherished that idea. Perhaps he would go overseas one day too, either to America or Canada. For now though, he was happy to be in Edinburgh, living this moment with Ann.

Edwin had very little experience with women which was unusual for a man of his age yet he had enjoyed his family life with his parents and siblings. That and work seemed to have filled his time. Now he was free and lonely. His roommate Tim from the brewery had little interest in doing much but drinking the beer from where he worked. It had been convenient to share a room so they could both save money. Fortunately they both worked different hours so Edwin did have some privacy, as far as one could in Borthwick's Close which seethed with residents.

Today the Gardens were fairly quiet perhaps because people were staying home to enjoy their Christmas at home. Most businesses were closed. Edwin suggested they walk to the end of the Gardens where a large Christmas tree had been set up. Queen Victoria's husband, Prince Albert, had introduced the custom of Christmas trees into Britain although not many people used them yet. Some cities set them up in the town squares. Edwin and Ann reached the tree and stared in amazement at its size and beauty. Trimmed with ribbons and paper ornaments the tree stood proudly in the Gardens, a giant silver colored star adorning the top.

Ann remarked that she had seen a small tree in the home of Sir Charles Mortimer for whose daughter Ann had recently made a dress. The tree stood in the drawing room and had a few wrapped packages underneath it. On Sir Charles' solid oak front door had been a wreath trimmed with red velvet ribbon. It must be nice to have so much money that you can get a decoration just for Christmas, observed Ann. Edwin could only agree.

It was chilly and Ann pulled her muffler tighter around her neck. Noticing that she was cold, Edwin suggested that they leave the Gardens and walk through Charlotte Square and along George Street before returning to Jamaica Street. Ann was a little concerned that her parents would be worried about her so she readily agreed on the route.

As they passed through Charlotte Square they noticed a carriage pulled up outside Sir Charles Mortimer's house. The door was still closed and they could see the aforementioned large wreath hanging on it. Then the door opened and out walked a young lady, dressed in a lilac muslin gown with a small fur cape. On her head she had a matching bonnet. Accompanying her was a tall, greying man whom they both recognized as Sir Charles. He climbed into the carriage after her and the carriage completed a full turn around the Square for the benefit of Sir Charles' neighbors before heading along George Street.

CHAPTER 9

In Borthwick's Close, a couple of miles away in distance, a world away in class, living standards and cleanliness, Tim McGregor stirred in his bed. He had worked late last night, Christmas Eve, and he had taken his free beer from the brewery where he worked and brought it home to celebrate. Edwin, his roommate, had been working too and was not there to drink with him so it had been a rather lonely and drunken occasion for Tim.

Tim remembered going out onto the High Street for a while and then taking a walk along Princes Street where the more wealthy were promenading. The comfortable appearance of the people only served to make him morose. He knew he really should not drink beer as he became sad and at times belligerent. It made him do things that he later regretted. Tim's father had been a petty thief and he had taught Tim well. Tim knew every slight of hand trick known to man and he occasionally used them to supplement his income.

Tim's head felt thick and his mouth tasted woolly. He was sorry he had drunk all his beer last night as his head hurt so much. Also, there was none left for today. Everywhere was closed for the Christmas holiday. Tim's family had left Edinburgh several years previously so Tim would be spending the day alone.

Yet he was not totally alone as Borthwick's Close had about 200 inhabitants. It was rarely quiet.

People lived six stories high in the tenements, with little light, air or water. In a nearby close there had been a fire recently and several people had died, trampled on in the panic to get down the stone staircases. The fire itself had not been bad. After all, these flats had not much in the way of furniture to burn, and the walls were stone. Yet when there was a fire everyone panicked.

Tim's flat was on the fourth floor which was satisfactory as he did not have as far to carry his water. There was a central pump from which to get water in the close but it was usually busy. Occasionally it even ran dry. It was even worse for those residents who lived close to the Castle as the water had to be pumped up the hill. Water outages for those residents were common.

Tim looked around the room and noticed that he still had a piece of rye bread on the table, along with a piece of rather stale cheese. That would have to do today for food. He had a piece of shortbread too that the young girl who lived across the Close had given him. Well that would serve just fine for Christmas dinner. It was better than some he had previously.

He had heard talk in the brewery that the price of bread might go down if the Corn Laws could be repealed but it had not happened yet. Tim was no politician but he knew that foreign grain could not enter Britain as the taxes were so prohibitive. That made the price of bread artificially high and it was people like Tim who received the hardship. It just did not seem fair to Tim that poor people could not reap the benefits of cheaper bread. Bread was higher now in 1842 than it had ever been. Hopefully that would soon change.

Spending the day on his own was very unappealing to him. A keen walker, usually by necessity as he could not afford otherwise, Tim decided to enjoy the unexpected Christmas sunshine and go outside. Walking through the Old Town was not so pleasant as it was frequently congested with people, animals, carts, and merchants. Instead Tim headed for New Town which was more spacious and orderly. No one paid any attention to him as he walked over North Bridge and turned left onto Princes Street. All the while he kept his eyes open for an opportunity to grab some food, or something even better, if it presented itself. He decided to walk as far as George Street before turning for home.

As he walked along, not anxious to go home as he knew he would be on his own there, he passed a rather portly gentleman, dressed in a frock coat and top hat, helping a woman in a lilac dress with fur cape, out of a carriage. The lady stumbled as she descended from the carriage and, as she did, the gentleman reached out to help her. In that second when the gentleman's attention was turned to the lady, Tim reached for a silver chain stretched across the man's waistcoat. In a trice he had the chain and the watch in his right hand and he was heading as fast as his feet could fly back to Hanover Street and onto Princes Street. He was so good at stealing that the gentleman did not even notice that the watch was missing.

Tim hurried home so he could examine the watch in the privacy of his room. It would not pay to bring out a watch like that on the street as Tim certainly did not look like its original owner. Tim dressed like a typical brewery worker, his cloth cap distinctly showing his station in life.

Now Tim looked at the watch. It was a Longine with a silver case which was engraved with a soldier holding a musket. It clearly belonged to a former soldier although the man he had stolen it from looked as though he had not served in any military capacity in a very long time.

He pondered his options of fencing the watch. He knew he could not ask Edwin, his roommate, or Edwin's boss, William Berridge. He had previously talked to Edwin about stealing, in a very generalized way, not wishing to tell Edwin that he was a thief himself. He received no encouragement from Edwin, and he realized that he could not confide in Edwin as Edwin believed that he could get ahead by hard work, an idea which did not appeal to Tim.

It would be difficult to fence this watch. It was quite distinctive, particularly as it showed that it had been a gift from Queen Victoria. Briefly Tim regretted taking it but he also knew that he was hungry and he needed more money than Scottish and Newcastle brewery could pay him.

Edwin, whom he now rarely saw, had landed on his feet. The two had worked together at Scottish and Newcastle but now Edwin had started an apprenticeship as a watchmaker. Some people get all the breaks, he thought, and pondered anew where he could dispose of the watch. He had a friend, a former neighbor, whom he had known from childhood, who would pay him for the watch. He knew that the friend, Charlie, always made very good money on the sale and even though he, Tim, had the difficult job of stealing items in the first place, he did not receive much money for his labors. Still, it was easier to steal than it was to try and dispose of the property later.

Carefully he put the fancy watch in his coat pocket. He would dispose of it tonight. He had no need for it himself. He had his own inner clock to tell him when to head to the brewery. When he came home depended on when his boss told him he could leave. His job was to move the heavy barrels and load the carts for distribution to the pubs. It was backbreaking work but he was young and could handle it far better than some of the older men with whom he worked. He sincerely hoped that when he got to their age that he would not have to lift those barrels.

So far Tim had managed to escape prison time but it was luck. He knew his luck might run out sometime, as it did for his father. His father had stolen two diamond necklaces and had received a sentence of nine years transportation. That had been three years ago. By now his father would have settled in Australia and begun a new life there.

Tim heard tell that the conditions there were even more brutal than in the prisons in Britain. No one seemed to care though. Put these criminals out of sight and out of mind was the general consensus of opinion. The problem was that there were just not enough prisons to house the criminals. Petty thieves were meted out harsh punishments, such as transportation to Australia, as there were not enough prisons to house them here in Scotland.

Tim had heard of one judge, James McIntyre, who would actually cry as he sentenced men to Australia. One woman had pleaded and wept as her husband was led away and the judge declared that he was sorry but he had no choice. She said she had no means of support if her husband left for Australia, that they had eight children to feed. The judge started to cry but would not change the sentence. There was no adequate place for the man to go. The prisoner had been forging coins, small petty thievery. The sentence was inappropriate, said the Judge, but he had to hand down that sentence.

Thievery was becoming harder too as the new police force started to achieve results. These 'bobbies', so named after Sir Robert Peel, the Home Secretary who had established the police force, were effective in reducing crime. Widely unpopular among the working classes, they were welcomed by the wealthier classes who felt safer on the streets since the arrival of the 'peelers'.

Tim chewed on his crust of bread and finished the piece of cheese while he considered his options. He thought he would probably be able to find his friend Charlie in a pub on Rose Street later that day. Meanwhile he decided to take a nap and get ready for the evening's business. Perhaps Charlie would buy him a pint this evening after he had seen the watch.

CHAPTER 10

The door opened smartly as Sir Charles' carriage arrived at the door of Sir James Forrest. A footman ran down the steps and opened the door of the carriage and Sir Charles promptly descended, turning around to assist his daughter, Mary, who had stumbled a little.

The footman closed the door of the carriage and led the way into the house. Inside, the butler took over and guided the Mortimers into the drawing room of Sir James Forrest. The room was unoccupied and this gave time for Sir Charles and Miss Mary to look around the room and examine the furnishings.

The room was handsomely furnished, reflecting perhaps a man's taste. The floor-length draperies which hung at the tall Georgian windows were of a rich burgundy silk and they hung in folds as they reached the floor. The two divans facing each other were covered in the identical burgundy silk. To one side was a gold colored love seat whose seats faced each other in an S shape. Several other side chairs with gold and burgundy stripes were scattered around the room. On a magnificent German-made sideboard various carafes of wine were assembled, with Waterford crystal glasses to one side. The room was dominated by an oversized marble fireplace which sported a large log fire, burning brightly and warmly.

At this moment the large ornate door at the end of the room opened and in stepped Sir James

Forrest. A rather robust gentleman whose corpulence reflected the excesses of his life, Sir James walked with a dignity which belied his necrotic toes, the result of his advanced diabetes. Despite the disappointing diagnosis of diabetes Sir James enjoyed a diet of whatever he wanted. He could afford it and he wanted it.

He walked towards the small wine cabinet and offered the Mortimers a pre-dinner sherry. Both accepted readily. Sir Charles had already had a glass of madeira before he left his house; he felt the need to relax. His anxiety was beginning to run rather high over his daughter's marriage possibilities. Unaware that her father was so anxious for her future, Miss Mary decided she would enjoy herself and have a sherry. It would probably help her get through the evening with yet another potential suitor. Finding a husband was becoming rather tiresome and in some ways undesirable. She was satisfied with her life; her mother had died several years ago and she and her father lived contentedly in Edinburgh.

As she took the first sip, the large ornate door opened again and in stepped Sir James' son, Albert. Slightly tanned, perhaps because of his having spent a lot of time in the South of France, Albert was of pleasant appearance. His mid-brown hair was arranged in the current style, his collar was fashionably high and the cut of his coat was clearly of Savile Row quality.

"Allow me to introduce my daughter Mary," said Sir Charles. Albert bowed to the appropriate depth and Miss Mary curtsied in her prettiest way. She was not unhappy to see Albert was quite handsome. If she had to marry then she would definitely prefer someone who was of pleasant appearance. If you had to share the breakfast table and one's bed with someone it would definitely be easier if he were good-looking.

Sir James invited everyone to sit and Miss Mary avoided the loveseat, opting instead for one of the divans, next to her father.

At this point Sir Charles reached rather surreptitiously for his watch. He did not wish to appear rude by doing so. He wondered how long it would be before they ate. He needed to gauge how much he drank. This was not an occasion to over-indulge.

He realized suddenly that his watch was not in its usual pocket. He tried to hide his panic. He reached into his coat pocket and it wasn't there either. The chain was missing too. By this time the disquiet reflected on his face, causing Sir James to ask what was the matter. Sir Charles replied that he had lost his watch; he had left his house with it but now it was no longer here. After a glance around the room and vestibule to ensure it had not fallen there, the carriage was sent for and inspected, all in vain.

Sir Charles and Miss Mary discussed how the watch could have disappeared, and Sir Charles then remembered that a rather poorly dressed young man had stepped near him as he was assisting Mary. He remembered the man brushing against him, barely perceptibly. He must have taken the watch!

All plans for Christmas dinner were delayed and Sir Charles was in a quandary as to how to deal with the loss. He did not want to wreak havoc in Sir James' plans but he needed to try to recover his watch. Sir James on the other hand remained calm and merely requested of his butler that a message be sent to the local police chief. Meanwhile other guests were still arriving, and, for several minutes, the new arrivals were busy shedding their wraps and coats and receiving introductions.

Sir Charles was disappointed that the final group was so large as he had wished for a more intimate dinner with Sir James and his son, yet he was glad to maintain his status in Edinburgh society. For a brief moment he was able to forget that he had lost his watch, only briefly though, as the loss grieved him sorely each time he remembered it.

Sir James offered his arm to Mary Mortimer and together they led the way into the dining room which had a large table already set with sixteen place settings. The centerpiece for the table was a large silver eagle of life-size proportions. It sat on a silver tray which extended the width of the table. Each table setting was naturally of silver too; the wine and water glasses were Waterford, as had been the sherry glasses.

Mary was seated to the right of Sir James in the position of honor. On her immediate right sat Albert. This was not an unhappy scenario for Mary.

She had momentarily been concerned that the massive eagle would have blocked her view and conversation with the Forrests. For her father's sake she wished to make a good impression on both men. Sir Charles was seated further down the table between the wives of two city officials with whom Sir James worked. He would have preferred a more favored position closer to Sir James but he was not unhappy to see that Mary had a good position next to Albert. He wished he could hear their conversation.

Albert enquired after the health of Miss Mary and her family. He personally had not known of anyone who had contracted typhoid but he knew that it was a concern in the south of England. So far it appeared that it was escaping Edinburgh. He himself had been studying art in Florence for a couple of months. Had Miss Mary been there?

Miss Mary replied, "Unfortunately I have not had that opportunity. Please tell me what you saw. I assume you went to the Uffizi?"

Albert was glad to discourse at length on the sights of Florence and from there he continued his story about his trip to Rome, which he had preferred infinitely more. Albert had enjoyed the antiquity of Rome, that you could find evidence of earlier civilization on almost every street corner in Rome. Mary could only marvel at how wonderful it must have been. She noticed that, although he was from Edinburgh, Albert spoke with an English accent, affected by many Scottish aristocrats. She asked him if he had spent time in England and he replied that he had been educated at Eton College and Oxford before embarking on his trip.

Sir Charles meanwhile was struggling to listen to his daughter's conversation and maintain discourse with the middle-aged ladies seated on either side of him. Having discussed the weather, the Christmas holiday, and the price of cotton these days, Sir Charles felt momentarily at a loss. He was somewhat preoccupied by the disappearance of his watch. Hopefully the police chief would come soon and he could report what he believed to be a theft. He did not hold much hope though of the watch being found; there was so much crime these days and, even though the sentences were severe, the lack of a large police force or militia meant that most crimes went unnoticed and unreported. It hardly seemed worthwhile reporting a crime if there was no resultant conviction. Yet Sir James had insisted and, given that he was the Lord Provost, perhaps the new police force might be better at tracking down the thief when they knew that Sir James had a personal interest in the watch being found.

Sir James sat at the head of his table and viewed the setting with satisfaction. His wife had died several years previously but he had no mind to replace her. It was just too difficult at his age to become accustomed to another woman and he had little time for one anyway. His staff kept him in the right place at the right time with the right clothes and that suited him well. His position as Lord Provost demanded that he be out of his home on six nights out of seven, and most of the day too, as he fulfilled the responsibilities of his position. He had been elected by the city council to the job and he was the leader of that council but he also had several ceremonial tasks in addition.

Only four Scottish cities had Lord Provosts, most of the cities had mere Provosts. This elevated Sir James to a comparable position to the Lord Mayor of London and obviously gave him contact with the Queen when she was in residence at Holyrood. All in all, he was very satisfied with his position.

He turned his attention to his son Albert and Mary Mortimer who were chatting together. That relationship seemed to be developing well. It was time for Albert to settle down to regular work and the position that Sir James had arranged for him with the Falkirk firm would provide enough income to allow Albert to settle down and marry. Mary Mortimer was pleasant enough; she was not the prettiest girl he had seen but she had a sweet demeanor and seemed eager to please. Her father would not be the easiest man to deal with but, given that Sir Charles wanted respectability in Edinburgh society, Sir James felt that Sir Charles would be compliant in any marriage between the two young people.   •

The gold charger plates had been removed and Royal Doulton china soup bowls replaced them. Into these was poured oxtail soup, a robust start to the Christmas meal. After those dishes had been cleared, several footmen came in carrying tureens of vegetables and one very large turkey which was placed in front of Sir James. He admired the turkey, for indeed it was a large one, and he picked up a silver knife and fork and began the process of carving the turkey. Clearly, even though turkey was expensive, he had done this on several occasions as he was adept at carving it neatly. He placed the pieces onto a silver platter which a footman promptly took away and started serving the ladies. A Chippendale sideboard was the working surface for all the tureens and the footmen were swift in offering all the delicacies.

As the gentlemen and ladies settled into the meal, conversation flagged a little as they concentrated on their food. The pièce de résistance though was the Christmas pudding which Sir James had bought at Jenners, the new department store on Princes Street. It had opened with much acclaim earlier in the year and many compared it to Harrod's of London although it was significantly smaller. It had an atrium in the center of the store which opened to four higher levels. The standard of service was impeccable and it was favored by many in the town - those who could afford to shop there, that is.

The Jenners Christmas pudding was served on a silver platter and, as was traditional, was flamed for effect and taste. As the footmen apportioned the Christmas pudding and the accompanying brandy cream, Sir James beamed contentedly at his table and his guests. His face was reddened by the effects of the wine and the warmth of the occasion. His nose had been deformed by rosacea but in the candlelight you could see the vestiges of what had been a handsome face. Sir James was a man comfortable in his own skin. He recognized his own importance and influence in the city and for a few years he was enjoying the fruits of his labor.

As the guests finished the pudding, murmuring compliments to their host, the door opened again and the butler announced that the chief of police was waiting in the drawing room to speak to Sir James and Sir Charles. A trifle irritated by the interruption, Sir James decided that he would continue with his usual habit of a cigar and brandy with the gentlemen. The women left the dining room to allow the men to smoke in peace. Sir Charles was anxious to talk to the police chief but hesitated to ask Sir James to see that man now. Clearly the chief of police would have to wait until Sir James had finished his cigar.

The police chief waited not impatiently in the drawing room. He was used to dealing with Sir James and the other gentlemen of Edinburgh society and recognized that his time was not his own. They could not be hurried. Finally the group of men finished their brandies and cigars and Sir Charles was free to meet the police chief upon whom he delivered a very exact description of his watch and also what he thought might have happened to it. The police chief could offer sympathy and take notes but was unable to promise it would be found. Petty thievery was so common that there was far more than the chief and his men could cope with.

It was time then to meet with the ladies who were preparing a musical evening. Mary Mortimer was an accomplished pianist and she began the evening's entertainment with a selection of Chopin sonatas. Albert stayed close by her side and turned the pages at the appropriate time. He was clearly interested in Miss Mary. Even though the evening was marred for Sir Charles by the loss of his watch he was gratified to see that a suitable gentleman was showing interest in his daughter.

Eventually they could leave the home of their host. Usually Sir Charles would have been one of the last to leave but this time he was still preoccupied by the loss of the Longine and he really wanted to return home and be by himself for a while. When conversation was continuing around him he could forget the watch, but when he had to listen to Mary and the other ladies perform then his mind wandered, and the loss caught him afresh and as painfully as when he first realized he had lost the watch. Certainly the police chief offered no hope that it would be retrieved.

On the return route to their home Sir Charles and Miss Mary omitted the tour around the square which they had conducted on their departure. There was no point, no one was looking out of their windows at this time of night. Besides, Sir Charles wanted to ask his staff to search for the watch even though he knew in his heart it was a fruitless request.

CHAPTER 11

Meanwhile Ann and Edwin had completed their walk and headed back to Ann's home. It was already getting dark as they arrived. Edwin decided to spend only a few more minutes with the Berridges before returning home. He did not want to overstay his welcome. William reminded him that the following day was a holiday too and he had a Christmas box he wished to give Edwin, marking Edwin's first Christmas as an apprentice. Edwin, who was not expecting anything, was intrigued and pleased even more because it gave him opportunity to visit with Ann again. He bade his leave, patted Toby on the head as he was forced to climb over the cat's prostrate body, and he headed down the stone staircase and out on to Jamaica Street. Toby was clearly resting before a night of rat-catching.

This time Edwin's footsteps flew as he headed for Borthwick's Close. The best Christmas box he could receive from William was being allowed to court Ann. Nothing could top that! He headed back over the Mound and turned onto the High Street, finally reaching Borthwick's Close, which was surprisingly quiet that evening. As he opened the door of his flat he called out to Tim but no one replied. Tim must still be out. Not actually surprising as the two did not really talk much together and they led very separate lives. Other than having worked at the brewery together they were very different men.

It was early but Edwin decided to turn in for the night. He would prefer to save his few candles for another evening. Edwin and Tim shared a room and Edwin's bed was neatly made on the left side of the room. Tim's bed looked as though it had not been made for several days. Edwin was neat in appearance and habit and it disturbed him that his flatmate was so slovenly but Edwin could not afford to live on his own. As he lay in bed he wondered how he could even afford ever to marry Ann. Perhaps because of the long walk and his full stomach Edwin fell asleep easily and did not hear when Tim arrived a couple of hours later.

The next morning was fortunately another cold, crisp day and Edwin washed his face with the cold water he had pumped the previous day. He had a single small towel with which to dry. Years of combing his hair without a mirror meant that he had a lot of practice and he easily made smart his appearance. He had only one change of clothes and it was clean so he changed yesterday's clothes in which he had slept and put on a clean shirt and trousers.

Edwin prepared a bowl of porridge, poured a little milk which he had acquired from the cow in the Close, and he used the last of the sugar he had bought the previous week. He was glad that he had developed a liking for this Scottish dish as it was cheap and filling. He did not know when he would have another meal, although he suspected that the Berridges might at least offer him some tea and perhaps a piece of cake. He had seen Lillias Berridge preparing a Scotch

Christmas bun which seemed similar to an English Christmas cake. Mrs. Berridge had said however that traditionally they waited until New Year's Eve, Hogmanay, to eat it. It differed from the English cake as the latter had a layer of marzipan or almond paste on top and, in the most fancy cake shops, a layer of white icing too. The Scotch bun had lots of currants and spices but was wrapped in pastry.

Edwin was a dreamer. His mother had always worried about his daydreaming. It was not escapism for Edwin, it was just the pure delight of his imagination. In his imagination he could picture marrying Ann in her kirk, working as a watchmaker, lots of children, and a small house with plenty of food in the larder and nice clothes for Ann to wear. He wanted only the best for Ann and he certainly aspired to get it.

Pushing his thoughts aside as his mother had taught him to do, Edwin cleared away his spoon and bowl, finished his cup of tea and headed for the door. He noticed that Tim was on his bed on the other side of the room, sprawled across it, on his stomach, his hand clutching his pillow. His mouth was open slightly and, perhaps he was dreaming, as his mouth curved into a smile. This prompted Edwin to smile at Tim even though Tim could not recognize it.

Edwin closed the door quietly and headed for the Berridges. He wondered what the Christmas box from William would be. William was a dark horse; although he had the demeanor of a professional soldier, he was a kind man, considerate of others and had been training Edwin well. Edwin pondered anew why the two sons of William would favor working in a factory to working as a watchmaker. Oh well, their loss, my gain, thought Edwin.

He completed his walk briskly, grateful that for once the wind had died down on Princes Street and he could enjoy the exquisite scenery without having to worry about hanging onto his hat or jacket. He arrived at 15 Jamaica Street and once again encountered a rather sleepy Toby guarding the Berridges' front door. Knowing that Toby liked to have his ears stroked, Edwin bent down and fondled the young cat's head. Toby responded by stretching his neck so Edwin could chuck his chin. This made the cat's eyes close and settle into the moment. If Edwin wanted to chuck his chin all morning that would suit young Toby very well. Unfortunately for Toby, Edwin was anxious to see Ann and he gave Toby one last stroke, and then he straightened, pulled down his jacket into place and knocked on the door. Ann answered, obviously as eager to see him as he was her.

Mrs. Berridge appeared behind Ann and the two ushered him in. William was sitting in an armchair perusing the "Scotsman". The weekly newspaper was a luxury which William afforded himself and he excused his extravagance by reading about Edinburgh society. He felt in his business that he needed to keep up with the happenings of his clients. The fact that the newspaper was considered liberal and rather anti-Establishment did not escape him but it was something he could afford and he looked forward to its purchase every week.

As Edwin entered, William looked up, folded up his newspaper for safekeeping and asked after Edwin's welfare. "Very fine, sir, thank you," replied Edwin.

"Let's go downstairs for a moment to the workshop, I have something for you there," promised William. Edwin obediently followed and the two entered the workshop. It seemed rather cramped and stuffy this morning as it had been closed up for most of the last two days. William did not seem to notice though and reached for a small drawer in the cabinet on the back wall. He pulled out a mainspring winder, which was set in a small, red velvet box, and he gave it to Edwin saying, "Here's your Christmas box. Thank you for your service. You'll be needing this when you qualify as a watchmaker. It's your most important tool and I'd like to be the first to give you one."

Edwin was touched by the other man's generosity. Assembling what he would need to set up his own business would be expensive and this was a start. The two men used mainspring winders almost every day when they cleaned watches and at times replaced the mainsprings. At this time of year in particular, they handled many watches whose mainsprings had broken due to a change in temperature overnight. A watch could be fully wound one evening and by morning would have stopped because of the cold. In some older watches the mainspring became tired or set and the watches needed to be wound more and more frequently.

Edwin was delighted with the gift. "Why, thank you, Mr Berridge! I'll certainly have a lot of use for this. It will be a good start to my collection of instruments. I'll guard it carefully." At that, he put the mainspring winder back into its red velvet box and put it in his jacket pocket.

"How are you spending the rest of the day, Edwin?" enquired William with a small smile, as he guessed that Edwin would probably want to spend his free time with Ann. He guessed correctly as Edwin indicated that he wanted to go walking with Ann if she were free. Both men headed back upstairs and Ann was waiting to see Edwin. She knew already that her father was going to give a mainspring winder to Edwin but she wanted to know if Edwin was surprised and pleased with it. He assured her that he was and suggested that they take a walk.

It was still morning and they had several hours they could walk so Edwin suggested that they walk to the port at Leith to see the ships coming and going along the river. Rather surprised at the distance that they were going to walk but nevertheless happy to go with Edwin, Ann put on her coat and bonnet and the two left, Ann's arm firmly hooked into Edwin's elbow.

They headed from Jamaica Street to Queen Street into Picardy Place. There Ann suggested they rest for a moment on a park bench before heading down Leith Walk. She was rather glad that her parents did not know that she was going to Leith as it had a rather unsavory reputation. She felt safe with Edwin but dock areas always attracted rather unruly types. Men had been to sea for months and when they came home they wanted to drink and carouse and there were plenty of people who were willing to part them from their hard-earned cash.

From Edwin's point of view, he loved the sea. He was fascinated by the opportunities it offered to explore. A rather restless spirit, the sea promised fortune and chance. He tried to explain this to Ann.

"I've always liked the sea and ships," he confessed. "I was born far from it but I remember the first time I saw the sea at Hull and I knew then that I'd like to go somewhere by boat. I like the idea of the freedom it offers. I think I would have liked to be an early explorer but now the world has been discovered and there is nowhere left to go. Let's go and watch the ships being unloaded. I like the sounds and the smells of the cargo. It makes me feel that I am in a foreign place even though I'm only in Scotland - which is foreign for me," he said, with a wink.

Ann laughed for he was indeed a foreigner in Scotland. Edwin liked to hear her laugh. She did it often and her laugh and joy in life spread to everyone around her, he had noticed.

Ann had never pictured herself as living anywhere else but Edinburgh. She loved her home city and could not imagine going to live in England, much less to another country, even if it were a British colony. She said this to Edwin, who paused and considered how different they were. By this point though he was so much in love with Ann that he did not consider the differences consequential. After all, they still had to work out the kirk issues.

Edwin knew that Ann wanted him to go to the kirk with her on Sunday. He did not mind doing this occasionally, although he preferred the Church of England trappings with the rich tapestries, brocades, and ornate garments of the clergy. He liked the stained glass windows and the dark lighting. It made one feel peaceful and almost timeless as you recognized that you were just a small part of a large scheme of things. In old churches you could think of all those who had worshipped before you and realize that others would follow you too in worship. It made Edwin feel almost as small as he did when he looked up into the sky and could not count all the stars he could see. He had learned to identify many but he knew there were some he could only see with one of the large telescopes from the Observatory.

The Church of Scotland was austere by comparison. The clergy wore drab clothing, the altar cloths were of plain material, and the churches were devoid of significant decoration. They preached predestination and predetermination, both of which Edwin did not completely understand, although he worried in some way that because he did not understand it he might not be included in whatever group they felt counted in. He would go to church with Ann the following Sunday though, but he was not about to make it a habit, even for Ann.

Finally they arrived at the docks and were fortunate enough to find a bench on which to sit and watch activities on the quayside. A clipper was docked alongside their bench. Edwin had not seen one before; he had heard of them, of course, as they were used to bring tea from China and they were renowned for their speed and sleek appearance. The sails were furled at the moment as it had recently docked and its sailors were in the process of unloading their cargo, which appeared to be tea chests. Edwin wondered how it would feel to be on such a sailing vessel, headed for China, with the sails at full mast and a breeze across the deck. That was of course the romantic version, he knew, as the sailors who were unloading the tea were clearly muscular and that came from physically hard labor. No, Edwin decided, life was better here with Ann and the promise of a great career.

CHAPTER 12

Tim awoke just after 11 o'clock in the morning, a couple of hours after Edwin had left. He noticed that Edwin had tidied up their room and made his bed before he left. Tim was grateful for Edwin and his neatness; he just could not maintain that lifestyle himself.

Tim had spent the previous evening looking for Charlie, the fence he hoped would buy the watch. This had required a visit to several pubs along Rose Street, not really a hardship for Tim. There was always the promise of a drink from Charlie as a tip if Charlie really liked the watch.

He met up with Charlie in "The Black Cat", one of his favorite pubs on Rose Street. Charlie had been standing at the bar chatting to the barmaid, a rather tired and overworked older brunette, who was clearly enjoying the attention from Charlie. Working in a pub gave her a lot of male attention, particularly as ladies did not frequent her establishment, which meant that most of the time she had no competition. As Tim walked up, the barmaid barely acknowledged his presence and continued smiling at Charlie, licking her lips slightly.

Charlie however recognized Tim and could easily guess his business. He ordered a drink for Tim, "A glass of stout for my young friend here," he said, "And have one for yourself." The barmaid served Tim and then set aside the money for the drink for her as she already had a glass of ale. "Cheers," she said, sipping on the ale.

Tim and Charlie went to sit in a corner of the pub and after a few minutes of idle chit-chat Tim introduced the subject of the watch.

"I've a watch here you may want to buy," he began, pulling out the Longine from his pocket. Charlie knew better than to ask where Tim had acquired the watch. Such questions were never appropriate in his line of work. He sat with his back to the rest of the room so no one else would notice what he was doing; he began then to examine the watch. He was impressed by the clear face and numerals and the fine black pointers. The silver engraved face with the design of a soldier was distinctive and was easily identifiable but he knew too that in the right hands this watch could bring him a lot of money. He noticed it was Swiss-made too which made it particularly desirable. He was excited by the opportunity but he also knew the watch was recognizable and would need just the right buyer so he hesitated for a while, which only served to increase Tim's anxiety. It also permitted Charlie to lower the price he would pay for the watch when he noticed Tim nervously scratching his pock-marked face.

Finally he made an offer of one pound for the watch. Tim had hoped for more but he was only making five pounds a month at the brewery and right now he could use the pound. He gladly accepted the proffered pound note; Charlie on the other hand tried to control his smile as he knew the watch would fetch ten pounds in the right hands. Charlie was used to dealing with people who were short of money. He knew that if he flashed the money before their eyes they could not resist. He pushed his lank, greasy hair out of his face, tipped up his beer and took a long draught. That enabled him to hide his satisfaction on the transaction. Then, after rubbing his rather long, thin nose, he absent-mindedly picked at a pimple that was beginning to erupt on his chin. He was considering how he was going to sell the watch. It would certainly be a specialized purchaser, someone who was, or had been, a soldier. Had been, he thought, as a current soldier certainly couldn't afford such a fine watch.

Charlie looked at the barmaid at the counter who was looking in his direction. He had been enjoying his conversation with her and so he said to Tim, "You had best be off now, it's best not to be seen together."

Tim was a little disappointed as he would have liked to savor his stout for a while longer and perhaps chat to Charlie, but he realized what was interesting Charlie so he quickly finished his pint and headed out the door. He could always go to another pub and spend a few pennies for another pint. He would try and get some food today too. It had been a while since he had eaten well. Charlie meanwhile took up his position at the bar, his mind half on the watch, half on the low-cut dress of the barmaid.

CHAPTER 13

William Berridge studied the watch on the table in front of him and then reached in his desk drawer for a mainspring. Much of his repair work involved replacing mainsprings. As he was reaching into the drawer the front door of the workshop opened. He looked up, expecting it to be Edwin whom he had sent on an errand to return a repaired watch, and he was surprised to see a stranger standing there. They did not get a lot of walk-in business, much of his work had been developed by word-of-mouth.

The stranger was medium height, dressed in a shabby frock coat which had seen better days. Covering his rather lank and greasy hair was a cloth cap, which had also seen better days. Having captured William's attention, immediately the young man advanced into the room, reaching into his pocket to remove a silver pocket watch.

"I have a watch here which I would like to sell, or perhaps you can tell me of someone who might be interested in it," said Charlie.

William took the watch and was startled to see it was a Longine which fitted the exact description of Sir Charles Mortimer's which he had repaired last autumn. He had returned it to Sir Charles at the end of October. It was now January 15 and the watch was clearly running and showed the time to be 11:14 a.m. Still running well, thought William, but of course it should be.

"Where did you get this watch?" he enquired, rather dreading the answer.

"Not quite sure, had it a while," said Charlie. "I buy and sell things to try and make a little money."

Berridge thought fast. He was sure it was the same watch he had repaired a few months ago. He did not want to buy the watch but he did not want to lose it either. He needed to check with Sir Charles Mortimer and see if in fact he had lost his watch.

"I will need a little time. I can't buy the watch myself right now, but I may have a buyer for you," he suggested. Charlie looked wary and asked if he could have the potential buyer's name. William swiftly said, "I'm sorry I can't give you that as my clients are very private people but I will check with him immediately and, if you can come back tomorrow, then I will have an answer for you then."

Charlie was not pleased with the answer but he felt he had no choice either. He had had the watch for three weeks and it had proved harder to dispose of than he had imagined. He normally would not have even asked this watchmaker to buy it but he was getting desperate and needed to sell it. He agreed that he would return at noon the following day. He would not give William the watch however so William pretended to take some notes about the style and quality of the watch. He also jotted down the watch's serial number, and then he returned it to Charlie, asking at the same time for Charlie's name.

Charlie answered, "Charlie McBain, at your service." Then Charlie headed out the door leaving William in something of a quandary.

A few minutes later Edwin Turner arrived to find William still at his desk, looking somewhat troubled. William explained the issue. Keeping meticulous notes of all the watches he repaired, William had checked the serial number of Charlie's watch against the serial number of Sir Charles' watch. Edwin remembered the watch too as that had been the watch which sparked his interest in watchmaking. He had also returned it to Sir Charles after it had been repaired. He offered to speak to Sir Charles but William felt this was a matter of urgency and importance with which only he should deal, so William left Edwin in charge of the shop while he headed to Charlotte Square to see Sir Charles.

On arriving at Sir Charles' house the butler rebuffed him, suggesting that he use the tradesman's entrance. Stiffly Berridge reported that he had seen a watch which may have belonged to Sir Charles. Swiftly the door opened and Berridge was allowed to enter but had to linger in the vestibule. He amused himself by examining the portraits of Sir Charles' ancestors which adorned the walls. There were fewer than usual in such a home, as Sir Charles had only recently come into money and prominence. Idly William wondered if the portraits were in fact of Sir Charles' family or if he had merely bought paintings to decorate his walls. He recognized one of Miss Mary, Sir Charles' daughter, and the artist had clearly done a fine job of highlighting her best feature which was her high cheekbones, and he had minimized the size of her rather protruding teeth.

The butler disappeared into the library and a few minutes later William was ushered into that room where he found Sir Charles sitting behind a massive desk littered with papers. The walls were lined, as William would have expected, with leather-bound books, many of them sets, probably mostly unread. He was aware that it was fashionable to have a library and stock it with classics yet few actually read the books.

Sir Charles opened, "Well, Mr. Berridge. I did not expect to see you. I understand from Edwards that you have seen a watch which may be mine. My watch was stolen in fact on Christmas Day. I reported it to the police chief but he had little hope of finding it. Where did you see it?"

William recounted the details of the man who had entered his shop and also the details of the watch, and finished by saying that he had compared the serial numbers and he had in fact seen Sir Charles' watch. Sir Charles was momentarily displeased that Berridge had not bought the watch as Sir Charles just wanted back his watch. On reflection though, he hoped that the thief could be caught and he decided to let the police chief know and perhaps Charlie could be caught red-handed tomorrow. The two men agreed that a policeman could hide in William's workshop and Charlie McBain would then be caught red-handed.

After William Berridge headed back to his shop, Sir Charles had his butler, Edwards, contact the police chief who, knowing that Sir Charles was a friend of Sir James Forrest, came speedily to Charlotte Square. They arranged to have a policeman in the workshop in the morning.

William Berridge was nervous about the arrangement but he had a keen sense of right and wrong. Even though he had no personal liking for Sir Charles whom he found arrogant and rather unpleasant to deal with, he did not want to see a thief go unscathed.

The next morning a policeman duly arrived and stood behind the door leading from the workshop up the stairs to the Berridge residence. Edwin quietly worked in a corner but was a witness to the whole event. At five minutes to twelve the shop front door opened and in walked Charlie McBain. Berridge and McBain greeted each other and exchanged pleasantries while Berridge wiped his hands and then reached for the Longine watch.

"I do have someone who would like to buy it and he has authorized me to buy it for him," began William. Charlie broke into a smile, but nervously picked at a couple of his pimples. One started to ooze and he pulled out a very dirty handkerchief to mop it. He had been fencing stolen goods for several years but it still made him anxious.

"He will pay you five pounds for the watch," continued William.

That was a little less than Charlie expected. However as he was now desperate to sell the watch he said, "That's fine, do you have the money now?"

"Yes, here it is," said William, reaching into his desk drawer and pulling out five crisp one-pound notes. Just as Charlie took them, the policeman stepped out, truncheon firmly in his right hand. At the sight of him Charlie dropped the money and headed for the door but Edwin was already there to impede his exit. A quick blow to the head from the truncheon and Charlie fell to the floor in a daze.

It had previously been agreed that William Berridge would deliver the watch and the five pounds back to Sir Charles Mortimer. After Charlie and the policeman had left for the police station, Edwin was left in charge of the shop again and William headed for Sir Charles Mortimer's house. This time he was not chastised for standing on the front door stoop and he was promptly escorted to see Sir Charles in the library. Sir Charles genially offered William a sherry which he declined. He then gave William a half crown for his trouble and thanked him profusely. It had been a successful day all round.

At the end of the day Edwin headed for home. He was not seeing Ann this evening as she was working and he was tired. Perhaps he could catch up on sleep. However, upon returning to Borthwick's Close, he found a crowd of people milling around in the courtyard. He noticed that most of the kerfuffle was actually coming from the flat he shared with Tim.

Before he could get to his door, Tim came out, handcuffed from behind, accompanied by a peeler.

Edwin tried to stop them but the peeler was not interested in lingering in the Close. He never knew when the crowd would turn unfriendly and defend "one of their own". Edwin tried to find out what had happened and the peeler would not answer but several in the crowd commented that Tim had stolen a watch from Sir Charles Mortimer. In a flash Edwin realized what had happened. Tim must have stolen the watch, fenced it to Charlie who then showed up at William Berridge's workshop. Charlie had obviously tried to pass on the blame by naming Tim. Edwin had known that Tim had a very secret life. The two had lived together but not shared confidences; it was solely an economic arrangement. He could not help but feel sorry for Tim though. Prison time was very harsh, transportation even worse. Justice often seemed more harsh than the crime committed.

Edwin walked into his flat but was detained by a policeman who was in the process of searching it. Edwin was momentarily upset that the policeman would do that without waiting to ask him but he knew better than to cross the policeman and he sat at his little wooden table while the policeman looked through Tim's things. Neither boy had many possessions and in a brief two minutes the search was complete with nothing else being found. Edwin was relieved at this but tried not to reflect his anxiety to the policeman. Perhaps the fact that Tim had nothing else here might lighten his sentence and he could claim it was a first offense, although Edwin rather suspected that was not true.

Fortunately for Tim, Edwin knew that records of crimes were not easily transferred from one parish to another and if he had stolen other things elsewhere the police might not have access to that information. His concern now was that the crime might warrant a public hanging. Edwin had witnessed one of these in Nottingham when he was six and he could still clearly remember it. His parents had taken him along as an encouragement not to commit crime himself; they wanted him to see the possible end result.

Edwin, even as a young child, was aghast at the carnival-like atmosphere of the hanging. Literally thousands came to watch it. The church bells tolled as the cart carrying the condemned man entered the square. As the man, dressed in a new white suit and white gloves, descended from the tumbril, the crowd roared in approval. This was a good morning's entertainment, an event worth getting up for. As the condemned man requested to say a few words the watching rabble hushed momentarily. They were there to support one of their own. Some had even brought flowers to throw at the condemned man. From what Edwin understood from his father, the man had merely stolen a few shillings. For this he received a death sentence. The good thing was, according to Edwin's father, that hanging was becoming less popular, partly because it was not preventive in stopping crimes. People were not horrified by the gallows, perhaps because it was traditional that the condemned person did not reflect his fear and dressed in finery for the occasion.

The alternative though, Edwin knew, was transportation and that brought its own share of problems. He could not imagine which would be worse, to be hanged or to be condemned to a life 14,000 miles from home without hope of return. The living conditions, work, and even the sailing to Australia were all deplorable. In his heart as a young child Edwin determined that he would never put himself into a position such as Tim had arrived in today.

By taking young Edwin to a hanging, Edwin's father had achieved exactly what he wanted - a distaste and fear of the Law.

CHAPTER 14

Edwin did not sleep much that night. Tim being taken away had filled most of his thoughts. The other residents of the Close hung around outside for a while and a few questioned Edwin about Tim but by and large no one was particularly surprised or upset by Tim's actions. The wealthier people called Tim and his kind the "criminal class" as if it were something that fitted into society, somewhere even lower than working class. Certainly there were enough poor people involved in criminal activities to categorize them in that way.

Edwin tried not to worry about what would happen to Tim. There was nothing he could do for him anyway. His two main worries now were telling Mr. Berridge that his flatmate had been the perpetrator; he hoped William did not imagine that he was of the same ilk. He would have to explain to William that they shared a room but not a friendship. How Ann would react worried him too.

His next concern was for his flat. He needed to share it with another young man, or perhaps two. He could not pay for the rent on his own and he did not want to leave it or share it with others. He knew that some in the Close shared ten people to a room and Edwin valued his privacy more than that, even if he had to spend a few more pence.

Round and round these thoughts spun in his head and he tossed until daybreak. Sometimes he missed his parents and his other family members so much. He had learned so much from his uncle and his uncle's boss. Edwin knew he had been more fortunate than many of the young people he saw working in Nottingham. He had seen many young children, ten years old or even younger, working long hours in factories or in the nearby potteries. They had no childhood, the hours were very long, the food limited, and the treatment from the factory owners was frequently cruel.

Edwin had been fortunate to get an education through his uncle's employer, Mr. Thomas Henderson. That gentleman recognized the benefit of education and he allowed Edwin to join the classes that a governess provided Mr. Henderson's son. The two boys had been close friends and Edwin was very protected from a regular childhood for someone of his social class. However, now that Edwin was older, Mr. Henderson had no position for Edwin. With kindness he gave him some money and food for his trip and gave Edwin advice on where to go.

Finally Edwin gave up, deciding that more sleep would be impossible that night. He realized that he had no food in the flat, not even milk. Another day without a decent breakfast. Edwin did not really worry too much about that. Sometimes Ann Berridge would offer him some fresh-made bread. He thought her bread was almost as good as the bread his mother had made. He thought back to his mother and her bread baking. She had a white metal dish in which she raised the dough. She always made brown bread and he had loved to watch her knead the bread. She was so strong and she kneaded the bread so efficiently. Afterwards she would cover the dough with a damp white linen cloth and she would put the dough in its dish to rise on the hearth in front of the fire. Anxiously he would wait for the process to be finished so he could sink his teeth into the thick crust. It tasted hot and yeasty and worth waiting for.

Cutting off thoughts of his family as that only made him sad, Edwin focused on the day ahead. He wondered how he could explain Tim's situation to William. William tended to see things in black and white, and this would make it difficult for Edwin to explain Tim's situation. Best to get it over with. He wondered if William would consider him guilty by association. He thought not but he was still learning to assess William Berridge.

Hastening to work he determined he would be at his post early, partly in the hope of catching a glimpse of Ann but also because he still wanted to impress William. Edwin liked this job, and he needed it too. So he was already working when William entered the shop. William looked a little surprised but said nothing.

Not able to sit on the news any longer Edwin just blurted out, "You remember Sir Charles Mortimer's watch yesterday?" "Of course," said William rather drily. He was aging but was not that old!

"When I got home last night," and at this point Edwin faltered. William looked askance at him and waited for him to continue.

"My flatmate has been arrested for stealing that watch!"

Now even William, who had been trained in war to not be phased by anything, looked shocked. He knew Edwin had a flatmate but Edwin never talked about him and he assumed they were merely sharing a flat for economic reasons. There appeared to be no real friendship between them. Nevertheless he was a little surprised and disturbed that Edwin had selected to share a flat with a thief. It did not reflect well on Edwin's judgment. Nevertheless, controlled in all his words and actions, William waited for Edwin to continue.

"I had no idea that is what he did. The police searched my flat but found nothing else stolen. I don't know how it happened. I saw Tim being taken away on the police wagon. I didn't have a chance to talk to him. I'm hoping that the police just made a mistake."

"Unfortunately there is no mistake. The man who tried to fence the watch with me yesterday gave the thief's name to the police. It does not look good for your friend."

"No, he's not my friend, he's just my flatmate. I met him when I was working in the brewery and I needed someone to split the rent with."

"What will you do now? "

"I'm not sure. Perhaps I should just find other lodging as I can't afford to keep that flat on my own."

William was quiet then and the two men continued to work. At lunchtime Edwin decided to step outside and William went to have lunch with Lillias Berridge who had as usual prepared a decent lunch for William. She always managed to take care of his stomach even when money was in short supply.

William pondered over Edwin's predicament for a moment, long enough that Lillias recognized that he had a problem. William was usually taciturn; he always thought through what he wanted to say before he said it. Finally he briefly told Ann about Edwin's predicament and then asked Lillias her opinion about Edwin. He expressed his concern about the company Edwin was keeping but, in fairness, indicated that Edwin and Tim appeared to only have a business arrangement in cohabitation.

Meanwhile Lillias had heard all manner of good things about Edwin from Ann and therefore she was sympathetic towards Edwin. William then continued, "You know he has to find a new flatmate or a new place to live. Do you perhaps think we could put him up here, at least for a while? He could sleep on a cot in the corner of the shop."

Lillias was never surprised by her husband these days. That is what came of being married for so long. She merely commented, "It's your workshop, your inconvenience. I think perhaps you should charge him a little rent, but a reasonable amount. If he decides to get married he will need to have all the money he can get."

William, being somewhat wise in the ways of women, knew exactly where that conversation was leading. He liked Edwin and would not be disappointed with him as a son-in-law, but these things take time, he decided. He therefore chose to ignore Lillias' comment and merely said that he would talk to Edwin that day.

So the matter was settled. Edwin was more than delighted that he could spend time closer to Ann of whom he was becoming more fond with each passing day. He liked the idea of sleeping on the premises and that he would no longer have to walk to work. At the end of the day he walked home and went to see his landlord who was less than pleased that he was losing a good payer. Edwin agreed to stay through the weekend and the two parted company.

On Sunday Edwin moved out of Old Town and into New Town and his life with the Berridges began.

CHAPTER 15

Tim had a fairly sleepless night. He spent it in jail, and he found he could not sleep because of anxiety for his situation and too because his cellmates were restless sleepers. One was a drunk who lay in the corner, oblivious to his urine-sodden clothes, snoring loudly. It would be a while before he knew where he had spent the night. Another young boy, clearly arrested for the first time, sobbed in another corner. The regular criminals ignored him. It was time for him to grow up. Yet another man paced the cell, unable to sleep. The cell, nine feet wide by fifteen feet, was full and there was no adequate place to sleep. Tim arrived after the one meal of the day had been served; he was hungry, but he was no stranger to that.

Tim pondered his situation. It was not his first contact with the police, but he was worried this time. He knew that the watch was valuable and, even though it had been returned to its rightful owner, the crime was considered serious. He was sure that the rich man from whom he stole the watch would be influential in determining the punishment he would receive. They were all the same, these so-called upper classes. The man had been something of a dandy. The watch probably meant little to him but that would not stop him from insisting on prosecution and severe punishment. Given Tim already had a criminal record it did not bode well for him. He knew he needed to recognize that at best he might be heading for

Australia in the next few months. At worst, hanging was a possibility too although these days it was not so common a punishment for petty theft.

Silently he considered his options. There were not any. He could only hope for a lenient trial. After all, there was no violence involved which would certainly guide a judge's thoughts when sentencing. He was young too and that would influence the judge's decision as to the nature of his sentence. He was young enough to be sent to Australia. He was 'the right age' for transportation. If he had to go to Australia he could live with that even though the conditions were horrendous. He knew that, once there, there would be no return for him. That is, if he made it through the long voyage, confined to the prison deck, subjected to brutality, little food and water, a lot of work, and plenty of dysentery and disease too.

Once in Australia, he knew that the prisoners were subjected to violence from the natives and, of course, from their captors. Definitely no picnic. The upper classes were not backward in letting the lower classes know what was in store for them if they misbehaved, and indeed it was a deterrent to crime. Justice was not meted out fairly and Tim knew that he could not expect it. If convicts could be sent to Australia then it removed the need for prisons in Britain, removed the perpetrators of crime forever and provided labor for wealthier employers. Such thoughts required more thinking than Tim was capable of, and he applied his time to thinking of how to escape or evade the pending punishment.

Right now he faced arraignment. At least he would know what would happen to him. He worried about getting food. He had little money and needed it to buy bread, water and, of course, gin from the warder. He knew he might be held there a long time. The gaolers were not anxious to feed their prisoners as lack of food after several days silenced most prisoners' complaints. If they died it was unimportant to them as they could sell the bodies to the local medical school and even get paid five pounds for it. It certainly did not entice most warders to take care of their prisoners well.

At that moment, Tim heard a clanking of keys at the cell door and then it opened to reveal two warders. They were armed with bludgeons and filled the doorway with their size.

"McGregor!" one of them called out. Although a fairly common name, Tim was the only one bearing it or willing to claim it. He stepped out and they led him down a long hallway, up two flights of stairs, and he was momentarily shocked by sunshine. He had only been in prison a day but he had already started to forget what the outside was like. The wind was bracing and despite the sunshine the day was very cold.

Tim was pushed onto a heavy wagon pulled by two large horses. There were already several others in the wagon. Tim had seen this before, indeed had experienced it as it was not his first brush with the law. There was no place to sit and so he stood and tried to maintain his balance as the wagon rolled slowly over the cobbled streets. Tim was not sure where he was headed but expected it to be the Sheriff's Court which usually handled cases like his. He would be given his choice of a trial by jury of fifteen people, or he could accept the judgment of the Sheriff. Tim, being somewhat simple, could not imagine putting his future into the hands of fifteen people. He thought he might stand a more sympathetic response from the Sheriff, although he would not be able to tell you how he came to that conclusion. He just knew he wanted his situation to end.

Slowly the wagon rolled along the Royal Mile and there were the usual selection of gawkers. Tim did not recognize anyone but tried to keep his eyes downward so he did not have to look at the passersby. Eventually the wagon swung into a large courtyard behind which was a fine Georgian-style building with archways, one of which marked the entry. On coming to a stop, Tim was hustled off the wagon and then had to wait outside a courtroom. He contented himself by looking over the other miscreants. They were a typical bunch, he would say. Some clearly had come in from the country, yet others looked like tradesmen. All looked unshaven and dirty.

Finally it was Tim's turn to enter the courtroom. He was momentarily taken aback by the opulence. Even to Tim's untrained eye he could recognize fine carving and furniture. The Sheriff himself sat in a long, bright scarlet robe, adorned with a shoulder-length grey powdered wig. On a day like today it would feel comfortable, Tim thought, conscious that he'd lost his cloth cap in the fracas last night. He was escorted to the dock and there his shackles were removed but there were guards close by to prevent his possible escape.

The Sheriff looked down at papers and did not even look up as Tim walked in. He then pushed his glasses down his nose so he could look over the top of them, and he stated to Tim the crime of which he was accused - grand theft. Tim was dismayed at this. He had hoped that the crime, which was really pickpocketing, would be considered petty theft. The watch must have been worth more than he had anticipated. His heart sank as, if he were convicted, then he would most certainly go to Australia.

"What do you plead?" barked the Sheriff, looking at Tim with distaste. Tim, by now, feeling no hope, decided that if he pleaded guilty that his sentence might be lighter.

"Guilty, Your Honor," he said without rancor.

"I see that you have been convicted of picking pockets on three previous occasions. Do you have anything to say for yourself?"

"I am very sorry, Milord. I did not mean to do it. It just happened."

At this the Sheriff snorted, scratched his wig as if it itched, and said, "No point in having a trial. You've already admitted it. I will remand you to the hulks, pending transportation to New South Wales, Australia."

At that, Tim was escorted out of the courtroom, dismissed by the Sheriff and by the rest of the world too. No one to notice that this had even happened to him and no one who would care. Even Edwin would not follow up on what happened to him. Tim's family had no interest. You took your chances in this life and if it meant imprisonment or banishment, so be it.

Tim was returned to the prison where he had been held overnight and he stayed there only a few days before being transferred to a hulk as the prison was already overcrowded.

Most of the hulks were docked outside London at Woolwich or Chatham, although there were some at Portsmouth and Plymouth too. He was unsure where he was to be assigned although he had heard that prisoners bound for Australia went to hulks in Portsmouth or to Millbank in London. Tim had not seen a hulk and neither was he desirous to do so. Tales of conditions on the hulks were legend.

As the prison population grew in Britain, the need for more prisons grew too, and Parliament had decided to house prisoners on abandoned Navy warships until the prisoners could be transported to America and then, in more recent years, to Australia. Since American Independence the new so-called Americans would no longer accept British prisoners. They saw no purpose in trying to integrate convicted felons into their new country and so Australia and

Van Diemen's Land, an island off the south-east coast of Australia, became the new home for thousands of criminals. Meanwhile, as these prisoners waited their turn to leave they were housed for years on the hulks. The hulks were no longer seaworthy, some of the masts and rigging were missing, but they could still float.

Several days passed before Tim found out where he was headed. He learned one morning that he would be transferred to London later that day as he was assigned to HMS *Euryalus*, docked at Chatham. He hoped life would be better there than the jail where he was now housed but he suspected it would not. He was right.

CHAPTER 16

January slipped into February and Edwin settled into his new life at 15 Jamaica Street. The move from Borthwick's Close had been an easy one although he still worried a little about Tim and wondered how he was coping. They had not been good friends yet it gave Edwin pause to think of Tim and how their lives which had intersected briefly had gone in such totally different directions.

He commented on this one morning with William Berridge as they worked companionably together. William was a very good mentor and Edwin was a willing student. He could already see the advantages of having a respectable trade which could support him for life.

"I met a friend from the brewery the other day when I was out walking," Edwin began. William waited, but indicated that Edwin had his attention.

"He knew Tim. You remember my flatmate Tim who stole that watch," he reminded William.

"He said that Tim had pleaded guilty and that he was remanded to a hulk before he went to Australia. Said he was on the HMS *Euryalus*." Edwin struggled a bit with the name as it was so unusual.

At this William looked up, somewhat surprised. "I know that ship," he said. "It was in the Battle of Trafalgar; in fact it was Admiral Collingwood's flagship for a while."

He then explained to Edwin what a flagship was as Edwin had never been in the military. He then proceeded to tell Edwin a little of life on the hulks. William was something of a man of the world and had met many different kinds of folk in the military and with his watchmaking.

"The hulks are Navy warships which have been decommissioned. I'm sorry that Tim has ended up there as I've heard that life is terrible on them. The ships are docked near London, close enough that the prisoners are taken off each day to work. Not sure what they all do but some are used to dredge the Thames. They are very overcrowded though. They've even added rooms like turrets to them. It's a wonder they don't sink as they are so top heavy but they do the job. No one can escape from them. I've heard it's even worse than being in prison as so many people are sick with dysentery. There's typhoid and scurvy too. I've heard that sometimes a body may lie dead on one of those ships for days until it's thrown over the side. It doesn't even count as time served either. Until you get to Australia the clock doesn't even begin to start ticking."

William smiled a little at his own joke, as he continued working on a pocket watch.

Edwin remained silent for a while. He was secretly horrified by William's description and privately grateful that he had escaped such a life. One thing was for sure, he was not about to pick a pocket, however fine a watch might be in it!

At this moment Ann entered the room. She was bringing tea for them. They did not stop their work; after all, William was a businessman and time was money. Edwin had even been surprised that he had talked so long today although William's hands had never stopped working.

William had other children but Ann was his favorite. He was pleased to see the secret glances the two young people had for each other. Ann could do worse than marry someone like Edwin, and maybe Edwin could take on this business in a few years. That would not make William or Lillias unhappy and would guarantee a secure life for Ann.

Edwin was becoming increasingly fond of Ann. As an Englishman he had been trained not to express his emotions much but he assumed that he perhaps loved Ann. Certainly whenever she walked in the room his heart leapt a little and he had a hard time not smiling all the time. He had noticed however that she had that effect on everybody. He suspected though that he was perhaps the only one who knew that she kissed sweetly and blushed prettily when he complimented her. He had few chances to kiss her, only when they walked to the docks at Leith to see the ships. Yet it really was not proper to kiss in public so he had only managed to kiss her in the stairwell at 15 Jamaica Street, risking discovery at any time by her parents. Doing anything beyond kissing before he married her seemed unlikely given the strict upbringing she had. He hoped though that if he married her he would find her as passionate for him as he was for her. Her kisses had promise and thrilled him.

Easter fell late this year, on April 16. Edwin had set that date in his mind as a wedding date. He did not want to rush things but he felt that Ann was of similar mind and the following Sunday he planned to ask her to marry him. He worried a little how he could support a wife, much less a family, but he felt that within the secure environment that the Berridges provided that it would work out all right. He did not care for children much but knew already that Ann wanted to have a large family and he wanted to give her what she wanted. Children seemed to come along whether you wanted them or not. You just learned to deal with them as they appeared. He thought Ann would make a wonderful mother. She would be gentle and loving, just as his own mother had been. He was sure that his mother would have liked his choice of woman.

Sunday came along but it was stormy so Edwin and Ann decided to cut short their walk to the docks and stop in at a little teashop they knew in one of the side streets from St. Andrew Square. It was warm and cozy and the tea was cheap. The waitress did not mind how long they sat together as there was not much business that day. Edwin had saved a few pennies and decided to splurge on an iced currant bun which he knew Ann particularly liked.

He began, a little hesitantly, "Ann, I've been wondering....we enjoy each other's company, I believe." He stopped for a moment and looked at her face trying to read what she was thinking, but she was giving nothing away.

"What I am trying to say is, perhaps we should set up house together."

"You mean live together? I don't want to do that!"

"No, of course not. I would not ask that of you. I mean to get married. I've saved a little of the money your Da has been paying me and I can get the marriage license. I will even get married in your kirk, if you wish. I just want to be married to you. You mean the world to me, Ann."

By now Edwin had been far more expressive than he had probably ever been in his life and he became silent.

"Yes, I will marry you," said Ann, and then giggled. "I always thought though that I'd marry a Scot who would wear a kilt when we got married. I suppose I shall just have to accept that you will wear breeks!"

Edwin had been in Scotland long enough to know that breeks meant britches to the rest of the world and he laughed too.

"Easter is April 16. Perhaps we could marry then," ventured Edwin.

"I'm not sure. That can be a busy day at the kirk. It would be nice though as there would probably be some flowers in the kirk already. It doesn't matter though. I have some ideas about a wedding dress."

Edwin laughed again as he knew already that Ann, as a seamstress, had made several wedding gowns. He also knew that was something about which young girls dreamed, along with their mothers. He personally did not understand the fuss but because he loved Ann he would tolerate whatever she wanted for a wedding. It was just another day to him.

He impulsively kissed her in the teashop and then explained to the waitress that they planned to marry, they were now engaged. She was rather dour but congratulated them politely. Finishing their tea quickly they decided to head for Jamaica Street to break the news to Ann's parents.

CHAPTER 17

Sunday, April 16, was an unusually warm day for April in Edinburgh. Edwin had spent the previous evening with a casual friend from the brewery as he knew that Ann thought it unlucky to see the bridegroom before her arrival at the church. They had both met with the minister who had talked at some length to Edwin about his faith, or lack of it. He was firmly admonished and given guidance on how to treat Ann but in the end Edwin turned over his half crown, the minister accepted it, and the wedding was set for the afternoon of April 16.

The venue for the wedding was St. Andrew's Church on the north side of George Street. The minister, John Bruce, was about to retire but he agreed to perform the service as one of his last tasks at that church. He had known Ann Berridge for several years and was fond of her, hence his rather stern admonishments to Edwin. There were few in attendance as Edwin had no relatives and he knew few people in Edinburgh. William was a conservative spender and he saw no purpose in splurging on his daughter's wedding. He was very aware that it was not the wedding that counted in a marriage, it was the year-in, year-out tedium that solidified a marriage.

Ann had been happy to make her own dress of pink muslin. It had a long tapered waist, puffy long sleeves and a demure high collar. It was trimmed with tulle around the neckline and the sleeves. Ann knew she looked pretty in the gown and she beamed with pleasure at her own reflection before she left her house for the church.

Lillias was thrilled and excited for her daughter and she had spent the previous evening informing Ann on what to expect on her wedding night and how to respond to her husband. Because Ann had lived in very close quarters with her parents for many years she was not surprised by the information but she listened attentively to her mother. She was not one to ever contradict her mother.

As Ann entered the church with her father she looked at it as though she were visiting it for the first time. It was a beautiful building with a tall bell tower and spire. The church was classical in design but what was magnificent in particular was the ceiling with its large rosettes. The air was cool and tranquil. Edwin looked apprehensive as she entered the door but as soon as she started to walk down the aisle he brightened and smiled happily as she approached him.

William gave away his daughter and walked rather stiffly back to where Lillias was already seated. Every inch the soldier, he was intent on standing tall even though his back was hurting him. Too many hours sitting at that bench, he thought. Hopefully he could cut back his work soon as Edwin learned more about watchmaking.

The minister concluded the brief wedding service. Both bride and groom were disappointed by the brevity. Ann wanted the service to last forever so she could treasure the memory of that day. She enjoyed the coolness and beauty of the building and enjoyed her wedding outfit which she had so painstakingly made. Behind her she could sense her mother smiling. Lillias had been happy in her marriage and wanted the same for her daughter. She thought that Edwin would make a good husband. He was willing to work, willing to learn, was respectful to all the Berridges and treated Ann with tenderness.

Edwin was finally able to kiss his bride, although it was only a brief kiss. There would be more later but propriety required that he give her only the briefest of kisses now. Mrs. Edwin Turner smiled shyly at her parents and they came and hugged her. After signing the license and registry in the church vestry everyone was free to leave. Because it was a beautiful day and Ann wanted to walk home to show off her wedding dress to the passersby, they all walked slowly back to Jamaica Street where Lillias and Ann had prepared a few refreshments for the family and their friends.

The following day was a workday for Edwin, besides which there was no money for a honeymoon, so the couple began their married life that night back in Jamaica Street. Edwin, who had been sleeping in the workshop, was now permitted to share Ann's bedroom next to his in-laws, and so they began their married life with little privacy but, none the less, significant passion. As Edwin and Ann lay next to each other, both nervous yet excited, Toby walked in and positioned himself by the door where he could carefully inspect both of them. He sat alertly, his golden eyes glowing brightly and attentively. After the marriage had been consummated, he jumped on the bed between Edwin and Ann and settled in for a short nap before going to look for rats. And so began a pattern of living for Edwin, Ann and Toby Turner which lasted several years.

CHAPTER 18

Meanwhile romance had been blossoming too with Miss Mary Mortimer and her beau, Albert Forrest, son of Sir James Forrest, the Lord Provost of Edinburgh. Albert, who had sported a nice tan after his European trip, soon became embroiled with his work with the law firm in Falkirk and the tan disappeared. Because of the distance between Edinburgh and Falkirk his father had deemed it appropriate that Albert find his own lodgings in Falkirk. This did not please Albert as he missed Edinburgh social life and, while Falkirk had developed as an iron and steel community and was a small thriving commercial center, it held none of the attractions of Edinburgh.

While on the continent, Albert had developed a penchant for gambling. One of the reasons he had shortened his tour abroad was because he had run out of money. His father, who knew of Albert's gambling habits, had refused to give him more money. In a few short days Albert had lost much of his savings in the Monte Carlo casino. This made marriage between Albert and Sir Charles Mortimer's daughter Mary seem more attractive to Sir James Forrest. He was a pragmatic man and knew that he needed someone who would calm his son down, and who could also provide for him financially. Unfortunately this would mean marriage to the daughter of an upstart, but needs must.

On Easter Day as Edwin and Ann were getting married, Mary and Albert were taking a stroll through the New Town. Mary was not really keen to walk far as her new shoes were pinching her. She was however anxious for others to see her beautiful lemon colored Easter bonnet, resplendent with daffodils and tulips. Her milliner had delivered it earlier in the day, and Mary questioned how long it would last before the flowers perished, but at this moment in time it looked beautiful.

As the two turned onto Frederick Street, Albert drew Mary closer to him. Ostensibly it was so that she would not be harmed by a passing carriage. Yet after the carriage had gone by he still maintained his hold on her and she did not resist. She liked how safe she felt when he held her. She also enjoyed how her hand felt on his arm and she clung to him somewhat possessively.

They walked along companionably, each wondering what the other was thinking. By this time Albert, persuaded a little by his father, had decided to ask Mary Mortimer to marry him. He did not love her, and perhaps never would, but marriage was a business, he thought, and he felt that they could have a successful partnership. His time in Europe had been a learning experience for him in the ways of women. He suspected that he would never know great passion with Mary who was conservative and unworldly. Yet he knew that he could find passion elsewhere and that would not surprise or perhaps even bother Mary.

Mary was also considering marriage to Albert as they strolled along Frederick Street. She had heard rumors of Albert and his gambling but he had never mentioned it. She did wonder if his interest in her stemmed from her money but quickly she thrust aside that thought. People married for all kinds of reasons and it usually worked out. If it didn't, then a couple would live separate lives but stay married. Mary hoped that would not happen to her but she had certainly witnessed it amongst her father's friends. She did know that she did not want to stay single for much longer. It was becoming embarrassing to preside at her father's dinner table with his friends. She felt like a dowdy spinster. Mary had no notions of having great beauty or intellect. Albert was attractive and that was good enough for her.

Albert suddenly enquired, "Is your father at home today? I have something I need to discuss with him."

Mary silently wondered if it would be a marriage proposal but she merely said that her father was at home and would be delighted to see Albert too. The two then headed back to Mary's house and, while Mary divested herself of her coat and fixed her hair, Albert went into the library where Sir Charles was seated at his desk working. He looked up as Albert entered and immediately offered him a glass of madeira.

Albert thanked him and accepted. He then took a seat across from Sir Charles and when Sir Charles looked questioningly at him, he began, "Sir, as you know, I began with my law firm in Falkirk a few months ago and the job is going well. I am told that if I work there for five years I may make partner with the other three solicitors. We deal with industrial law and it seems to be a constant source of business in Falkirk, and in Glasgow too. As you perhaps do not know, I do have a trust left by my mother, which I can access when I am thirty."

Taking a deep breath, he continued, "With that in mind, I now feel I can express my feelings to you. I have become increasingly fond of your daughter Mary. We enjoy each other's company very much. I would like to ask your permission for her hand in marriage. It would delight me a great deal, and I believe it would her too. If we were to marry I would make arrangements so that I could spend most of my time in Edinburgh and we could live here. I know that living in Falkirk would not be so desirable to her and I want to make her happy."

At this he stopped, figuring he should allow time for Sir Charles to consider the matter. Sir Charles, who had thought of this marriage for a significant amount of time already, needed to linger no longer on that thought and he readily agreed to the marriage. It then only required that Albert discuss the marriage with Mary. He had considered asking her before meeting with her father but he was reluctant to play all his cards at once and had determined that if Sir Charles did not agree, he would not pursue Mary further. It was not a love match and he knew they both could recover from the situation in a fairly short time.

After a few more pleasantries Albert left Sir Charles, who immediately poured himself a celebratory glass of madeira, delighted that he was stepping up socially by his daughter's marriage. Albert found Mary on the gold brocade love seat in the drawing room. Quickly he sat down next to her and took her hand in his. Miss Mary at this point was not really surprised and she could anticipate the next step. She was not given to fainting or even pretending to faint and so she turned her gaze steadily on Albert. On reflection Albert thought it best that he kneel for this as he knew that was considered a requirement among many young women of the upper classes. He then began to speak,

"Miss Mary, you must have wondered why I spoke to your father." She said nothing.

"Miss Mary, as you know I went to work for the law firm of Russel and Aitken in Falkirk and business is going well. I expect to make partner in five years and I've already received a sizable salary increase. In addition I do have a trust left by my mother which I can shortly gain access to."

Perhaps because Albert Forrest wanted to put forward his best foot he neglected to say that the trust was a small one and not nearly enough to support him in the manner in which he would like to remain accustomed.

He continued, "These last months have been so special to me and I believe they have to you too. I really would like to share the rest of my life with you. We could live in Edinburgh so you wouldn't have to live in Falkirk."

Taking a final deep breath he continued, "Would you please marry me, Mary?"

"Oh yes, Albert. I would be very happy to."

Mary beamed and her rather prominent front teeth did not seem so obvious when she smiled. Albert took her gently by the shoulders, kissed her tentatively on the cheek and then more boldly on her lips. This made Mary beam even more. Albert really was a handsome young man and she felt fortunate that he had asked her to marry him.

Because it would be a big society wedding, the date was set for October 18. This would give the couple and Sir Charles Mortimer opportunity to plan. Sir Charles only had one daughter and he certainly wanted to make this wedding a very grand affair. In addition, as Lord Provost, Sir James had commitments for months in advance and the wedding had to be planned into his calendar too.

CHAPTER 19

The next year passed very fast for the two lovers, Edwin and Ann. They never ceased to enjoy each other's company, and the fact that they worked and lived in the same house was a source of joy to them. It was no surprise to either them or the Berridges when Ann became pregnant only two months after she and Edwin had married. This would be a first grandchild for the Berridges and both were elated at the news.

William continued to mentor Edwin. He enjoyed the younger man's enthusiasm and optimism. Edwin was prepared to work hard and he was learning the watchmaking business very fast indeed. Much of the work was repetitive yet it required considerable dexterity to perform it well, and Edwin had a knack for that.

The baby was due in March 1844, less than a year after the two were married. Ann was glad that the baby would be born at that time and she would not be so big through the Edinburgh summer. True, it never got really warm but she had friends who assured her that it could be pretty stifling when you were nine months pregnant, and the houses became stuffy.

Christmas 1843 was a happy time. Edwin looked back at the last year and how his life had changed. A year ago he had been living in Borthwick's Close with Tim. He briefly thought about Tim and was concerned for him. He had heard that Tim had gone to the hulks at Portsmouth and had recently shipped to Van Diemen's Land, the island off the south-east coast of Australia. Edwin had heard that conditions there were even worse than in Botany Bay. The natives were unfriendly and a large animal known as a kangaroo was particularly aggressive. Many people did not survive the journey by ship; others died of disease when they got there. Altogether an adventure to be avoided.

Edwin enjoyed watchmaking. At the moment he was still learning to repair watches but he spent time each day watching William assemble watches. That is what Edwin aspired to do. He would one day like to see a watch that he had made himself, engraved with his name, Edwin Turner. Part of the attraction of watchmaking, besides the detailed work, was the casing which one could make very ornate and in character with the owner of the watch. Sometimes too Edwin was able to deliver watches to the big houses whose owners sometimes had several watches. He enjoyed looking at these homes. He wished he could provide such a home for Ann but she was content. She enjoyed being with her parents, and with him, and her cat Toby. Ann was easily pleased with her life.

On Sundays Edwin and William continued to go from time to time to the Observatory where they had first met. They enjoyed talking about astronomy. Both women appreciated the men's friendship and interest as neither woman had a strong interest in astronomy and enjoyed the men discussing it together and not with them.

Hogmanay came and went and they all enjoyed a celebratory drink at midnight. This New Year promised much for everyone, particularly with a new baby due in a few weeks. Those weeks passed by very fast; Ann continued her sewing jobs and also made a couple of outfits, artfully embroidered, for the new baby.

March finally came and on the 8th of that month they were all sitting around the fire after supper when Ann suddenly gasped and clutched her very pregnant belly. Immediately Edwin jumped to her side and her mother laid aside her sewing. William watched silently; he had been through this sort of thing before and he knew it took a long time, particularly with the first baby.

Lillias busied herself heating water and finding some towels she had set to one side for the event. She also sent Edwin for the midwife who lived a couple of streets away. Fortunately she was available and came promptly, which lessened Edwin's anxiety somewhat.

After a couple of hours of increased pain experienced by Ann, both men left the house and decided to head for Rose Street to get a beer. They were uncomfortable being around the women and the women did not want them there. Edwin would like to have stayed but William assured him that was not the correct thing to do and so they went to the George and Dragon and ordered pints of bitter.

After two pints though, both men were ready to leave the pub and head back to Jamaica Street. On arriving there they found they were still not welcome and so they went to sit on the front stoop. It was a clear, cold, starry night and so they amused themselves by talking about the stars. Not long after, they heard a baby's cry and Edwin lost all calm and rushed upstairs where Lillias greeted him triumphantly.

"It's a little boy!" she cried.

"How is Ann?" asked Edwin, delighted that he had a boy but more concerned about Ann.

"She's fine, just a little tired. Go on in."

Edwin entered their bedroom, casually noticing that Toby was in one corner and had clearly witnessed the whole event. That cat was certainly very privileged.

Baby Turner was wrapped in a sheet. Lillias had already cleaned him up and he was looking at the world through dark blue eyes, a little unsure of where he was. He was red and wrinkled, just as Ann had warned him he would be, but he looked perfect to Edwin who carefully counted all his fingers and toes to see that he was all there. Ann smiled tiredly at Edwin but also managed to look proud. She took her baby and held him to her breast to which he latched on fast. Edwin thought he had never seen Ann look more beautiful.

William then came in and joined the group. He had never had a strong interest in children; he was a soldier first and foremost and there was no time in his younger years for them. He loved Ann though and he shared in her excitement over his new grandson. He looked fine, he was a baby; they all look alike, thought William.

After considerable discussion the baby was named Alfred. Lillias and William had strong opinions on what their first grandson should be named and it seemed difficult to please everyone so, rather than displease anyone, Edwin and Ann called the baby Alfred. Very soon that name was shortened to Alfie.

Six weeks later Alfie was taken to the kirk to be christened. By this time James Bruce had retired but, because Ann was very special to him, he agreed to return to the church to christen young Alfred. Afterwards the small family and James Bruce returned to Jamaica Street for tea and cakes.

Alfred was an unusually happy baby who rarely cried except when hurt. Edwin and Ann felt very fortunate and in just a few months Ann was pregnant again and Alfie, at 11 months old, was now older brother to Will. Edwin had become very attached to William as a father-in-law, a friend, and as an employer. It seemed fitting that a child should be named after him. William delighted in both children. As a grandparent he had more time for his grandchildren than he had for his own children.

CHAPTER 20

Edwin was rapidly learning how to repair watches with speed and skill and was doing a fine job of learning the business side of watchmaking too. He had already started designing his own watches also, which was his long-term goal. Edwin noticed that William was slowing down somewhat in his work. He did not want to mention it to William as he did not want to offend him but he did mention it to Ann.

"Ann, I'm worried about your Da. He doesn't seem well right now. Has your mother said anything to you about him?"

"No, what have you seen? I'd noticed that he doesn't seem himself and even though he eats everything on his plate he looks a bit thinner."

"Yes, I'd noticed that too. Perhaps he's working too hard. We're really busy right now. Our business is just increasing all the time. I know I'm tired and he's older than I am!"

"I know he worries about my brothers. We don't hear from them these days and Da wishes they would visit us occasionally. I know it is hard to get from Dumfries but it's not that far!"

"I wouldn't worry too much about them. They are doing what they want to do. I know your Da would rather they worked here but they don't have any interest. From my point of view, that's very good."

At this, Edwin stood up, walked across the room to his wife and kissed her on the cheek. She was

135

such a lovely woman, he thought. How lucky I am! Ann looked up and smiled at him. Edwin was a good father and he certainly was a good husband. Ann had friends whose husbands went to the pub every night after dinner, returned home late and then beat up their wives. She'd seen the bruises and black eyes of her friends, and Ann was very aware that Edwin was always loving and kind to her. She was indeed fortunate. Her father was a good man too and she had chosen her husband wisely, based on the model set by her father.

Ann decided to ask her mother about her father. She was worried about him as she had noticed that he didn't seem interested in his food even though Lillias always prepared food that he liked. Perhaps he was just preoccupied with business. She had also heard him coughing late at night. Long, hacking coughs that made the listener want to cringe and leave the room. She had heard her mother try to quieten him and had seen her rub his back in an effort to relieve his discomfort. Her mother was always so patient with him even when William, in his frustration at his coughing, would scold her. William, ever the soldier, wanted to be tough and did not want a woman fussing after him. Yet he was beginning to look gaunt, particularly after a bad coughing spell.

Ann found Lillias sitting sewing in front of the fire. She sat quietly with her for a few minutes and then asked her solemnly, "Ma, I've noticed Da's cough. Is there something wrong with him?"

Ann was always direct in her approach. She disliked circumspection. However from Lillias she drew only a worried look and it stopped her from insisting on a direct response. Lillias merely said that she had bought some cough medicine from the widow in the next flat and she thought it was doing some good.

Yet it did not. One morning, two months later, Edwin was in the shop, working alone. William was usually prompt in coming downstairs but this morning he had not yet appeared. Edwin had brewed some tea for him and it was already turning cold when Ann rushed through the workshop door and burst out, "Edwin, come quickly! Da cannot get out of bed and he has coughed up blood!"

Swiftly Edwin dropped the watch and the tweezers he was holding and ran upstairs behind Ann. Ann could certainly move fast when she needed to. Even though he was concerned for William he still managed to notice his wife's nicely turned ankles as she sped upstairs ahead of him.

There he found Lillias wiping up blood by the side of William's bed. William was lying back on the pillow with his eyes closed, his face ashen grey. His breathing was shallow and ragged. He opened his eyes when Edwin entered but said nothing.

"Would you like some porridge, William?" asked Lillias, not really sure what she could give William that would help him.

When she saw the blood this morning it confirmed what she already suspected. Living in close quarters with so many people in Old Town and now, even in New Town, you became accustomed to illness and death as you or your neighbors confronted it so regularly. Nevertheless it struck fear into Lillias. It was still different when it was your own family, and particularly your husband. William had not wanted to discuss how badly he felt as he did not want to scare her. Now she was at a loss as to what to do. Perhaps the apothecary would have some medicine for William. She knew of a doctor but they really did not have the resources to pay for one. She also disliked the idea of bloodletting and was concerned that if she sent for a physician that would be the treatment for William. Lillias had seen that happen before with a friend and there was not a good outcome.

"Edwin, could you go to the apothecary and talk to him about William, please?" requested Lillias, absentmindedly pushing aside her hair away from her face as she leaned over William to mop the side of his face.

William lay with his eyes closed, aware of her being there, tolerating it but clearly feeling very ill. Edwin went into his room to find his coat and then headed outside into Jamaica Street. He then turned right onto the first street and walked into the apothecary's.

Normally he would have enjoyed lingering in the store. He loved the jars with their colored powders and their Latin names. He liked the idea of making medicines and enjoyed watching the pharmacist make some medication. He knew too that the apothecary was well revered within the community as a man of learning. He could cure sometimes and it was far better to take some of the rather noxious potions which he concocted than to undergo surgery at the Royal Edinburgh Hospital in Morningside. He had heard that hospital was rated highly by people who went there, but being cut open did not seem like a good option to him.

The apothecary appeared from a door at the back of his shop. He was a short, grey-haired man, stooped over by hours of compounding drugs. He was genial though and welcomed Edwin warmly even though the two had never met.

"How can I help you?" he prompted Edwin, his voice a simple Scottish lilt which ensured his education and station in life.

"My father-in-law William Berridge is very sick. I think he has been ill for some time as he is getting very thin. This morning he coughed up blood and he's in great pain. Do you have something for the pain and to stop the bleeding?"

"What does his skin look like?"

"Well, he's rather grey looking and he looks tired all the time but he works long hours."

"Yes, I know Mr. Berridge. I bought a watch from him some years ago. He lives just around the corner, doesn't he?"

"Yes, at 15 Jamaica Street."

"Does he have a fever?"

"I don't know. I don't think so."

All the while the apothecary was opening jars and searching through his stock of medicines. He then prepared a tiny package which contained laudanum. Edwin quickly said, "I thought only ladies took laudanum."

"Generally speaking that's true but it's a good painkiller and will give Mr. Berridge some relief. That's what he needs now."

Edwin looked in his pocket for his money, handed over to him a sixpence, and quickly took the package, thanking the apothecary even as he ran out of the door. Never one to linger, Edwin was back up the stairs and by William's bedside in just a few minutes.

William lay still, exhausted by his racking cough and willing the pain to go away. Edwin handed Lillias the laudanum and took a seat in the corner of the room so he was readily available if Lillias needed him. Meanwhile Ann stood weeping by her father's side. She was used to seeing him as a strong man, who was never sick and who never flinched at pain. It unnerved her to see her father so debilitated.

They all decided to stay with William through the night and take turns staying awake. No one wanted to sleep until they knew that William was getting better. He soon settled when the laudanum took effect. By the next morning his color had returned and for now the illness had abated.

CHAPTER 21

Edwin enjoyed the increase in responsibilities as William tried to regain his strength. Very often William would come into the workshop and just watch what Edwin was doing. These days he needed to offer very little advice to Edwin. Edwin was well on the way to being a watchmaker.

One Monday morning not long after William's sudden onslaught of illness, a young man opened the front door and stopped in front of Edwin's desk, temporarily blocking the light which Edwin needed. This forced Edwin to immediately look up, which had been Albert Forrest's intention. He was used to getting what he wanted from life.

As promised to Sir Charles Mortimer, his father-in-law, he had moved back from Falkirk to Edinburgh. Mary had not settled in Falkirk; it was far too provincial for her taste even though the new train service between Edinburgh and Glasgow did stop at Falkirk. Albert was doing well with his law firm. He enjoyed commercial law and was already becoming an effective barrister. Mary secretly wondered if part of his interest in being a barrister was the wig and gown that he sported when in court. He would spend an inordinate amount of time, she considered, looking in the mirror, adjusting the wig until it was to his satisfaction. Mary was however secretly proud of her husband and his appearance and she did not really mind his vanity.

"Good morning, sir, may I help you?" inquired Edwin politely.

"I hope so. My father-in-law, Sir Charles Mortimer has a pocket watch with a soldier and musket on the casing. He recommended that I talk to Mr. Berridge about it as I would like something similar."

Albert Forrest revealed his aristocratic upbringing by speaking with an English accent instead of his native Scottish one. Edwin had noticed this before with several of their clients. As an Englishman he was surprised as he thought the Scottish accent with its softness and lilt exceedingly beautiful. Yet he knew the cultured English accent did show breeding and education.

"Sir, I am familiar with Sir Charles' watch and I know it is Swiss-made. It is a Longine. Mr. Berridge did not make that watch, although we do make watches here, and we are able to duplicate the quality of that watch," said Edwin rather grandly, hoping in fact that he could make as fine a watch as the Longine.

"Well, what I had in mind may be more simple anyway," responded Albert. "I am a barrister and I would like the casing to reflect my profession. I was thinking perhaps of a set of scales, with books weighing down the scales. Is Mr. Berridge available, however?"

"I am sorry, sir, but Mr. Berridge has been quite sick recently. I have been taught by Mr. Berridge though and I am confident that I can make a watch which you would be proud of." Edwin held his breath for a moment as he knew that he was treading in unknown territory.

Albert Forrest looked Edwin up and down. As a barrister he had seen many young men stand in court, accused and frequently guilty. He was confident of his ability to judge people. His assessment of Edwin was that he was eager, confident, and charming. He seemed like the kind of man who would take chances but he seemed honest enough.

Albert then suggested, "Do you think you could draw up a design for the casing for me? I could come in again in a week's time and if I like it we can discuss price, materials and so on."

"Yes, sir. The only thing I need to know is what material you would like the watch made of. It would affect the design somewhat as some metals work better than others for molding."

Albert had not considered this but he decided rather promptly that he would prefer gold. He did not want his watch to resemble too much that of his father-in-law, and he certainly knew he could afford a nicer one than Sir Charles Mortimer whose watch was silver.

At that, the two men shook hands and Albert departed, agreeing to return in a week's time to review the design. After he left Edwin could barely contain his excitement. He hoped that William could offer him advice but he felt it was time to be making watches on his own.

William sometimes accused him of being overly confident, but Edwin knew that he wanted his work to be challenging and he thought he could muddle through any situation if necessary. He told William as much although he did not describe his work as muddling. He knew that word alone would unsettle William. William merely shook his head rather worriedly. He was content with Edwin as an employee, apprentice, and son-in-law, but at times Edwin took chances that others would not. He would regularly promise work would be completed and then not be able to finish it. This upset his clients and it was bad for business.

Edwin settled down again to the watch at hand but, as he was working, he was thinking about the design he would make for Albert Forrest. The books sitting on the scales would be the most intricate and difficult part of the job as they needed to be recognizable as books and be of different sizes to create interest. The scales would fill the whole face of the casing. He would need to put at least three books on the scale, preferably identifiable as law books. That would be the tricky part.

Just as he was finishing the watch with which he was working, William came downstairs and entered the workshop. He inquired, "Did I hear a customer?"

"Yes," replied Edwin, rather triumphantly. "A new one. He is Albert Forrest, the son-in-law of Sir Charles Mortimer. He has seen Sir Charles' watch - you remember, that Longine with the soldier and the musket - and he would like something similar in gold.

He'd like me to design a casing with a set of scales and books on it as he is a barrister."

At this William looked concerned and asked when the design was to be ready. Having been told, he merely said, "Please show me the design two days before that in case we need to make some changes. I will help you with it. Please don't do any work for Mr. Forrest without me taking a look at it. I'm sure you'll do a good job and he will be pleased but this is an important account. The Forrests and Mortimers know all the influential people in town and I'd hate to upset them."

William now took a look at what Edwin was working on and he clearly approved of it. Edwin really did have a knack for detailed work and he clearly enjoyed watchmaking and repairs. As Edwin's watch repair was completed and it was ready to be delivered, William decided to stay in the shop and do a little work. This gave Edwin some freedom to deliver the watch and enjoy a walk outside. Edwin decided to ask Ann to accompany him. She herself had a delivery to make of a new dress which she had just finished so, while Lillias looked after the children, Edwin and Ann walked through New Town to drop off their packages.

Edwin excitedly told Ann about the commission of work he had just received. Ann was happy for him. She knew that he needed to get experience fast. Her father was really not in good health. The apothecary's medicine seemed to have slowed down whatever was ailing him but he had not gained weight and he still looked gaunt and grey, often falling asleep in his chair in front of the fire. Ann was not used to seeing her father behave like that.

Ann herself had not been feeling well recently. Pregnant once again, Ann found herself wondering if this would be the last baby. She certainly hoped it was but knew that Edwin had said before they were married that he wanted a large family. Business was brisk but Edwin was still an apprentice. When he finished his apprenticeship then perhaps things would be easier. She knew that even William, who had an established business, fretted over the bills. Sometimes these rich people, even though they had money, did not like to pay their bills and there were weeks when her father had to work hard to come up with the money to pay for food. With this new baby she wondered just how much harder it would be for them all.

CHAPTER 22

Two days later William Berridge sat alone in his workshop and looked at his accounting books. He had kept meticulous records of his accounts and he was worried now as to what to do. To this point William had been storing some of his money in the Royal Bank of Scotland. He had banked with them for so long he could not remember why he had chosen that particular bank. For sure there had been plenty of banks to choose from; they each printed their own money, arranged their own loans and accepted their own deposits. He remembered when the Royal Bank of Scotland had moved its offices to Dundas House on St Andrew Square. That must have been in about 1821, he thought, but he was not sure of the date.

William was aware that it was not like this in England where the Bank of England controlled everything. He rather favored what Scotland was doing. Each bank accepted other banks' notes. At times it was a little confusing as each bank also printed several versions of its own banknotes. They were certainly colorful and that was perhaps why the banks did it. He didn't know.

Last year the Prime Minister, Sir Robert Peel, had enacted a new law where a lot of the banks were to close and only three banks in Scotland would survive. Fortunately William kept what little he had saved in the Royal Bank which was to survive this change in the banking system. It worried William though. Banks had always concerned William, partly because they seemed to print a lot of money in different styles and he worried that the value of that money might go down. Yet it had not. The bank accepted his deposit, gave him a little interest, and a long time ago had even given him a low-cost loan.

Now though William was concerned about the power of the English Parliament. When they tried to change Scottish banking that was beyond the pale. William was aware, because he had traveled, that Scots were viewed as misers. Well so be it, at least they were careful. Now, being careful, William decided to withdraw what money he had in the Royal Bank of Scotland and hide it in the workshop until he felt once again that his money was safe in a bank. He knew he now had only three to choose from - the Royal Bank of Scotland, the Bank of Scotland and the Clydesdale; the latter he considered to be an upstart bank as they had not been around long enough. He was very aware that there could always be a burglary but hiding it would only be a temporary situation anyway.

It was already getting too dark to work so William decided to head to the bank and withdraw his money. He would not tell anyone except Lillias. He knew Edwin was of the new age and if he had money to spare, he knew that Edwin would probably put it with the Clydesdale Bank as he was attracted to new things. Young people of today just did not cherish the old, they valued only new and fresh and different.

Edwin would definitely not approve of him hiding money in the workshop or under his mattress.

Walking at a fairly brisk pace William Berridge headed along George Street towards St Andrew Square. He did not usually take short cuts or linger to watch the crowds but his health had slowed him somewhat. Disgusted at himself that he had to walk more slowly, William purposefully thought of other things. He watched others as they paraded along the street, conscious of the appearance they projected as they strolled. Others walked with determination and purpose, intent on their business. The carriages rolled by too as William walked. He recognized some of the occupants as his customers and occasionally he doffed his hat upon recognizing a familiar face.

Shortly he was at the Royal Bank of Scotland on St Andrew Square and he found it unusually busy. The clerk behind the counter looked rather drawn and frenzied. When William questioned him as to his welfare the clerk pushed back his green visor and wearily said it had been a long day. As William requested the funds from his account the clerk stated that several people had been closing their accounts recently. He knew it was because of worry over the impact of the new Law and he assured Mr. Berridge that there really was no cause for concern. Some banks had closed but the Royal Bank of Scotland was firm and would be part of the future for decades, no, centuries to come.

Not feeling as reassured as he perhaps should have been, William decided to go ahead and withdraw the money as he had planned. When things settled down again then he could put the money back in the bank again. Meanwhile it would be safer in the workshop. He had a safe box there where he could stash his money. He asked for his money in gold as he did not trust the variety of colored banknotes that the banks were printing. At least you knew that gold had a value.

Putting his gold sovereigns into his pockets he carefully made certain that the money was not visible to anyone and then he headed slowly to the door, opening it for a gentleman who was exiting at the same time. He recognized him slightly, and touched his brow before putting on his top hat. Then with dignity and a feeling that with his money safely in his pockets, he was a man who was secure in himself and the world, he walked slowly home.

When William arrived home Edwin had closed the shop as it was already almost dark. Swiftly William put his gold coins in the safe box, locked it and hid it again in a locked desk drawer. Even Edwin was unaware of its existence.

William wanted to look at Edwin's design for Albert Forrest's watch but it was not lying on the workbench. Well, that would just keep until tomorrow. Time to go upstairs and eat some supper. Lillias would be waiting for him.

CHAPTER 23

Lillias and Ann were both waiting for William. Edwin had gone for a walk. He was inclined to do this sometimes to clear his head. He was excited about the design of the new watch and sometimes he just had to work off his extra energy. Walking cleared his head and enabled him to sleep better. Ann found it rather strange but she was used to it. Sometimes she would walk with Edwin but mostly he would walk on his own while she put the children to bed. Right now she was worried about the new baby growing inside her. She had confided to Lillias that she was worried about the expense of another child. Lillias did not share Ann's worries. The idea of a new grandchild thrilled her.

Ann commented to Lillias, "I'm sure it's a girl this time. I just feel a little different from when I had Alfie or Will."

Lillias replied, "I hope so! I'd like to have a girl for a change. It would be nice later too to have another pair of hands to help us. I'd like to be able to make her some really pretty outfits. We spend our time making nice dresses for these rich women and it would be nice to make for our own!"

Ann heartily agreed. She enjoyed making the fancy dresses for the Edinburgh aristocracy but sometimes she just wished that she and Lillias could wear some of the outfits that they made. Yet that would be impractical. They had nowhere to go in them and they were so expensive too. It was a juggling act just trying to get the bills paid to buy the new materials. Their customers may be rich but they certainly did not like to be parted from their money. It was so hard to make ends meet at times.

With the new baby, there would be another mouth to feed. Alfie and Will were both too young to work. Ann had heard that children could no longer work in the textile mills until they were nine but there were plenty of other things that they could do as young little people. Idle hands were admired by no one. "Teach a child in the way he should go and he will not depart from it." Ann had heard this at the kirk yet she wondered if that was really what the Scripture meant. She was not very learned in Scripture. There was a big black family Bible on the living room table but she had never seen anyone open it except to record the births of Alfie and Will. Soon it would be opened again for this new baby.

Ann still attended the kirk with her mother every Sunday. She found calmness and peace there. In fact, she could not imagine her life without God in it. She enjoyed meeting the other women and participated in the altar guild where she helped set up the altar with flowers and special cloths each Sunday.

She was disappointed that Edwin did not attend but he was a good husband and so she had to learn to live with it. He just did not find what she did in the church and he would get upset if she ever told him she was chosen by God. Edwin would say that it made no sense that God would create all these people only to let some of them perish. Ann did not understand that either but knew it would all be sorted out by the time she arrived in Heaven. She did worry about Edwin though. He was a good husband and she loved him dearly.

At the thought of Edwin she smiled a little. He was so enthusiastic about his watchmaking. Lillias had told her that William was very pleased with his skill and Ann was proud. Edwin was a good father to the boys too. He dandled them on his knee each night. She was glad that he was not a man to run off to the pub every night as she had observed happen with others. William and Edwin were a lot alike in that regard.

Slowly she stood up, mindful of the need to keep her balance. As she walked to the stove she held her aching back with her right arm. She would be glad when this pregnancy was over and yet again she wished to herself that there would be no more. Ann was still worried about the cost of a new child. Yet Edwin always reminded her that cost only lasted for a short time and then the children could make money of their own.

This had been the way it was for her. She started sewing when she was five and by age six her mother was selling some of the things she had made. Ann had seen some of these fancier homes where they even had a nursery and a governess to educate the children. What a dream that would be! Going to school must be wonderful, she thought. Ann had learned to read and write because her father had taught her and she knew she was lucky in that regard.

At this moment, as her mind was wandering, Edwin entered the room. He had finished his walk earlier than Ann had anticipated and the supper was not quite ready yet. The meal was to be shepherd's pie and Ann had been able to procure more beef than usual so it would be more than the usual mashed potatoes and a bit of cheese. It was one of Edwin's favorites though and she wanted to make this particularly tasty.

Edwin declared excitedly, "Ann, Lillias! I have finished the design for that watch! I can't wait to make it."

"When is Mr. Forrest coming to see the design?"

"Thursday, I hope. I do hope too that he brings some money so that I can buy the supplies. We can't make the watch if he doesn't give us an advance."

"I'm sure he realizes that," soothed Lillias, who really was not as sure as her sentiment indicated. "May I see the design?"

Edwin proudly laid out the design next to the old family Bible on the table. It really was a nice pattern and highly appropriate for a barrister. There was so much that you could put in a design for a barrister but the space was small and the idea of a few books sitting on a scale was almost all there was room for on the watch casing. Edwin had laced a laurel wreath around the rim of the casing and on one of the books he had put Albert Forrest's initials. For the back cover of the casing Edwin had designed a wig and pen.

Already Edwin was considering the face of the watch. It should be white mother-of-pearl, he decided, with black Roman numerals. He would also use a second hand. They were still not very popular but he recognized Albert as being a man of the world who would want the most up-to-date watch.

Tempus fugit. Edwin had seen that on a watch and did not know what it meant. William had explained it was Latin for Time Flies. Edwin could vouch for that. It already seemed like many years since he was living in Nottinghamshire with his parents. How different his life had become, and how much better. He was glad not to be involved in farming anymore. It was a fine and useful job, provided you had no other options. Now Edwin was going places. Perhaps when William retired, Edwin could step in and take over the family business. Certainly Ann's two brothers had no interest in it. They rarely appeared in Edinburgh and showed no interest in the business except to get handouts from William.

As a soldier William believed in standing on one's own two feet. When the boys exhorted him to give them money he reluctantly gave it but it was personally ingrained in him to be independent. That is what he admired about Edwin. Edwin was his own man. He had accepted work from William but he earned his keep and never asked for help. He could manage money well, William observed.

Lillias and Ann looked at the watch design which Edwin had placed on the table near the fire. Ann loved to see Edwin's enthusiasm. She liked his design too. If Albert Forrest did not like that, she remarked, he would be clearly a man of poor taste. Edwin laughed at her but he was pleased that she supported him.

He looked at Ann now, pushing her hair behind her ears, and looking carefully at his work. She was beautiful even in pregnancy although he secretly hoped this would be the last baby. He worried about having to support a large family. He had always wanted one but the reality of already providing for two children had reshaped his thinking in that regard. The problem for him was that he found Ann as attractive as when they first met. Their children had been conceived in love and he found it difficult not to want to make love to her even when she was nine months pregnant. She looked up at him and, as happened so often, she could read his mind. She laughed at him and Lillias looked inquiringly at both of them who just laughed more but did not enlighten Lillias as to why they were laughing.

Suddenly they heard slow footsteps on the stairs. It was William. He was clearly tired but he managed to smile bravely at them all.

"Have you finished Mr. Forrest's design yet, Edwin? I was hoping you would have it ready."

"Here it is," offered Edwin, handing over his paper. William sat at the table and looked over the design carefully. Edwin watched carefully and waited for some reaction. William, ever the soldier in control, looked noncommittal. He knew Edwin was waiting for a response and he rather savored this moment. Finally he looked up, rubbed his eyes, and then said rather dourly, "It will do."

Crestfallen, Edwin was silent for a moment. Ann looked at him and wanted to reach out to comfort him. Suddenly William burst into laughter, "Got you! It's very good indeed! I think Mr. Forrest will be well pleased with it. I know I would be if I were getting a watch like that."

CHAPTER 24

Albert Forrest stepped out of his carriage and told his man to wait for him as he entered the workshop. Edwin was already at the workbench. William stayed out of the way while Forrest was in the shop but he made sure he was in earshot. This was a big account and one he did not want to lose.

The entertainment of the night before had left Albert feeling financially secure and adept in his dealings. After a short absence from gambling when Albert first married Mary, Albert had taken up his old habits. Sir Charles Mortimer was disappointed in this aspect of his son-in-law but he had recognized before the marriage that gambling was a part of Albert Forrest's life. He recognized too that he would indirectly have to support the habit if he wished to keep his daughter happy.

When Albert had money in his pocket he exhibited a certain swagger. This morning he had decided to dress in one of his kilts. He was proud of his Scottish heritage and at dinner parties he was prone to bring into the conversation that his Sept had fought with Bonnie Prince Charlie against the English. Accordingly he had no love for the English now but sometimes you just had to put up with them, as in the case of this watchmaker standing before him now.

As an Englishman Edwin viewed the kilt with some fascination. He was secretly glad that he did not have to wear one as they looked cold and impractical.

Yet it must feel good to be a part of a clan or family that is so strong they have their own tartans for different occasions. Edwin did not know much about it but Ann had explained to him that there were ancient tartans, and dress tartans, and hunting tartans and it seemed there was a tartan for every occasion you could imagine. It became even more complicated when each clan had several sub-groups with different family names. They were called septs and they had their own tartans too.

Now Albert Forrest stood before him wearing a Forrest plaid. He was mindful that the Forrests were a sept of the Forrester clan but he preferred to sport a Forrest tartan. He wore the traditional short black jacket, wool stockings, black slippers and a magnificent bearskin sporran in which he kept a small amount of change. Albert had figured out early in life that it was better not to carry much loose cash with him, and this enabled him to enjoy meals at friends' expense, run up gambling bills without immediate payment, and so on. It worked well for him. Today he was carrying more money than usual as he had been advised by the watchmaker that he would need to provide a deposit so that they could buy the materials for the watch.

"Good morning, sir," ventured Edwin politely. Forrest did not respond immediately, merely taking off his hat and nodding briskly.

"I came to see the design for my new watch," Albert then responded, assuming as his kind were wont to do, that what he had ordered would indeed be ready on the requested day. Edwin was, of course, prepared and rather proudly showed the design to Forrest, although he held his breath in case Forrest rejected it.

Forrest did not, however, and beamed with pleasure at the design. He particularly liked that his initials were on one of the books on the scale. A nice finishing touch, he decided.

"How long will it take to make?" inquired Forrest. "I was hoping to wear it in a month's time for a special reception I am holding."

"That should be no problem, sir. We will of course need a deposit towards the cost of the watch. Five guineas should be adequate. Here is an estimate of the finished watch," said Edwin, passing him a paper. Edwin was still uncomfortable directly asking for money but could manage better if he had a written estimate.

Forrest rather reluctantly opened his sporran and silently counted out the five guineas. He also signed where Edwin requested on the estimate. In all he felt that the watchmaker's fee was quite reasonable. Last night's winnings would pay for the watch and he would have a rather fine timepiece to display to his friends. He hoped the watch would be as fine as the Longine which his father-in-law used. Swiss watches were very good, there was no doubt, but Forrest liked to favor a Scotsman whenever he could.

At this point Ann's cat Toby walked into the shop and looked with disdain at Albert Forrest.

Edwin was secretly amused but said nothing. Forrest looked at the cat with equal disdain but found himself having to climb over the cat to get out of the door. Satisfied that he had been a nuisance, Toby stretched and then walked back upstairs to visit Ann.

Toby was paying careful attention to Ann right now. He believed there was another baby on the way. Last time he had seen her like this a baby appeared. The last thing we need, decided Toby, and he found a corner to curl up in where he could sleep undisturbed.

Meanwhile William entered the shop, slapped Edwin on the back and then coughed rather alarmingly. He used his handkerchief as he coughed but Edwin did not escape noticing that there was blood on it as William put it back in his pocket. William took the five guineas and told Edwin that he would attend to getting the supplies Edwin needed. After Edwin left the workshop William added the five guineas to the sovereigns which he had already hidden in the safe box carefully placed in a drawer.

Chapter 25

Two days later Edwin was awakened by a cry from Ann. She was sitting bolt upright in bed, and she was rubbing her stomach. Edwin was not surprised as Ann had been unusually busy the last few days and seemed to have a frantic energy. William had warned him about that during the first pregnancy as Lillias had cleaned the house very busily as each of her children was born. Ann seemed to have acquired the same habit in childbirth.

This time labor was easier and shorter for Ann. Toby took his usual position in the corner of the room, and Edwin and William took their usual position on the stoop and waited until the midwife summoned them. Not two hours had passed before she did call them. "A girl, Mr. Turner, you have a girl!"

Edwin had hoped for a girl who would be able to help Ann. His first thoughts as always though were for Ann and he rushed to see her. Ann was lying back, tired but happy. She was pleased to have a girl. That was what everyone had wished for this time.

"Edwin, we never talk about what we are going to call the babies before they are born. We are both a wee bit superstitious about that. I really like the name Lydia. What do you think?"

Edwin looked at the baby and then looked at Ann and said, "I think that's a fine name. We've not had one in the family yet. She's pretty and it's a pretty name."

William and Lillias came into the room at this point and asked, "Can we see the wee one?"

"She's Lydia."

"Lydia, for sure that's a bonny name!" exclaimed Lillias, rather pleased that the new baby was to be given a name similar to hers. Lillias scooped up baby Lydia into her arms and rocked her comfortably. It was nice to have a baby girl after so many boys in the family. Lydia had a surprisingly full head of hair, dark like Edwin's. She was going to be a beauty like Ann, decided Edwin, rather aware of his bias. Ann, who had two bald babies previously, was also delighted with the child's hair. She thought Lydia looked like Edwin. Lydia's face crumpled suddenly and a loud wail came from her tiny mouth. Toby stood up rather disgustedly, recognizing that for now he would not be the center of attention in the Turner-Berridge household.

At this moment William started coughing uncontrollably. The medicine he had been getting from the apothecary was not taking care of his problem and Lillias' attention went immediately from Lydia to William. She was worried about him. He was just not getting better and refused help. As she went to him he rather roughly said, "Quit fussing, woman! I am fine!" He abruptly left the room and his absence brought a chill to the room's occupants.

Although Edwin was delighted with his new daughter he had grown fond of William and hated to see his mentor and friend in such distress.

"Is there anything I can do, Ma?" as he now affectionately called Lillias.

"I don't think so, Edwin. He's so stubborn that I canna talk sense into him," said Lillias, lapsing into her Glaswegian accent which she did when she was tired or stressed. "But that medicine isn't working. He needs to see a doctor but he refuses. Doesn'a want to spend the money."

Lydia started to cry at this point and once again the family's attention was turned to her, not before Lillias vowed to get William to see a doctor.

Her plans were overridden during the night however. In the middle of the night they were awakened by the sound of glass being smashed. The sound came from downstairs. Grabbing a cudgel that he had kept under his bed for years, William called quietly for Edwin who always slept deeply. He did not want to disturb whomever was downstairs in the workshop. Edwin had heard the noise. Unable to sleep because of the excitement and because Lydia had awakened them earlier with a lusty cry, begging to be fed, Edwin was fast on his feet. Having lived in Old Town he was not unaccustomed to break-ins but he had learned to sleep more deeply since he had moved to Jamaica Street.

Ann looked petrified. She drew Lydia close to her and looked over at Alfie and Will who were still fast asleep. "Be careful, Edwin," she whispered. "Perhaps you shouldn't go down there now. Best they take what they want. I don't want you hurt!"

Ignoring her plea, Edwin met William who was waiting for him, his cudgel in his right hand. Edwin was surprised to see it as he figured William for a quiet restrained man despite his military background. Maybe William was more a man of the world than Edwin had realized. Burglaries were not uncommon in Old Town but he had heard of very few in New Town.

The two stepped slowly and carefully downstairs trying not to make a noise on the stone staircase. At the door to the workshop they waited, trying to hear if anyone was talking from within. They needed to know how many people they would encounter.

They waited a moment longer. Edwin quietly whispered, "Two, I think." Given there were two of them and hoping for the element of surprise, they flung open the workshop door. Edwin was unarmed but he had learned to be good with his fists. William grasped his cudgel tighter. What they saw though caught them by surprise.

There were not just two men in the workshop but four burglars. One was guarding the door, two had emptied the drawers, throwing instruments to the floor. The last was holding the safe box in which William had deposited his gold sovereigns.

At the sight of his gold sovereigns and all his wealth being stolen, William flew into action, flailing his cudgel but failing to strike anyone significantly. As he did this he began to cough again and he stopped for a moment to catch his breath. Recognizing that the older man was struggling for air, the two men who were raiding his drawers seized the opportunity to punch him in the stomach, winding him even more. Then a fist cracked his nose, emitting blood. In his surprise William, all military training temporarily forgotten, reached for his nose, shocked that it felt broken. He dropped his cudgel. Seeing this, Edwin grabbed it and swung it as if it were a tabor, intending to crack it on the nearest victim's head. Too late. The men were leaving the shop, all four heading in different directions. One carried the safe box.

CHAPTER 26

Mrs. Albert Forrest set down the Royal Doulton teacup she had been pensively holding as she gazed out of the drawing room window. She wondered when her husband would return home. She knew he disliked to answer questions about his whereabouts and she had long since stopped inquiring where he was going when he headed out in a carriage most evenings. She suspected the servants knew but she was not about to ask any of them. Her personal maid, Aileen, was discreet but Miss Mary hesitated to ask her where Albert went each evening. She feared the answer.

Albert would return home late at night or very early in the morning. He would sometimes crash into the furniture and on occasion he had approached her in bed, smelling of alcohol and perfume. She had feigned sleep and he had stumbled away into his own bedroom. Good riddance, she thought.

Albert had not turned out to be the husband Mary had hoped for. He did work steadily at his law firm and had been made a partner recently, yet he still could not manage on his law income. She knew her father was giving him handouts and she cringed at the idea. She was ashamed but then Daddy had plenty of money so perhaps it did not bother him too much. She knew her father well enough to know that he was interested in social climbing, some of which he had been able to achieve, thanks to her marriage.

The drawing room was her favorite room. Decorated in burgundy brocade and Chippendale furniture it reflected her good taste, she decided. She chose not to notice that it was similar in style to that of her father-in-law whose house reflected the epitome of good taste. Certainly her drawing room compared favorably with some of the drawing rooms to which she was invited regularly.

As she looked out of the window she was surprised to see the family brougham pull up to the front door. It was a fine carriage, shiny and black and decorated with the Forrest coat of arms. Mary was aware, as her husband had pointed out many times, that this brougham was the latest style. It was even named after Lord Brougham whom Forrest respected as a judge. Mary enjoyed riding in the carriage, particularly as it had windows in the front from which she could look out and also be seen. It had only one step with which to get into the carriage which made it significantly easier to enter. All in all the Forrests were delighted with this gift from Mary's father, Sir Charles.

To her surprise, Albert stepped out. He was home early today. Immediately Mary reached for the bell on the wall for a servant so she could order tea for Albert. Albert strode energetically up the steps to the house and entered the house, calling for her.

"I'm in the drawing room," she responded, arranging her dress prettily around her knees. "You are home early," she said before realizing that was best left unsaid.

"Yes," he responded tersely, heading straight for the drinks cabinet where he poured himself a large Scotch and without further ado gulped it down in one swig.

"I've ordered you some tea," said Mary mildly, picking up her embroidery but watching her husband carefully to assess his mood.

"Tea! I don't want any!" Albert poured another large Scotch from the Waterford crystal decanter and sat down rather carelessly on the loveseat. Mary waited for him to explain the reason for his mood; she knew if she waited he would tell her. He did.

He had ordered a new watch like Sir Charles' from a watchmaker on Jamaica Street who was favored by Sir Charles. Sir Charles' was a Longine but Albert believed the new watch would be as nice and Scottish made, not Swiss. He had planned the design and the watchmaker had done a good job on that design. It was to reflect Albert's standing in the community with a scale and law books. It was initialed too. Albert had gone to the store today to see how the work was progressing. It was not to be ready yet as it was to take a month. He had paid a five-guinea deposit a few days ago and wanted to see that work was really progressing.

When Albert arrived at the workshop on Jamaica Street he found the shop window was boarded up, clearly the glass had been broken. Inside he found Edwin straightening the shelves and sorting his instruments. He had looked very uncomfortable when Albert asked him about his watch. He muttered that the work would be done but the shop had been robbed the night before and some things were missing.

"But do you have my five guineas, my good man?" asked Forrest. Looking uncomfortable and unable to meet Forrest's gaze, Edwin said that he would have the watch ready on time and he returned to sorting out the instruments, clearly willing the conversation to end. Exasperated as Edwin would not respond directly, Forrest looked for the older watchmaker but was informed that he was gravely ill. Recognizing that no more information could be gleaned from this young watchmaker, Albert decided it was best to leave and return again in a few days. He was irritated that he could not get a direct answer, irritated even more as he suspected that the five guineas might have been stolen.

Albert knew the chances of recovering the money and whatever else was stolen was unlikely. The justice system was significantly flawed. He defended criminals who could afford his services. He knew too that the odds of the watchmaker getting a thorough investigation for this loss were unlikely. Thievery amongst the lower classes and even the trading class was very common. Peel had done well in creating a police force but it was early days and there were just not enough trained "peelers" to take care of all the crimes which were perpetrated.

From dealing with criminals daily Forrest knew that burglaries were committed sometimes out of sheer necessity. He had decided long ago that poverty drove people to do nonsensical things. It made no sense to the intelligent mind that anyone would steal a watch and risk transportation to Australia as had happened to the felon who had stolen Sir Charles' watch. The penalties handed down were inappropriate for the crime perpetrated, yet they were necessary to control the poorer classes. This was the law and for the most part it worked well.

Only last week though Forrest had witnessed a case in which the judge cried as he gave out a sentence. A man had forged a sixpence. It was the second time that he had been caught. The man's wife was a pitiful creature. Dressed shabbily, and not too clean either, she had begged the judge for a lighter sentence. She had five children and without her husband she had no means of supporting them. If he went to Australia there was no hope for her but to go to the workhouse. The man was sentenced to seven years transportation. There was no alternative punishment, the prisons were inadequate and full. Yet it also made no sense that a family ended up in the workhouse because they had lost the breadwinner. He had even heard of cases where the wife had also committed a crime so she could be transported with her husband. At least things seemed to be improving with this Prime Minister.

Disgruntled with his situation but happy that he could complain to someone about it, Forrest took a long swig of his Scotch. He looked at his glass contentedly. Lagavulin from the isle of Islay. He was glad that his father-in-law had similar taste in malt whiskies and was not unhappy to pay for a fine one. Forrest kept the Scotch in the house for his father-in-law yet he ended up drinking most of it himself even though Sir Charles had paid for it.

Mary asked, "What are you going to do about it?"

"There's not a whole lot to be done yet. I want to see the old man but he is very sick. I just have to trust him. I had wanted to have the watch for next month and now that doesn't look good."

"At least the poor man has his tools so he can still work."

Albert did not see this as much consolation but he chose not to argue with Mary. He was hopeful that he could stop by her bedroom later that day. They were both very mindful that they had still not produced an heir to the Forrest fortune. Both sides of the family were starting to notice and comment, which embarrassed Albert exceedingly. He did not know how Mary felt about it. She tolerated him quite well but seemed quite occupied with her social life among the ladies. It sometimes surprised him the sort of things that interested women and he congratulated himself occasionally that he had not been born one.

He decided to stay in this evening and keep the company of his wife. He noticed how she was always eager to please him and he was anxious to spend time in her bedroom. He knew that other women were easy to find and just as easily dispensable - he had plenty of experience in that area - but he was tired too of frequenting the brothels of Old Town. He was physically tired too. The hours that he worked for the law firm were taking their toll. Yet again he wished he lived in Falkirk but that was a closed subject for his wife. He looked at Mary carefully, examining her dress, her shiny hair, and her trim figure. Yes, he'd stay in tonight.

CHAPTER 27

Edwin was worried. Very worried. Since the burglary William had taken to his bed. He sometimes complained of chest pains and the wracking cough was getting worse. No one could ignore the blood on his handkerchief. Lillias was distraught and wrung her hands regularly. Edwin noted rather callously that wringing one's hands serves no purpose, but mostly he felt sympathy for Lillias as she had spent many good years with William and she clearly loved him deeply.

Ann was busy with the new baby. Lydia was a joy to the whole family. She was a beauty and no mistake. The other two children, because they were still young, seemed oblivious to the problems facing the family.

Edwin was very aware of them though. He had gained a lot of experience as a watchmaker and William had done a very good job of mentoring him but Edwin did not have all the experience necessary to run the shop. Then too, with William not working, he was not producing income. There was still plenty of work although Edwin knew that they would lose some when regular customers realized that William was incapacitated. How could he hold it together?

Yet Edwin was optimistic. That was just his nature. He also had a lot of self-confidence and he was sure that he could keep the shop going until William was back on his feet. Yet there was a cash problem for the business. When Edwin visited with

William the evening before, William asked the women to leave the room and then he told Edwin about the missing sovereigns and Albert Forrest's missing guineas. They were penniless but they could still work.

Although Edwin was young enough that saving money did not fit in his plans, he could feel William's keen sense of loss for the money which he had carefully saved for years. He was dismayed for William and shocked to learn that William owned the sovereigns in the first place. He did not understand why William would take his money out of the bank yet he knew that older people distrusted banks. This new Law created by the English the previous year was certainly worrying to many Scottish tradesmen.

Edwin had not developed a strong sense of business but the idea of hiding money in the workshop did seem foolish. There was so much crime in the city that a watchmaker's business seemed to him to be an easy target. There were times that they had several watches in the workshop on which they were working. Sometimes the watches had been repaired and their owners had not picked them up; others waited until Edwin could take time to hand-deliver them. It was remarkable to him that some of the richer classes were so careless about their possessions. He knew there were two watches in a drawer in the workshop which belonged to sea captains who had left them there several months ago, and now the men were presumably at sea. Edwin had no idea when or if the captains would return to claim the watches.

Fortunately the burglars had not found the watches before they were disturbed, or perhaps they thought the watches would not be easy to dispose of. Watches were easily identifiable, gold sovereigns not so.

The five guineas for the supplies for Mr. Forrest's watch were gone too. Edwin had been embarrassed when Mr. Forrest asked him about the guineas as he suspected they had been in the stolen box. After Forrest had left, Edwin had checked with William and found to his dismay that his instinct was correct.

Yet even though Edwin was worried about the future he was hopeful too. He had a bottomless sense of optimism; some would call it the optimism of youth. They would make it through this crisis. He had reported the loss to the police but the policeman had barely noted the details and shrugged halfheartedly when asked by Edwin as to the possibility of retrieving the gold. He looked at Edwin with an expression which clearly indicated his derision and then he picked up the bun he was eating and turned back to his cup of tea, which held more interest to him than Edwin. Frustrated, Edwin left the police station and decided to make some inquiries on his own. He figured he might hear more about it in one of the pubs on Rose Street. If Tim had been around he might have asked him but Tim had of course gone to Van Diemen's Land.

Edwin had heard that the government in New South Wales was unwilling to take any more convicts. They had their fill of them, as had previously, the Americans. Instead, convicted felons were being transported to Van Diemen's Land, an island off the coast of Australia. Conditions were worse than in New South Wales. Edwin idly wondered if Tim had made the voyage satisfactorily. Many convicts did not. Disease was rampant on the ships and there was little supervision of the prison deck. By the time they arrived, others had sometimes become diseased.

There had to be a better way of handling criminals than transportation, thought Edwin, as his mind lingered on Tim's plight. Certainly Tim had stolen a watch and that was wrong, yet the punishment was harsh.

There was a prison attached to the police station on Constitution Street in Leith, Edwin knew, as he and Ann had passed by it when they were courting. Yet it was inadequate. Strange, he pondered, that there was money enough to build a fancy monument on Princes Street for a poet yet not enough to build better prisons for criminals. A poet, no less! These Scots certainly made a great deal out of honoring their more famous citizens. It was a fancy building for Sir Walter Scott, and that's for sure.

At this moment, Ann came into the workshop, Lydia resting comfortably on her right hip. Lydia was asleep, her long lashes resting on her chubby cheeks. She was a beauty and no mistake, thought Edwin.

"What are you doing, Laddie?" Ann asked him affectionately. Ignoring the fact that he was always working on watches, Edwin responded by showing her the watch he was working on. He had to tell her about the burglary and the loss of some of the money but he made little of it.

"Ann, there's something that's bothering me but I think I have it all worked out."

"What do you mean?"

Looking concerned, Ann moved the baby to her other hip but did not take her gaze from Edwin. It was unusual for him to worry about anything.

"You know when the burglars broke in they took some of your Da's money. The man whose watch I was making, you remember, Forrest, he gave me five guineas as a deposit on the new watch."

Ann's anxiety showed on her face. She was the worrier of the family. She waited though for him to finish, which he did with some difficulty.

"Well, the five guineas are missing. We don't have the money to buy what I need for the watch and I don't have it to give back to him!" He finished in a rush, glad that the truth was out as he did not like to keep secrets from Ann.

"I do have a plan though. I have three watches here to be repaired. If I can get those done and returned then I will have enough money to buy the supplies for Mr. Forrest's watch. I just hope we get paid right away though for the other watches."

"Perhaps instead of waiting for the customers to come back for their watches you should return them immediately and ask for payment," volunteered Ann.

"I'll do that for sure. I just hope I can get the money. I have to go to the tradesmen's entrance and sometimes I don't even get inside the houses and I certainly don't see the owner of the watch unless there is a particular need to talk to the owner about the watch."

Ann placidly said, "Then you will need to find something to discuss with the owner."

"I will. We'll get through this, Ann. And your Da will get better and be able to work again," said Edwin, not convinced himself of the veracity of his words.

"I know we will, Edwin. Tomorrow is Sunday. Why don't you go up to the Observatory tomorrow? Tell Da you are going and see if he wants to go with you. The walk would do you both good. As far as the money, Lillias and I are making some dresses now and they will be ready in a couple of days. If we get paid for those we will be all right again. At least we get paid faster for our work than you do yours. These fancy women want to keep getting new dresses and they know they must pay as they go if they want any service from us."

She continued, "I really think watchmakers are the slowest to get paid of any trade. They are even slower than dentists. No one wants to pay the dentist as it always hurts. Hurts to have a tooth out, hurts to pay for it. And people think they can do without their watches for a while, and when they do get them back it doesn't even enter their heads that you might want to get paid."

Edwin had heard this before from Ann. She had grown up with this argument from her parents. He let it slide off him. Normally he was not bothered by a slow payer, but right now he needed his customers to pay for his work. He sighed and then reached out for Lydia who had awakened and recognized him. She was definitely a Daddy's girl. Too small to do anything but look at him gravely she seemed nevertheless pleased to see him. In no time at all she'd be smiling at him and charming him, he thought. He decided that he would take a break for a while. Ann was right, he did need to get some fresh air. If it were nice the next day he would head up Calton Hill, hopefully with William.

At dinner that night Edwin asked William to go with him to the Observatory the following afternoon and William considered and then agreed that he would enjoy that. They had not done that recently and he had missed it.

CHAPTER 28

It rained overnight but as William and Edwin headed along George Street towards Calton Hill the sun appeared and brightened the street, the houses, and the shops. Edwin savored the scenery. He had loved Edinburgh from almost the first day; he enjoyed the contradictory warmth and dourness of the Scots, and he loved the scenery. True, parts of Edinburgh were squalid and overcrowded, yet the design of the New Town was decidedly elegant. He felt fortunate to live now on this side of town. He even liked the newly minted Scott's Monument although he had thought the money spent on it could have been put to better use. He had said as much to William.

William replied, "Aye, I could find better ways to spend my money than that but then I've never been much for book learning and reading. Certainly never had any interest in poetry!" He said this with a slight scoff in his voice.

The two walked slower than usual, because of William's health, up the hill towards the Observatory. Both of them enjoyed each other's company. Having lost his own parents, Edwin had been glad to be accepted into the fold of the Berridge family.

William was panting now even though the climb was not very steep. He had done this walk so many times that it dismayed him how unfit he felt. As they headed for the entry he looked briefly at his pocket watch. It was exactly 2 o'clock. Both of them were reminded of how they had met there just a few short years ago. How life had changed for all of them - a new career and family for Edwin, marriage of his daughter and grandchildren for William and, not least, a successor to his business. As William puffed and panted up the hill he thought of how grateful he was that Edwin would take over the business. He was in despair that he had lost so much of his savings yet he felt he could rely on Edwin to take care of Lillias after William had passed away. At least it was free to enter the Observatory! He could enjoy it without worrying about the cost. From now on he would have to watch all his pennies. Many times he had heard tell of how you needed to watch your pennies and the pounds would take care of themselves and never was a statement so true to him now.

They entered the cool vestibule of the Observatory. There were few other visitors. It always seemed strange to both of them that there were not more visitors to the free exhibition, yet they knew that they had been fortunate in learning about astronomy.

By tacit agreement they went to see the German-made Transit Circle first. That had been their habit for a while now. Neither failed to be impressed by the German engineering and the ability of the telescope to see celestial bodies. From there they followed their traditional route through the telescopes. It surprised both of them that they were allowed to touch the telescopes and each of them liked to do that, feeling by touching them that they could be closer to that other starry world.

They looked out over the city. Edinburgh was changing fast now. Waverly Station had recently opened. The Queen herself was scheduled to arrive there this summer by train. There was already a regular Glasgow-Edinburgh rail line. William's sons, Henry and Hugh, had visited them recently using the train. The whole family had gone to greet them at the station. It was a large cavernous building sunk into the valley. There was even talk of building on top of it but for now the street led deep down into the station. From the entry the tracks branched right and left of the road, the one on the right heading north and west, the one on the left heading south.

When the train entered the station with a great noise and clamor, the smoke had belched out of the stack, covering close passersby with soot.

Horrified when she looked at her white blouse, Ann had exclaimed, "If this is the way the trains run, I will just use a stagecoach. At least I still arrive fairly clean."

Placidly Lillias reminded her that the blouse would be easily washed and really the train was just the best way to travel. It was faster than using a stagecoach and it looked to be just as comfortable. At this point, Ann's brothers, Henry and Hugh, stepped out of the carriage, waving their caps in victory to the family.

"How was the trip?" asked Lillias, trying to hug both boys at the same time. "Alright," said

Henry, his face not able to hide his enthusiasm at the new mode of transportation. "It was jolly fine but it was a bit hot and dirty."

The family had all walked out of the station, back up the hill to Princes Street where Hugh noticed the Scott Monument had now been completed. Dryly William commented that it had been open for a while, indirectly pointing out that Henry and Hugh had not been home for a long while.

The two brothers had stayed only a few hours as they had only one day off work. Work was going well for them in Dumfries but there was trouble with the union and the factory owners. William disliked unions and personally saw little value in them. He was disturbed that his boys were so active in the union as he believed no good could come of it. Everyone, including Henry and Hugh, were glad when the visit was over. There had been one unpleasant incident as they walked through the workshop and Henry casually picked up some of Edwin's instruments to examine them and then threw them down on the bench very carelessly. Edwin was incensed as he valued his instruments greatly. William thought they were going to come to blows but Ann managed to steer Edwin's attention away and the act of provocation was ignored.

After William and Edwin had finished their tour of the Observatory they stood at the doorway, enjoying the view of Edinburgh. Neither tired of it.

Lillias would sometimes describe Scotland as "God's Country" and both men would laugh and then

William would say that if God did exist then perhaps He spent most of his time there. It had become something of an inside family joke.

There was a bench outside the Observatory and William suggested sitting there a while. This was a departure from their normal behavior but Edwin realized that William needed to rest. As they sat there, William coughed again and pulled out a handkerchief, neatly embroidered by Lillias. It had been a birthday present from her and he treasured it. He was dismayed to see that he had covered it in blood, partly because Lillias would have to wash it and partly because this constant show of blood was testimony that he was seriously unwell.

Edwin noticed it too. To take William's mind from it, he addressed the subject of bills.

"I've been thinking of how to manage the money so we can get through this bad patch. I have three watches that I am working on right now. I think I will deliver them as soon as I've finished and ask for payment. That should give us the money for the Forrest watch."

"I don't want to hear that, Edwin. I hate to ask for money as if we are really desperate."

"But we are! I know how you feel but I can't do that Forrest watch unless we get some money."

"Well, do it and just don't tell me about it. You know I don't like to hound the customers."

Edwin's philosophy was somewhat different. He felt that if he asked for payment that he was only asking for what he was owed and he was not stealing.

He was merely prompting the customers to do right by him. He knew his and William's work was good and that they should get paid for it. He did not want to upset William though who was old school and had what Edwin considered old-fashioned manners.

After five minutes William checked one of the watches that he had just synchronized in the Observatory and he suggested they head for home. The walk home was even slower. By the time they reached Jamaica Street Edwin was holding William by the elbow to steady him. Perhaps going to the Observatory had been a bad idea, he thought, although William had clearly enjoyed it.

Slowly they climbed the stone stairs of their house, William clinging to the iron railing to help him climb. One hand in front of the other ever so carefully. When they reached the Berridge door, Toby was there, seemingly guarding it. He awakened as the two approached. Looking very much like a man whose sleep had been disturbed, he kept blinking, trying to orient himself. He then looked the two up and down and allowed them to enter the household, carefully wrapping himself around their legs, rubbing against them and thereby marking them as his.

After dinner of haggis and neeps, a favorite for William, he went to bed saying that he needed to rest.

At two in the morning Edwin and Ann were awakened by Toby who was pacing through their room. Normally this was hunting time for Toby yet, blessed by feline intuition, he had decided to stay home and see how William was doing. Instinctively he knew that William was very ill; pacing before the Turners was his way of indicating that there were issues for them to deal with. Ann leapt up; she knew Toby well and she went to see her Da to see what was the matter with him.

She found William reclining against a pillow, his face ashen and his eyes closed. Lillias was by his side, tears running silently down her cheek. Blessed with Scottish stoicism, Lillias rarely cried. She had learned that crying did not always help, but now she stood, crying copiously, unable to take care of William more.

William's breathing had become shallow and uneven. As Lillias adjusted his blanket he did not stir. Neither did he stir when Toby jumped on the bed. Lillias shooed away the cat angrily. Ann stood mutely unable to do anything but pray. Edwin stood at her side, offering silent support. The children slept on, unaware that they were about to lose their grandfather.

Two hours later, without opening his eyes again, William died.

CHAPTER 29

Three days later Edwin was back at his workbench. Usually cheerful, today he was worried and despondent. The enormity of his situation was overwhelming. Now he had the whole family including Lillias to support. William had not worked much in a while and they were becoming accustomed to reduced income. As he had already discussed with William, Edwin had a plan. William had not approved but he was no longer there to criticize it. Edwin would have given anything though to have William working alongside him. The two men had grown fond of each other and the loss of William was to Edwin the most grief he had felt since his own parents died.

Ann was distraught. Trying to take care of three children, one of whom was still a baby, stretched her limits. She was fully occupied yet still had sewing to do. Lillias had been married so many years to William that she was taking the loss badly too. These were early days. The reality for the women had not sunk in yet. They still expected William to walk through the door, erect and dignified, and address them in his soft Edinburgh brogue.

For Edwin work was a consolation. You had to concentrate so much when working on watches. It required his full effort to work on the intricacies of the watches. He could not afford to make a mistake. Time was becoming a valuable commodity. As the so-called Industrial Revolution spread around the country and mechanization became available in so many businesses that had previously been cottage industries, businessmen became mindful of their time. "Time is money" began to be heard in the workplace.

Time had no value to Edwin unless it were accurate. There was no point in having a watch if it did not tell to the second the exact time. Time gave order to life, a measurement that one could easily use, a simple way of marking the hours and seconds and even give value to life. Edwin never thought too much about the loftier thoughts in life. William had been the one who had book learning and was something of a philosopher. Now Edwin faced his own time issues.

He had to work harder, work longer, work better to make up for the shortfall due to William's passing. "I'm young, I can do whatever it takes," he determined. Yet he knew too that you really couldn't repair a watch any faster. He would just have to work longer, he couldn't work faster.

The workshop door opened and in stepped Albert Forrest. Concerned that he perhaps had lost five guineas to the watchmaker, he thought he would remind the watchmaker of the debt and his responsibility to produce a fine watch. Dismayed to see him, Edwin stood up and greeted him politely,

"Good morning, sir. May I help you?"

"Of course. I am wondering if you have purchased the supplies for my watch yet?" As an after-thought he then enquired, "Have you had any success at retrieving your things?"

Edwin replied in the negative to both questions but assured Forrest that he would shortly buy the supplies. Unfortunately Mr. Berridge had died and Edwin had not been able to work for a few days.

Now Albert Forrest let out a gasp of dismay but recovered fast. Ever mindful of his manners he expressed his regret at the passing of Mr. Berridge. He would definitely have preferred the older man to be around while Mr. Turner made the watch but that was not to be. Briefly he considered whether he should retract the order. Tapping his cane on the floor, something he did whenever he was perturbed, he gazed at his fine leather shoes with their silver buckles, and then he told Edwin about the deadline to prepare the watch. Confident at this time that he could complete everything on time, Edwin rubbed his chin carefully, considered his situation but hastily assured Mr. Forrest that his watch would be completed by the deadline.

Satisfied that Edwin recognized the importance of making the watch well, Albert Forrest tapped his cane one more time and then turned on his heel and opened the door to exit, not bothering to wish Edwin good day.

Edwin did not even notice that Mr. Forrest had left rapidly. His concern now was to acquire the money to buy his supplies. He knew that he could make a watch that would delight Forrest. For the umpteenth time that day he wished William were there. He would have known exactly what to say to humor the man. Edwin had already noticed, and in fact had mentioned it to Ann, that Mr. Forrest was more polite and respectful to William Berridge than to Edwin. He supposed it was his lack of experience and his youth that prompted Forrest's behavior towards him.

At least one of the watches with which he was working would be ready tonight. He would have a chance to deliver it before dinner. He could work on the other two watches tomorrow and hopefully he could repair and return them the following day. Yes, this was a plan that would work if the timing were correct. His next job then would be to make the Forrest watch. That would be slow but the payment would pay for William's funeral expenses which were due too.

Edwin was not given to sighing but the vivid memory of William's funeral caused him to sigh deeply. Lillias had very proper ideas of how the funeral should be and Edwin certainly did not want to disappoint her. He had discussed with the undertaker the arrangements and the cost and he agreed to pay off the debt after the funeral. The undertaker had offered eight levels of funeral arrangements and, although Edwin had been inclined to get the cheapest, he had been persuaded by the two women to arrange for something better. It was not that Edwin wanted to be cheap but he also knew how hard he would have to work to pay for it. Women! They had such set ideas on how weddings and funerals were to be conducted.

The least expensive funeral offered an elm-lined coffin, a horse and carriage, pallbearers, a coachman and attendant complete with black hatbands and gloves. This would have only cost three pounds. However, there were appearances to keep up. They were tradespeople, yet on the way up in the world, or wished to be seen as such. So to that list of accoutrements Lillias had added an outer layer of lead to the coffin, four pages, and twenty black ostrich feathers. Burial had been in the graveyard of the family church and Lillias had ordered a magnificent granite headstone with a cherubic angel sitting on top of the stone. Edwin had not seen the final bill for that. He had loved William as a father but truly could not see William in that angelic light. William would have been amused; Edwin did not dare contest the women on this issue. He hoped that the stonemason would be late in delivering the headstone and he could pay for it later in the year.

Ann entered the shop with Lydia on her arm. Ann had assumed the traditional mourning dress which she would wear for a year. It made her look more tired, and older too, thought Edwin, but again he held his tongue. He had no love for the ubiquitous crepe that women in mourning wore these days. Fortunately Ann had made dresses for both women to wear and that helped the family a lot.

Letters of consolation from relatives and customers had started to arrive and Ann had been busy responding to them. She had come to see

Edwin as she needed a break from her grieving. Edwin could always lighten her spirits.

"Would you like a cup of tea, Edwin? I've some shortbread which Mrs. Brodie brought."

Edwin had no real desire for tea but always enjoyed a biscuit, particularly if their neighbor Mrs. Brodie had baked it, and he readily accepted the offer. Ann disappeared upstairs and returned a few minutes later, having left Lydia with Lillias and the visiting Mrs. Brodie. She carried two beakers of steaming tea in her right hand and a plate of biscuits in her left.

She set them on the workbench, carefully avoiding the watch on which Edwin was working and then she perched on the stool her father used to use.

"Have you almost finished, Edwin?" she asked hopefully.

"I wish! No, I will finish this soon but I need to deliver it and get paid. I plan to deliver it myself this evening. Hopefully the owner is at home and can pay me at once. I hate to ask for the money but somehow I have to get it!"

"Is that the one belonging to Dr. Archibald Cockburn?" Ann inquired, pronouncing the name correctly as Coe-burn. Dr. Cockburn was gaining fame in the city as a surgeon even though he was still a young man. It perhaps helped that his father was Lord Cockburn, a well-known lawyer who had been Solicitor General for Scotland in the 1830's.

"Aye," said Edwin. He loved to imitate the Scottish accent on occasion and it always made his wife laugh. "Aye, that it is. I wish your Da could see this pocket watch. He would have loved it. It's a beauty!"

Ann politely looked at the watch Edwin was holding and she admired it. She enjoyed his enthusiasm for his trade; it matched that of her father. As a seamstress she enjoyed detail work and could easily understand what fascinated Edwin about watches. She would never have believed that she would find a man who so closely mirrored her father's interests.

"I'll let you finish then and we'll see you later. I need to put Lydia down for a nap now."

Edwin soon finished Dr. Cockburn's watch and set the time. He would have preferred to go to the Observatory, as William had been wont to do, and set the watch there, but time was of the essence now, he thought rather wryly. Quickly he put on his coat and cap and headed out of the door, paying careful attention to the lock. He could afford no more losses.

Briskly Edwin walked along Jamaica Street and headed towards George Square where Dr. Cockburn lived. George Square was an area favored by lawyers. It was where Dr. Cockburn had grown up and now he chose to live a few doors down from his father.

The weather was only cool today and Edwin was thankful that Lillias had persuaded him to get a warm jacket last winter. It had seen a lot of use since then. He found he still needed it even in the summer sometimes. He was thankful too that he enjoyed walking as his path took him slightly uphill into the southern part of the city.

Even though George Square was not a part of New Town per se, it was a recent development and was favored by the aristocracy of Edinburgh. Characteristically it had Georgian homes with their long sash windows and elegant colonnades at each shiny front door. It was at one of these that Edwin knocked.

A butler promptly opened the door and looked at Edwin with some distaste. He had made an instant assessment of Edwin based on his appearance and decided that Edwin did not belong on the front stoop of Dr. Archibald Cockburn. Rather stiffly he told Edwin to go to the tradesman's entrance and directed him to the back of the property. A minute later Edwin arrived at said door. This time a footman opened the door. He looked Edwin up and down but did not shoo Edwin away this time.

"I have repaired Dr. Cockburn's watch and I would like to return it to him, please," said Edwin pleasantly.

"That would not be possible," said the footman, without explaining the impossibility.

"I would like to discuss the mechanism with him, and would appreciate getting paid too," continued Edwin, mindful that he did not want to return without the money. "Would there be a better time to see him?"

"Dr. Cockburn left for India yesterday. He will be gone a few months."

"What about the watch then?" said Edwin, quite shaken by this information.

"What about it, then? Dr. Cockburn has other watches and he certainly won't be needing one for this trip," said the footman with rather an aloof sneer.

"I don't know what to do then," Edwin said. "Is Mrs. Cockburn at home?"

"There is no Mrs. Cockburn yet. So no, she doesn't want the watch."

"Is there anyone, the butler or his valet, who will take the watch and pay me for my work? I've spent hours on this watch and I can't wait so long for the money."

"Sorry, nothing I can do. We don't have money to pay all Dr. Cockburn's bills to whomever shows up at the door."

The footman had clearly been schooled correctly in English grammar as his diction, though Scottish, was exacting. At this he closed the door, leaving Edwin holding the watch in his right hand as he wiped his brow worriedly with his left.

Slowly Edwin turned on his heel and walked away. He looked absent-mindedly into the square and watched the children playing there with their nannies. He sometimes wished that Ann had extra help to take care of the three children and her sewing too. She worked so hard but never complained.

He walked home more slowly than he walked to George Square, well aware that there was no money jingling in his pocket. His mind was in turmoil now but there was hope too. He had a couple of other watches to repair and be paid for too. Edwin was not so easily defeated and this little setback would not deter him. He would get all his bills paid even if he had to work halfway into the night to do it.

CHAPTER 30

Mrs. Brodie sat comfortably in the best armchair, clearly settled in for a long stay. She was a good baker and knew that she could always find a warm welcome and hearth if she delivered her shortbread. She particularly enjoyed visiting a family after someone had died; she tried to be sensitive to their needs but also tried to introduce some Christian theology into her conversation. She attended the same kirk as Lillias and Ann and the three would sometimes walk together to the morning service. Mrs. Brodie lived on the floor above the Berridges but even though she was upstairs she knew very well the comings and goings of the household beneath her. She did not go out much but spent a lot of time at the window surveying the busy street scene.

Now, with William gone, Lillias was trying to cope with the loss and entertain Mrs. Brodie too. She did not think she would ever get over missing William and it was difficult to watch Mrs. Brodie sit in what had been William's favorite chair.

"Would you like another cup of tea, Mrs. Brodie?" she enquired politely, gesturing to the Brown Betty which was still by the hearth. "Indeed, I would! Thank you so much," replied Mrs. Brodie.

She continued, "That was a lovely service, Mrs. Berridge. Mr. Berridge would have enjoyed it himself, I'm sure."

"Aye, that he would, although he was never a one for funerals or a big fuss. He always wanted something very plain but I just couldn't do that. I wanted him to have the best. He was a good man and no mistake."

"That he was. I always thought he looked after you very well, Mrs. Berridge. He was a brave man too. When he had one dram too many one time he told me about what he did in the war. You must be so proud of him, my dear. That funeral service must have cost a pretty penny too."

"Aye, he was a good one and that's for sure."

Lillias nibbled on her shortbread to avoid talking more. She ignored Mrs. Brodie's comment about the cost of the funeral. She was not about to tell Mrs. Brodie what it cost. Mrs. Brodie was a nice woman but at times she was less than polite. Sometimes it seemed she did not know the meaning of decorum.

The remark did however make Lillias think of money again. She was a little concerned as she knew Edwin had not returned. Ann had told her that he was delivering a watch to someone and he hoped to get paid for the watch right there and then. It was almost suppertime. She hoped Mrs. Brodie would leave soon so she could find out a little more from Ann. The two women sat in silence for a few more minutes, each lost in their thoughts.

Lillias checked the stove to see how dinner was cooking and then looked around for the two young boys, saying "It's dinner time. Time to come to the table."

Not so much because they were obedient but because they were starving as young boys tend to be, Alfie and Will ran to the table. Ann was coming up the stairs from the workshop. She had been looking for Edwin but the shop was in darkness and the outer door was locked.

Edwin was not used to being out late and she wondered what had waylaid him. Meanwhile Edwin had set off for home but, as he did, his steps got slower as he realized that for once he did not have a solution to the money situation. He knew he could still collect money for the repair on the other two watches. He might even get some more watches in for repair but he worried that he might get the same reaction as he had just experienced. He wished again that William were here to finesse the financial negotiations. He had been far better than Edwin at getting people to pay their debts. It was perhaps his stature and military bearing or his age that prompted people to open their purses. He had tried to teach Edwin how to collect payments and, better yet not extend credit, but Edwin was still uncomfortable dealing with others from significantly higher class than he was.

He was thirsty now too. It was unseasonably blustery and cool but Edwin had walked hard enough to shed his jacket. Perhaps a pint would do the trick, he thought. Turning into "The Drunken Duck" Edwin went up to the bar and ordered a pint of William Younger strong ale. He did miss his daily allotment from his work at the brewery. That had definitely been the best benefit to working there. The only one, he chuckled to himself, although he did miss some of the camaraderie of the other fellows.

It had been a long time since he had drunk the strong ale. Certainly the beer had the reputation for one only needing to drink one pint as it was so strong. Predictably it went to Edwin's head and he left the pub after only the one pint but his steps became even slower as he headed for home.

Leaving "The Drunken Duck" Edwin walked only a hundred yards before he arrived at "The Cat and the Bell". It was new to Edwin so he thought he would try out this pub too and he walked through into the dark, smoke-filled saloon noting that it was very noisy and very full. There were no seats available so Edwin stood at the bar and supped on his beer, all the while watching the barmaid as she served drinks, laughed and joked with the clientele, occasionally deflecting some unwanted attentions from the pub's patrons.

The barmaid paid him no attention as she chatted with the regulars and after downing this second pint Edwin felt morose. He knew that he could ill afford the beers he had just finished and he decided it was best to head for home. Standing with a drink in a bar had never held much attraction to him although it was clearly the pursuit of much of the male working class. He touched his cap to the barmaid who barely noticed him leave. Promptly someone else took his place at the bar and he went outside and the dark swallowed him up, mirroring his gloomy mood.

Wishing he had not stopped for a drink Edwin set off for home. He was usually home at this time and the women would be worried. Picking up his pace he decided to take a short cut past Greyfriars Graveyard and the Covenanters Prison. He had heard tales from some of the fellows at the Brewery about the religious freedom prisoners who had occupied the Prison, a part of the churchyard. He knew people were afraid to go past the churchyard as tales of bodysnatchers and ghosts were rife. Superstition and myth were rampant among the locals. It made for good stories at the pub at night but he knew there had been sightings.

Thinking that perhaps he should have had another pint to send him on his way, he valued his time and decided to run through the churchyard as fast as he could. As he darted his way around the gravestones he tried not to look left or right. The yew trees stood tall looking askance at him.

Finally he reached the other side of the cemetery and he paused for a moment.

"You are getting to be a coward, Edwin Turner," he told himself. "What would Ann think of you if she could see you now?" He tried to smooth down his unruly wavy hair so that he did not appear so disheveled. No one noticed him walking along. The passersby were preoccupied with their own lives and paid no attention to the red-cheeked young man who was likewise uninterested in whom he passed.

For a while the beer had softened his worry over money but the cool evening air was taking away the warmth and comfort which the beer had offered him. Reality was setting in and he unconsciously reached for Dr. Cockburn's pocket watch. He liked its shape and smoothness. Exasperated though, he remembered again that he had the watch indefinitely until Dr. Cockburn decided to return from his voyage.

Depressed at the idea that he could not make ends meet and heartily wishing he had not wasted money in the pub, he continued on his way, ready for a good scolding from his mother-in-law, who in the last few days had given out several uncharacteristically strong tongue lashings.

When he finally entered 15 Jamaica Street he found Mrs. Brodie ensconced in William's chair and Lillias looking at Mrs. Brodie and at him with some dislike. She was clearly stressed by the length of Mrs. Brodie's stay and at Edwin's late arrival. Mrs. Brodie seemed however not to notice this and she concentrated on watching Edwin carefully. It took her less than a minute to realize that Edwin had been drinking, partly by his speech and partly by his beery breath. He tried not to breathe near her but Mrs. Brodie was skilled in observation and she missed nothing.

"I see you've stopped on the way home," she commented, looking down her nose at him, and sniffing with some disdain.

Edwin chose to ignore the comment and was relieved to see Toby walk in the room. Toby was no friend of Mrs. Brodie and he was skilled in irritating her. He jumped up on her knee before she realized what was happening. Immediately she jumped up, brushing him off. He was used to this and used also to her departing forthwith. Satisfied that he had achieved his goal Toby took his place at the hearth. The family looked at him with affection. Sometimes this orange cat was worth his weight in gold.

CHAPTER 31

Ann was worried about Edwin. She had noticed as did Mrs. Brodie that he had been drinking. It was not the quantity that bothered her but rather the fact that he drank and it was so rare for him. Something was clearly bothering him and she surmised it was not just her Da's passing.

Later that evening as they settled down to sleep, she looked at Edwin carefully. Propped on her right elbow and shoulder she gazed at his dark wavy hair, his freckled face and rosy cheeks, and she congratulated herself yet again that she had a handsome husband whom she loved very much. Right now though he seemed very detached. She had tried to initiate lovemaking but he clearly had no interest, claiming only that it had been a long day and he was tired. That definitely was not like her Edwin either. He was usually delighted if she indicated her desire for him. Ann tried to ask what was bothering him.

Edwin and Ann had never been reticent with each other to share each other's worries. Edwin was unlike many of the Scotsmen that Ann knew who were dour and stoic to a fault. Edwin as an Englishman was rarely seen to exhibit much anxiety or public emotion. Yet in private he was willing to share his life with Ann.

"It's the workshop, Ann. I have plenty of work right now but now that your Da is not there to work too I cannot manage it all. I wish he were here to see we get paid. My trip to Dr. Cockburn's on George Square was a waste of time. He has gone for several months and I am left holding the watch and don't know when, if ever, I'll get paid. He may even forget in that time that he has a watch. He's gone to India!"

Ann was shocked but tried to be resourceful. "Do you have any more work where we can get paid?"

Edwin replied, "Thank goodness, there's more. Most of the work is for cleaning watches. It's pretty routine but I do have a couple of watches which are going to take a good amount of time to do them. I should get well paid for those."

He continued, "The thing that's bothering me now is that I have spent hours working on the plans for Mr. Forrest's watch. He gave me five guineas for supplies but I didn't get them before all the money was stolen. Now he wants his watch and I have nothing but a design on paper!"

Ann really had no suggestions for him. She was comfortable that he would get everything sorted out. She trusted him implicitly. Kissing him briefly on the lips, she turned over onto her left side, turning her back to him, leaving him to mull over his situation, and wishing that he had had a third pint of beer.

After a very restless night Edwin got up early the next morning and decided to miss breakfast and start work on the repairs with which he hoped would garner him the funds he so desperately needed. There was little to eat in the house anyway. They had provided food for friends and neighbors for the funeral and most of that was gone. He wryly thought that the reason some people came to a funeral was for the party afterwards. Edwin's father used to say that the measure of a man's worth was not the numbers of mourners at his funeral as that was frequently dictated by the weather. However the Scots were a hardy bunch and could tolerate all kinds of inclement weather. An unusually cold, rather blustery day had not prevented William's friends from coming to his funeral and partaking of the refreshments later.

Edwin sat at his workbench and pulled out the two watches he needed to work on. He was surprised to see that Sir Charles Mortimer's Longine needed repair again. He opened up the casing and examined the springs carefully. It was still barely light and he silently cursed the darkness. No wonder William complained about eyestrain. Edwin could picture himself in a few years complaining about it too.

Methodically he worked on the watch, admiring again the precision and the design of the watch. Longine was becoming very well known in the watch marketplace and for connoisseurs he could see why. Time passed and he whistled softly as he worked. His resilience had reappeared this morning. He had a slight headache but nothing that would deter him from his goal of finishing these watches and returning them to their owners by the end of the day.

A couple of hours later Ann came with a cup of tea for him and a bread and butter sandwich. He looked up from his work, grateful for the interruption. He laid down the instrument in his hand and reached for the tea. It was good and strong, just as he liked it. He loved Ann's homemade brown bread too. He always enjoyed seeing her kneading the dough and then setting it to rise in front of the hearth. The anticipation of eating good hot bread was something that he looked forward to every day. This morning's bread though was yesterday's and it was already drying out. At least it was food and he did not need to buy more. Credit at the local grocery shop was questionable, he knew.

Ann was observant and noticed the Mortimer watch which she had seen previously. Edwin showed her what he was working on and she listened with half an ear, listening too for Lydia who was inclined to cry as soon as she awakened. Receiving that alarm from Lydia a moment later, Ann left and Edwin continued to work on the Mortimer watch.

Once finished he resisted the urge to take it immediately to Sir Charles Mortimer's house and he turned to the next watch. It belonged to Charles Jenner, the founder of the very fine department store on Princes Street. Interesting and perhaps representative of the cutting edge type of retailing with which Jenner was famous, Jenner had purchased a French watch from a brand new upstart company called Cartier. It was the first that Edwin had seen and he was surprised that Jenner would favor a watch, firstly from a French company, and secondly a new one at that. Perhaps he was starting to establish a new style. Certainly the Cartier company would have interest in having their watches sold in the finest department store in Scotland.

The watch was charming and definitely different. Set in gold the face was mother-of-pearl with very clear black Roman numerals. On the outer perimeter little boxes marked off each second but there was no second hand. On the contrary at the base of the face there was a small circle containing the second hand and it was there that the seconds were counted off. In addition there was the day and date in the center of the face. Inscribed in italics "Cartier" advertised its fine quality to the world. The casing was rather plain but the large heavy gold winder spoke to its value, as did the connecting hook used to attach it to the watch chain. Inside Edwin noticed its serial number engraved in ornate numerals, along with the owner's initials, C.J.

For a moment Edwin gazed at the watch and recognized its beauty. Then he opened up the back and reviewed its inside. He had been surprised that such a new watch would break down but he suspected it only needed a cleaning, as indeed it did. He looked in the drawer for his tools. Edwin was neat in his work habits and William had taught him to return his instruments to the same spot each time, even if he were to need them a few minutes later. That advice had been very handy on occasion.

By the time he finished working on the watches he looked at some minor work which he needed to do on two other watches. The watches themselves were functioning well but one had a broken chain; the other had lost its winder. Sighing because that was yet another item that he would have to purchase rather than craft, Edwin decided to deliver the first two watches.

Fortunately both Jenner and Mortimer lived in the smart part of town on Charlotte Square which was not very far for Edwin to walk. He gathered up his coat and cap and headed out without stopping to tell Ann where he was bound, so intent was he on getting paid for the watch repairs. Arriving at Sir Charles Mortimer's first he knew better than to knock on the front door. He went to the tradesman's entrance and waited somewhat impatiently until the door was opened.

"Good morning," he began politely. "I am returning Sir Charles' watch which I have repaired." The footman reached for the watch and Edwin retracted his arm.

"I am sorry but I need to be paid now," Edwin said, hoping that he sounded confident and a man to be reckoned with.

"Then you will have to wait. Sir Charles is in London and we don't know how long he plans to stay. There is family illness," said the footman rather vaguely.

Distressed but unable to do anything about it, Edwin turned on his heel, putting the watch back in his pocket.

Across the square he found Mr. Charles Jenner's house. It was freshly painted with a dark blue shiny door and shutters. He avoided the front door however and went around the back to the tradesman's entrance, which he found in considerably shabbier appearance. The door opened promptly as he rang the bell and Edwin explained the reason for his presence.

Rather stiffly the footman replied, "I am sorry but Mr. Jenner is on a shopping tour in Europe. We do not know when he will return. You can leave the watch with me though."

Edwin declined immediately, but was now shocked that his three major sources of income this week were out of town. He had no idea now when he would be paid. Aghast at the situation but controlled in his response as he was English after all, Edwin set off for home, somewhat in a daze. His mind turned over how he could come up with money to pay the current bills which were pressing on him.

As he turned onto Jamaica Street he noticed the local pawnbroker's business. It was something he rarely paid attention to as he had been raised by his parents to never use a pawn shop. While living in Edinburgh though he had noticed that pawnbrokers were a very popular business here, more so than in England. For many it seemed a way of life although it had made no sense to him because he had learned from William that the interest rate was 1.66% each month, making it 20% per year, and the interest compounded too.

He tried to brush the idea from his head but then, almost on a whim, he decided to get the third watch, Dr. Cockburn's, and take all three to the pawnbroker at the end of Jamaica Street and just see what he could get for the watches. It would only be temporary, just so that he could pay a few bills and get the materials for the Forrest watch. The watch owners would not even know what he had done as they probably would not return until after he had claimed back the watches. No harm would be done and it would set him right with his bills.

Quickly Edwin unlocked the door to his workshop, retrieved Dr. Cockburn's watch and headed towards the pawnbroker, all before Lillias or Ann even knew he had returned. He really did not want to worry them or deal with their disapproval. He was quite sure that William had never pawned a watch in his life. There seemed to be no alternative though. In a few days he could retrieve the watches again and no one would be any the wiser.

The transaction went smoother than he had expected. There was a middle-aged balding man behind the counter who looked at him blandly until Edwin showed him the watches. They had seen each other on the street but had no conversation to this point.

Even now the pawnbroker, Bill Nesbitt, had no interest in chatting. He was clearly very interested in the watches though and he explained his terms to

Edwin. He would give Edwin two guineas for each one. Although this was a lot of money to Edwin he also knew that the watches were worth three times that. Two of them were 18 karat gold, the other a rose gold. With six guineas though he could at least buy the supplies for Mr. Forrest's watch. Then after that was complete he would look into paying the other bills. It would be close but they could manage. He knew that the rent needed to be paid; that would take a shilling a week. With six guineas in his pocket, 126 shillings in fact, he felt that he could live for a while quite comfortably.

Hopefully the five guineas he had received from Mr. Forrest would not be required in its entirety and he could start to make a profit on the watch even before he had made it.

The gold had to come from a registered goldsmith. After it was finished Edwin would then take it to the Assay Office to have it hallmarked. It was not a legal requirement as it was for silver but Edwin knew that it impressed the buyer if he could see the authentication on the watch. William had always used William Cross as a goldsmith. He was experienced, coming from a family line of goldsmiths and he lived conveniently at 51 Hanover Street. Competition was surprisingly fierce amongst the goldsmiths and the Goldsmiths' Guild set high standards for apprenticeship and mastery of the craft.

With the money jingling in his pocket Edwin was quick to forget that he had pawned the watches. Always confident, he was sure that it would all work out. He checked to see if he had the Forrest watch design in his pocket. Assured that he had, he set off for Hanover Street at a trot, intent to order the casing and gold from Mr. Cross. That man had a small shop window, similar to the Berridge shop window. It was a bay window with dimpled glass. The signage on the black board above the window was characteristically in gold. It announced to the world, Cross and Carruthers. Edwin knew that John Carruthers was a jeweler who lived together with William Cross and their combined ten children above the workshop.

Upon Edwin's entering the shop Mr. Cross looked up from his desk. He greeted the young man cheerfully and looked at the watch design with interest. He assured Edwin that he could make the casing and that it would be ready in two weeks. Edwin had hoped for a week as he still had to assemble the watch. It meant that Forrest would not get his watch back when he wanted it. Nothing to be done about that now, he thought. He turned over three guineas to the goldsmith, realizing that his money was disappearing fast. After paying two weeks rent though there would still be enough for food. At least he had a job and a skill. No need to worry.

Edwin knew that unemployment was running high in Edinburgh and the surrounding countryside. Britain was changing dramatically; you could see that just as you walked around the city. In the hope of getting work in the city, farming families were moving there and were trying to get a foothold in the industrial revolution which had swept through the land.

It had created many problems because of shortage of housing and skilled labor, and the churches were stretched to keep up with the demand on their resources. Because of this, a Board of Supervision had been established to investigate an applicant's need for poor relief. Edwin hoped never to see the inside of a workhouse although he knew that relief in Scotland tended to be what they called outside relief which meant you did not need to be "incarcerated" into the workhouse. Edwin had heard tales of the workhouse and in fact had met several people who had applied for aid. Many of his former neighbors had been recipients of charity and aid. Again he thought, "At least I have a job and a skill!"

CHAPTER 32

Edwin arrived at 15 Jamaica Street and decided to see Ann immediately. She and Lillias were sitting by the fire, and Lydia was in a cradle by Ann's side. As usual she was fast asleep. Absent-mindedly Edwin kissed the baby's forehead and turned to Ann with a beam.

"Here's the rent money for this week and for last. At least our landlord can't complain anymore. We are up to date again!

"Here's ten shillings too for food. Spend it for what we need but there won't be anymore for a while."

Ann was definitely pleased to get it but inquired why there was not more as she knew the watches he was working on. Edwin replied vaguely, "I'll give you more later. That's all for now."

The two women looked at each other, and Lillias raised her eyebrows but neither said anything. Ann wished she could know more of her husband's business but it seemed that he did not wish to provide more information and she knew better than to ask. Despite Edwin's cheerful nature he had a quick temper and took poorly to criticism. It was time to eat anyway.

Later as they were lying in bed, Ann leaned on her right elbow and looked at Edwin carefully. "I really thought those watches would bring more money. Do you have the money now for Mr. Forrest's watch?"

216

"Yes," said Edwin, ignoring the comment about the anticipated revenue. He turned over on his side and promptly went to sleep. Certainly a few pawned watches were not about to upset him. He did feel uneasy when he thought about William as he knew that William would have disapproved strongly. You do what you have to do, he thought, carefully rationalizing the situation.

Within a week Edwin's usage of the pawnbroker had slipped his mind as he worked on some of the other watches that needed minor repair. There was one he particularly admired, made by Charles Taylor of Bristol. It was in 18-karat gold and had a fusee movement, very traditional yet very successful in keeping good time as the conical shape pulley had a chain which was attached to the mainspring barrel. As the watch ran down, the fusee equalized the uneven movement of the mainspring. This particular watch had a broken fusee chain that had whipped around the mainspring and damaged other parts of the watch. Nevertheless, even though this was complicated to repair, Edwin liked the fine gold plain casing. Even the hallmark reeked of money. It had the casemaker's initials, WW, and a crown above 18 which indicated that it was 18-karat. The letter "q" indicated that it was made in 1831. William Berridge had always liked this kind of mechanism even though it made the casing more bulky. He said it made the watch feel more solid and weighty.

Edwin had not heard whether the watch owners had returned and needed their watches. Mr. Albert Forrest had checked in with him a couple of days ago and Edwin was happy to tell him that work had started on his watch although he had the rather unhappy job of telling him that the watch would not be ready to meet Mr. Forrest's deadline. Disgusted and enraged, Mr. Forrest left the workshop quickly, trying unsuccessfully to keep his temper under control. It did not help that he had gambled and lost money again the previous night and unfortunately his father-in-law was in London at the moment and could not reinforce his coffers again.

Happily though Albert Forrest had just heard the news that Miss Mary was indeed pregnant. He hoped fervently for a boy but was relieved at this point that there was a pregnancy. Miss Mary seemed preoccupied with the pregnancy; her father Sir Charles Mortimer was delighted and at least for a while there was a promise of more funds from Sir Charles as he expected his first grandchild. This trip to London offered only slight delay to the cash flow, hoped Albert.

Ann was coping well with her new child. Lydia was a good baby, cried little and cooed a lot. The two older children enjoyed having a sister and they cuddled her often and regularly. Ann had started sewing again although she lacked the time to do as much as previously. Even with a good new baby, her time was tied because of extra feedings and lack of sleep.

Lillias too was not sewing as much. Her vision seemed impaired. She did not complain much but she found that she could not sew for long in a dark room. They were not short of work because they had developed a reputation for fine embroidery and stitching.

The following day Ann left Lillias to mind the children while she went and paid the bills. She also stopped in the Lawnmarket to buy cloth for a new dress she was making for a lady on Frederick Street. The selection of cloths was wide these days and she lingered for a while just savoring the colors and smells of the new fabrics. She wished she could have chosen one of the light blue chambrays but she knew she needed to settle for a black taffeta as the unfortunate lady had been recently widowed.

As she was buying the taffeta she decided to buy more material so she could make a dress for Lillias. That would cheer her up, she thought. She wondered though how she could manage to make the dress in secret so that Lillias would not see it before it was finished. Well, once the material was bought, there was no going back. She could not return the fabric and Lillias would just have to have a new dress. Lillias dressed plainly but had always wanted to wear dresses like those she made for her clients. She had never felt that she could. Besides, William had controlled the purse strings and Lillias was definitely unaccustomed to asking for what she would like.

Having selected the fabric Ann moved on to the ribbon stall. Again she knew that she would have to buy black and she ended up choosing a rich black velvet which she planned to use on the sleeves of both gowns. A few stalls further up the street she came upon buttons for sale and there she selected some small pearl buttons to decorate the collars.

Mindful that the ten shillings was disappearing very fast, Ann decided not to linger there. She also knew that at home the children would need some attention and these days it was hard for Lillias to give them the attention they needed. Her final stop was Fleshmarket Close to buy some meat. As she approached the Close she was almost overwhelmed by the noxious smell. Some of the city's abattoirs were still here although she had heard tell that many were moving to Fountainbridge. That was too far for Ann to go today. Besides, she had a favorite butcher here though she rarely ate meat as it was too expensive. Today though she wanted to make a steak and kidney pie for Edwin. It was his favorite dish.

Her butcher was Harry Crowe. Butchering had been the family business for many years and Harry knew how to treat his customers well and not surprisingly there was a line of women at his counter waiting for his service.

Harry was a stout man, short, with a thick head of greying hair that had once been quite red. His complexion was fair and his face was rather red, his nose showing the first signs of rosacea. Around his rather ample girth was a white apron reaching to the floor. He also wore a navy blue and white striped coat, the traditional sign of a butcher.

Harry had his back turned to the waiting women as he worked on his large wooden chopping table. He had been at work early and had selected a side of beef from the nearest abattoir. Then it became a race against time to quarter and section the beef so that the meat was prepared for his customers when his shop opened a couple of hours later. Harry had been running late this morning but that did not stop his cheerful demeanor.

As he worked, the women talked amongst themselves, not too quietly. They liked to tease Harry and he enjoyed the repartee. Today, as usual, they were complaining about the price of meat. Harry ignored them. He was used to that kind of talk and he agreed with them that it was getting very expensive these days to eat well. Some of the women were cooks from big houses and they did not seem to worry about where the money was coming from. That drove up the price for people like Ann who was very conscious of every penny she made and spent.

Finally it was Ann's turn. She placed her order and watched carefully as Harry cut and weighed the meat and kidneys. There would be more kidneys than beef as they were cheaper. Fortunately everyone liked kidneys and they gave good flavor to the pie. Ann had known of butchers who also managed to weigh their fingers as they weighed their meat but Harry was not one of these.

Pleased with the quality of his meat, Harry showed the selected pieces to Ann who considered them and the pennies in her hand before handing over her coins. Harry carefully bundled up the meat, asked after Ann's new-born and then took her coins in his blood-stained hand. He put the coins in his pocket, wiped his hand on his apron leaving a stain which added to the ones that he already had.

Ann stepped away from the stall carefully as the ground around it was frequently slick. Now, with both hands full, she headed for home. She would have time to make the steak and kidney pie before beginning work on the dresses.

Tucking one package under her arm Ann checked her pocket to make sure that the remaining money was secure. There would be just enough left to buy a piece of candy each for the boys and perhaps for Lillias and she could give the rest of the money to Lillias to start paying the funeral expenses. Another stop at a sweet shop on Princes Street to buy some pear drops - the whole family loved the half-pink, half-yellow sweets - and Ann headed for home, pleased with her purchases but eager too to start making the next dress.

Chapter 33

Two weeks passed and life started to settle down after the funeral. Edwin found it difficult to work alone. He had always been chatty and even though William had not talked so much he enjoyed the company of the older man. He worried that work would slow down once people realized that William was no longer at the helm. It was hard to tell how customers would react. Some just returned to the same spot where they had previously had their watch repaired, confident that the watchmaker there could do the work. Others though were more selective as though they were choosing their doctor or dentist and would not be swayed merely by the location and familiarity.

The day before, William Cross had finished the casing for the Forrest watch. Edwin had returned to the Cross workshop on the day it was due to be completed but was still half-surprised to see it ready. Not so pleasant a surprise came though when Cross told him that the watch would cost five shillings more than anticipated as it had taken more gold than expected. Edwin was irritated and immediately his temper came to the fore. He angrily leaned on the counter and told Cross that he had no more money. Placidly Cross backed away slightly. He had seen this kind of scene before. He knew he was on solid ground for getting his money as he had the casing which Edwin wanted.

After pacing a little in the workshop, Edwin stopped as he realized he looked rather ridiculous as the shop was so small, and he knew he needed the watch. He dug into his pocket, retrieved the five shillings which he reluctantly handed over to Cross, threatening at the same time never to return. Again Cross was regretful but he basked in the knowledge that he was a good craftsman and he knew that Edwin would be back.

Once Edwin got back to his own workshop he sat at his bench and examined the casing. He had to admire Cross' handiwork. The man knew his craft well and the design of the scales and books looked perfect on the gold. He had engraved it skillfully using the proportions suggested by Edwin. The circumference of the casing had a laurel wreath design exactly as Edwin had suggested. All in all it was a fine piece of work.

Now it was time to construct the innards of the watch. To Edwin that was the real skill but to the owner they were always impressed by the outer appearance as that marked with distinction a man. If the watch did not operate as efficiently as it should then to most men of the time it was unimportant. Edwin knew however that this was a watch that he would need to take to the Observatory to synchronize the time, just as he and William had done with other watches on several occasions. Gladly he had an excuse to go there although it offered less joy now that William was not there to accompany him.

Suddenly he heard a scream upstairs, and forgetting what he was working on and neglecting also to lock the front door, Edwin ran up the stone stairs to the floor above, leaping up the stairs two at a time. The door to the flat was opened just as he arrived and Lillias was rushing out, intent on finding him. Ann had been heating water on the stove and had accidentally scalded her right hand with the boiling water.

By the time Edwin found her she was seated in her rocking chair nursing her hand, tears streaming down her face. He reached for a pan of cold water and promptly put her hand into it to soak. It gave little relief but it was the best he had to offer. Edwin decided to wait with her until the pain subsided. Then he would go to the apothecary and get a salve for her hand. Lillias stood looking in sympathy at her daughter but unable to offer more comfort. She offered Ann a cup of tea but Edwin suggested they pull out the Scotch which they had been saving for Hogmanay and take a sip of it now. He knew from his own point of view that would calm him and it would calm her too. Not being drinking women both women were skeptical but tried the Scotch. After a few minutes Ann was calm again but her hand was already blistering badly. She would not be able to use it for quite some time.

As Ann sipped her Scotch, Edwin waited with her, distraught to see her pain. He really could not bear anything bad to happen to her. Downstairs the doorbell to the workshop announced a customer and

Edwin realized he had left the door unlocked. He made his way downstairs a little slower than he had ascended but was surprised to see that there was no one in the shop. Puzzled, he opened the front door and at first saw no one waiting there. Fifty yards up the street a young man was darting through the crowd. Immediately Edwin looked at his workbench and realized that the gold casing was missing. Shocked and aghast at the loss, Edwin ran out of the shop and followed the man who appeared to be heading for Old Town.

Although Edwin was fast on his feet the other young man was faster and the distance between them lengthened. By the time they both reached George Street Edwin was winded because of the hill he had just climbed, and he could no longer give pursuit. He tried to shout to get someone to stop the man but his pleas were ignored. Unfortunately robberies were commonplace. With unemployment being so high many had turned to a life of crime. No one wanted to get involved now.

Edwin leaned against an iron railing and contemplated what to do. The casing was of lesser value as it was not part of a watch and the design on it was so specialized that it would not suit anyone except a lawyer, a judge, or perhaps a professor. He was sure the thief wanted it only for the gold. An ounce of gold was selling for three pounds six shillings. For a fleeting second he realized that his design would probably be melted down. More powerfully though came the thought that he had once again been robbed and this time he did not know how to deal with it. Stop putting the cart before the horse, he thought, I can work this out.

Edwin realized though that he would have to tell Ann everything. She still was unaware of the pawned watches. Before he did that, he would visit the police station and at least let them know his casing had been stolen. Ruefully he realized that he was becoming a regular at the station. When he walked in though he was not recognized by the policeman at the desk. There were just too many crimes and Edwin's loss did not stand out from others, some who were more important personages. Dutifully however the policeman noted what was lost but again, as previously, offered no hope of it being found. He did suggest that Edwin check on different jewelers in the next few weeks to see if a watch with that design appeared. Knowing the value of gold Edwin really did not expect that to happen but he thanked the policeman anyway.

As he walked home he considered his options. He had pawned the watches yet had no way of retrieving them as he had spent the money they had raised. He had planned to sell the Forrest watch but there was no casing and no watch and he had no money to order another casing. Worse than that he could not even refund Mr. Albert Forrest the down payment on his watch. The little family was keeping its head above water with rent and food but some of the funeral expenses were still owed. Edwin realized that was one worry that he could delay until later. He was not expecting to use the funeral director again any time soon so that man could wait for his money.

More pressing was how to deal with Forrest's watch. It was time too to tell Ann about the pawned watches. He dreaded that even more than he dreaded dealing with Mr. Forrest. At times Ann could be very conservative and he knew she would disapprove of pawnbroking even though it was a common way for many in their class to acquire needed funds at a moment's notice. He just hoped that she would understand. Her love and respect were his most valuable possessions.

CHAPTER 34

A couple of days later Albert Forrest entered his dining room and sat down to his usual Scottish breakfast of porridge followed by sausage, black pudding, fried eggs and potato scones. He sat at the head of the table and waited as his footman loaded his plate from the sideboard.

The bi-weekly newspaper, The Scotsman, was lying by Forrest's right hand. It was not favorite reading material for him, he found it very liberal, but it did allow him to keep up to date with Edinburgh establishment. Its editor, Charles Maclaren, was a neighbor of his father-in-law. They had met a few times socially but in general Forrest avoided much contact with the Whigs. He had been dismayed when the Whigs pushed for franchise reform and now the electorate included some of the middle classes. Even as a young man Forrest did not welcome that kind of change.

He glanced through the paper idly as he waited for Mary to appear although it seemed she was going to get her breakfast again on a tray in her bedroom. Since the pregnancy began Albert had seen less of Mary as she rested much of the time. Albert was delighted with the pregnancy but would be glad when it was over. Mary looked tired and out of sorts much of the time. He had noticed that some women seemed to glow with pregnancy but that had definitely not happened to Mary.

As he flicked through the pages he looked for the criminal reports. As a lawyer he was always interested in seeing how judges applied the law. It was useful to his own work and planning for court appearances. He suddenly noticed in the long list of reported crimes that the watchmaker on Jamaica Street, Berridge and Turner, had been robbed again. The paper did not detail what had been stolen. Forrest hoped his watch was not affected by the loss. Momentarily irritated, he added milk to his tea and two lumps of sugar. Directly after breakfast it would be time to pay Mr. Edwin Turner a visit.

Half an hour later he climbed in his brougham and made the short trip to the watchmaker. He found Edwin sitting at his workbench but clearly not working.

"I just stopped by to see how my watch is coming along," he began.

Edwin was clearly distressed by the question but replied, "I am sorry....I had the casing but we were robbed again last night and it was stolen."

"Well, don't worry. I really don't want to wait any longer for it so you can just repay me my deposit money."

Edwin looked sick to his stomach but managed to tell Mr. Forrest, "I am very sorry but I cannot repay you. I spent the money for the casing and I don't have any other money. I have some watches which I have repaired which will bring me some money but I don't know when. I will definitely repay you when I can."

"I am sorry for your problems but they are yours and not mine," replied Mr. Forrest a trifle imperiously.

"If you cannot repay me within the week I will be forced to file legal action against you. As you are no doubt aware, I am an attorney and am quite familiar with this type of situation. You should have done a better job of taking care of your property. This is the second time within a month that this has happened. Most people would have figured out after the first robbery how to protect themselves from any future threats."

At this Edwin was tongue-tied. He was young and inexperienced enough that intimidation worked quite well on him. He could merely stare at Mr. Forrest, his mouth slightly open, perplexed as to how to answer. As he was stammering that he would try and get the money, Albert Forrest turned on his heel, exited the shop and climbed back into the comfort of his brougham, leaving Edwin in dismay.

Edwin sat at his workbench for a while trying to weigh his alternatives. He could try and borrow some money but really had no collateral. Worse than that he owed money to the pawnbroker and he still had not cleared the debt of William's funeral. For once his confidence began to pall.

As he was still sitting there, the workshop door opened again and this time a servant of Sir Charles Mortimer stepped in. Word travels fast, thought Edwin wryly. Forrest must have gone instantly around to his father-in-law's house and told him of the news. Sure enough Mortimer's servant wanted the watch of Sir Charles. That gentleman had completed his business in London and had returned the previous evening. He wanted his Longine. Was it ready?

Heavily Edwin replied, "Yes, it is, but I don't have it now. It's not here."

"Where is it then?"

"I was short of money after I was robbed the first time. I thought Sir Charles was gone for a long time so I pawned it. I thought I could get it back before he needed it."

Shocked at the audacity and truthfulness of the young watchmaker, Mortimer's servant suggested that Edwin retrieve the watch immediately. He would stop by later in the day and pick it up.

Hoping that the pawnbroker would be sensitive to Edwin's situation, Edwin agreed that he would be there later in the day with the watch. With luck the pawnbroker would give him the watch and allow him to pay later after Mortimer had paid him. As soon as the servant left the workshop Edwin locked the door, neglecting to put on his coat, so concerned was he with his new problems. Arriving at the pawnbroker's he realized he had also managed to lose the ticket for the watches.

Undeterred Edwin entered the pawnbroker's and described to that man what the watches looked like.

"Without a ticket I can't give you anything. How would I know they were yours?" asked the pawnbroker, smirking slightly. He had done this before on several occasions. He well remembered the watches. If he could persuade Edwin that with no ticket he could get no watches then he, the pawnbroker, could sell the watches for a nice, fat profit. It happened all the time.

Edwin clenched his fists. He tried to reason with the older man but to no avail. A quick right jab and the pawnbroker was flat on the floor, blood streaming from his nose. Equally quickly Edwin was over the counter and going through the drawers in search of his watches. They were however not to be found.

Trying to keep his head straight, Edwin left the older man on the floor and rushed out of the pawn shop. There was nothing to do there now. He slowed down after a few minutes and tried to collect his thoughts. This time he was stumped. With a lost pawn ticket and three watches pawned which could not be repaid, and money owed to Mr. Albert Forrest, there really was no solution.

Edwin became increasingly frantic. He did not know how to explain this to the women. There seemed to be no solution. The idea of taking the family and running away entered his head, not for the first time. Perhaps they could get a fresh start. It was too far to go back to his neighborhood in England. They could perhaps move to Dumfries where Ann's brothers worked and start again there. He was not sure they could move fast enough to escape his current problems. Edwin regretted hitting the pawnbroker but suspected that it was not the first time the man had been punched.

The town was busy today. He had to dodge around people just to keep moving. It was market day and the street was lined with stalls. Normally Edwin enjoyed seeing the makeshift stalls, hastily erected for one day's business. The tables were covered with fruits and vegetables in the summertime. In the winter because of the scarcity of fruits the vendors sold cakes and sweets. The fragrance of the fresh bread always enticed him although he preferred to eat Ann's homemade bread. The stall owners were bantering as usual between themselves and their customers. A cheerful group, they were always eager to make a sale or tell a joke. It took a special kind of person to become a stallholder; you needed to be ready to work hard, tolerate bad weather and an uncertain market. Edwin was a risk taker but he preferred more solid kind of work.

Finally he reached home and then he slowed down, letting his heart calm a little before ascending the stairs to the small flat. Ann was seated as usual in her rocking chair with Lydia on her knee. Her hand lay idle by her side, still wrapped in rags. It was still painful even though the salve Edwin had bought for her had helped a little in the healing process. She looked up as Edwin came in the room and immediately noticed how pale and worried he looked. Her father's death had affected them all so deeply, she thought, once again struck with a new shaft of pain as she realized that her father would not be there for her again.

Putting her own troubles aside, Ann said, "Edwin, what on earth's the matter? You look as if you've seen a ghost."

Edwin sat heavily down on the little stool by her side. He looked at her afresh, very aware of how he had let her down. That made it all the harder to tell her what had happened. Fortunately Lillias was out at the moment as Edwin could not face her occasionally sharp tongue. He felt badly enough as it was.

Taking Ann's good hand in his two, Edwin began to tell her the story. Ann's face showed no emotion at first. She was good at hiding what she felt. Her father's Scottish upbringing had taught her to be reticent in her feelings. Fortunately she had not inherited her mother's rather sharp tongue and temper. Telling her the tale of their lost finances helped Edwin. He always felt better after being open with Ann. Unfortunately though she had little to suggest. She was not used to making financial decisions and certainly not used to making decisions about where they would live or possibly move to.

Poverty was rampant in Edinburgh although Ann had personally not been exposed to it. Her father had a respectable and steady business so she had never had to fear being without food, or worse, living in the workhouse. She enjoyed a lower middle-class existence and had lived a step up from the working classes who had surged on the cities looking for work in manufacturing. Unemployment and lack of food had never been part of her experience so when Edwin spoke, she had little sense of potential insecurity.

Rarely did Ann venture into Old Town. It was not an environment in which she wanted to live or even see. The squalor, the smell of rotten food, the garbage on the streets, the lack of paving and the overcrowded alleys were not for the faint of heart. She knew Edwin had lived there but had been glad when William had offered Edwin steady employment. Even when they were courting Edwin had not taken her into Old Town. He had not wanted her to see the filth or recognize that 50,000 people lived in close quarters without sewage, furniture, or running water. If the wind was in the right direction the putrid smell from the Old Town floated over the Princes Street Gardens and that was close enough for Ann. Certainly none of her sewing clients came from there. People in the Old Town frequently had only one set of clothes to sleep, work, and eat in, if they were lucky. 'The Scotsman' had reported only a week ago of a family dying together in one room, the mother covered only in feathers and rat bites, the children huddled around the starved family dog.

Edwin struggled on with his story. Ann's eyes grew wide but she said nothing, allowing him to continue without asking questions. Finally, after he had finished his tale, she merely said, "I know it will work out, Edwin. That's what my Da saw in you. He knew you could work hard and would do your best."

Edwin could only sigh at this as for once he wished William were there to help him and he knew it would take a lot of luck to get out of his current mess. He wondered how long it would be before Mr. Forrest took legal action against him. He didn't have to wonder long as a knock at the door revealed a policeman.

Chapter 35

Just as Edwin had anticipated, Albert Forrest had lost no time in notifying his father-in-law of the demise of the older watchmaker and suggested that Sir Charles Mortimer take action against the young man. It really looked as though there was little that Albert could do to retrieve his money except make the life of the young watchmaker even more miserable than it already appeared to be. He doubted Edwin had many possessions that he could sell to get back his money. It would certainly pay Sir Charles Mortimer to ask for his watch now.

Later the same day Sir Charles' footman returned to the workshop, verified with Edwin that Sir Charles' watch was still at the pawnbroker's, and then reported to Sir Charles that his Longine had been pawned.

The footman had even gone to the pawnbroker that Edwin had used to see if the watch were there. Of course it was not. The pawnbroker was nursing a badly bruised nose and had plenty of colorful words to describe what he thought of Edwin Turner.

All this the footman reported to Sir Charles and his son-in-law, Albert Forrest. They were both sitting comfortably in Sir Charles' drawing room, sipping Scotch and looking forward to a generous dinner. Albert always enjoyed the fare at Sir Charles' table and the idea of pheasant and roasted potatoes tempered the anger he felt at the loss of his money.

He hoped that because of his early advisement to Sir Charles of the potential loss of his Longine that Sir Charles would see fit to advance him some money to cover his own gambling debt of the previous evening.

However Sir Charles was not thinking generously towards Albert at this time. The young man had proven to be a leech and Sir Charles despised that. The price one had to pay to be part of Edinburgh society, thought Sir Charles. Sometimes it just did not seem worth it, if society included men like Albert Forrest. At least Sir Charles had found a husband for his daughter and, better yet, the promise of an heir.

After the footman had stepped out, Albert turned to Sir Charles and suggested, "I think it would be a good idea to have this young watchmaker, Turner, or whatever his name is, arrested. There may be claims from other people and we should make our claim first."

Sir Charles thought for a moment. He loved the Longine and hated the idea that he would not see it again. Yet to what purpose did it serve to arrest the watchmaker? If he were thrown in prison or, worse yet, sent to Australia, then Sir Charles would never see the watch again nor the money he had spent on it.

"I am not sure that's what I want to do. I am so annoyed right now I'd like to burn down his shop. I loved that watch and no one else had one like it. That's the thing that bothers me most. You know I got it from the Queen."

Albert Forrest knew that. He had heard tell of the occasion several times. It was a story that Sir Charles liked to recount. He ignored the comment as he did not consider it relevant to the issue. Albert pressed on, "I could handle the paperwork. Work at the firm is quiet at the moment. I'd like to take care of it for you."

Sir Charles was shrewd; he knew what was coming next. He had not become wealthy by being stupid and he recognized Albert's type. He suspected that Albert's pro bono work on the case would not really be pro bono to him. Well, the young man ought to work for his supper, thought Sir Charles.

"Very well. I don't see that it will serve us particularly well but we may get something back. We really shouldn't let these people rob us of house and home. It will send a stern message to Turner, if nothing else."

At that he sent for the footman who was despatched to the police station in Leith. The police station had been established on Queen Charlotte Street, adjacent to the Council building sitting on the corner of Constitution Street and Queen Charlotte. Very conveniently, within the Council building there was a court and cells for the waiting prisoners.

It was an elegant place, reflecting the power of the magistrates and city council over the unfortunate miscreants who were tried there. The contrast between the circumstances of those about to be tried and those who ran the courts was stark. The magistrates enjoyed comfortable padded seats and sat in regal finery amidst portraits of their predecessors, hung upon oak paneled walls. The window furnishings reflected the latest quality and style too. Many a man or woman would enter the courtroom and be left slack-jawed in front of such finery. Unfortunately that did nothing to impress the magistrates who sometimes mistook the awe of the prisoner for a person of low intelligence. Or worse, it made the magistrate aware of the social differences and made him realize how very dangerous these prisoners might be in their thievery.

The footman waited until a constable could return with him to see Sir Charles. Meanwhile Sir Charles and Albert had eaten their pheasant dinner and were amiably drinking port as they awaited the return of the servant and policeman. Finally the footman arrived in a hurry. He really disliked going into Leith at night even though at this time of year it was still fairly light at night and one could easily see the faces of passersby. He was smartly dressed and clearly worked in an upper class household, and he felt that made him a target for thievery, even if accompanied by a police constable.

After the footman left the room, Albert Forrest, leaning back in his chair almost casually, introduced himself to the constable, and did not offer that man a seat. The constable pulled out a piece of paper and a pencil and slowly began to record the details of the crime committed by Edwin Turner, known watchmaker of 15 Jamaica Street. Edwin had misappropriated a fine Swiss watch which he had been entrusted to repair; he had also taken money from Albert Forrest and had not produced services for it, tantamount to stealing. Satisfied that he had enough details to conduct an arrest, Constable McGlashan repeated all he had heard, making sure he had his facts correct. He really did not like this kind of work, particularly so late at night. He had been planning to stop in at Madame Fleur's establishment on his way home and this disrupted his intentions.

After he left, Albert and Sir Charles sat back somewhat contentedly into their chairs. No one could feel happy knowing that he had been robbed but at least they could feel vindicated knowing that the young offender would now be in jail.

The young constable set off to Jamaica Street. He was unhappy with the job at hand. He knew well Sir Charles' "sort". He lacked the class and distinction of an upper class gentleman. New money, he expected, and a Sassenach too. Born and bred in Leith, McGlashan's father had been a seaman who was rarely at home; his mother had cleaned houses for the wealthy and she had taught him how to behave around them. That had helped when he got this job. That and the fact that she had brought him up with a moral upbringing and he had avoided crime. Now his career brought him face-to-face with criminals every day.

When Constable McGlashan reached Jamaica Street he found the door to the workshop locked. He had expected that as it was late but he knocked. Some of the neighbors looked out of the window to see what was happening. In this neighborhood criminals aroused interest as most of the people were hardworking and law-abiding. He was glad yet again that he was doing an arrest here rather than in Old Town where he might get pelted with rotten vegetables if he entered one of the wynds to arrest someone.

Edwin opened the door himself and ushered the constable into the workshop. He did not want Ann to witness this interview. He offered the Constable a seat at William's bench and then he sat down at his own.

"I have been sent by Sir Charles Mortimer and Mr. Albert Forrest to investigate a missing watch of Sir Charles and missing money owed to Mr. Forrest. Could you tell me what happened?"

Edwin sat upright at his bench. He had expected this to happen yet it chilled him to realize he was in this situation. He had never in his life expected to be investigated as a thief. He had always been able to make ends meet even if he had at times gone hungry. He really didn't know how to explain well what he had done even though he suspected the constable would be sympathetic.

"This was my father-in-law's business but he died recently," he began. "I got a bit behind in paying bills, the funeral and all. My wife has just had a baby too and she hasn't been able to work. She's scalded her hand to boot too and she hasn't been able to sew as she usually does. She's a dressmaker."

The constable remained silent and continued to look at him intently.

"Just before William, that's my father-in-law, died he was robbed and so the bills piled up. Lost his life savings. Took them out of the bank and kept them here and now they are gone. Stolen. Mr. Forrest had given me five guineas towards his new watch so I could buy supplies. That money was stolen too. I had three watches I repaired but when I tried to get paid for them the owners were gone. Sir Charles was in London and then I had repaired two other watches from Mr. Jenner, the department store owner, and Dr. Cockburn. They were both out of the country. I didn't know when they would come back but thought it would not be soon. Because I couldn't get paid right now I pawned the watches - just so as I could make ends meet."

This was a far longer conversation than Edwin was used to giving but he knew he needed to continue as the constable was sucking the end of his pencil with a quizzical air.

"You mean Dr. Cockburn the surgeon?" he enquired. This case promised to be even bigger than he had imagined.

"Yes," replied Edwin. It did not matter to him who was the owner, the most important matter was just that it was missing.

"I tried to get Sir Charles' watch back from the pawnbroker but he claims he never had it. I can't find the ticket and so I can't prove it. But I don't have the money either to pay for the watch and so I am just stuck!"

"Aye, that you are," agreed the constable. He had heard of this kind of case before, many times. The young man seemed genuine enough but that did not help. To add to it, it now appeared there were three watches missing, not just one. When the constable heard who owned the other watches he knew that they would also file charges. It bothered the constable as the watches were not really stolen, just "borrowed" but that would not sit well with the magistrate.

"I am sorry, but I will have to take you to jail for the night until you can see the Sheriff in the morning."

"Is there no way around this? It will kill my mother-in-law, and my wife can't cope on her own right now with the babe and her bad hand. Can you just come back for me in the morning, or can I just come down there?"

Wide-eyed and desperate, Edwin unconsciously ran his right hand through his hair. He wondered if he should try and make a run for it. He knew he could get lost in Old Town. The police were just not popular there and he knew that people would protect him, if only to save him from the police. He certainly knew his way around the closes and wynds and could easily hide. Many of the police did not want to enter there because of being accosted. Armed only with a baton, rattle and lantern they were no match for the hungry and at times desperate residents who had little use for authority.

Running away would not help Ann and Lillias though. The enormity of his situation began to sink in on Edwin. It could only end badly. He knew he was not guilty of stealing but he still could not produce either the money or the watches.

"No, I can't. Mr. Forrest and Sir Charles Mortimer are demanding justice. I don't know if you're aware, but Mr. Forrest is the son of the Attorney General. That puts me in a tough spot. You need to come with me now. You can tell your wife where you are. I'll wait long enough for that but you have to come with me now."

Constable McGlashan stood up, directing Edwin to follow and the two slowly mounted the stairs to the flat above. Edwin could not help notice that the staircase now seemed alive with his neighbors who peaked through cracks in their slightly opened doors. He ignored them though and entered his own front door.

Ann, Lillias and Toby were all sitting close to the fire. It was a small one, as they had very little firewood to burn and they were trying to use what they had very sparingly. Toby, who had been lying next to Ann, moved away to a corner of the room when the constable entered and observed the proceedings from a distance.

Ann looked startled when the constable walked in but offered him the seat upon which she had been sitting. Seeing the small fire and wanting to feel a little warmer the constable chose to take the seat but waited until Edwin had explained what was going on. Immediately tears rolled down Ann's face; she reached for Edwin and tried to cling to him. He bowed his head in shame but tried to put a bold face on it by saying, "I'll be back tomorrow, you'll see. It's all one big mistake. No need to worry yourself about it."

Ann nodded, not reassured but knowing she needed to play along to make Edwin feel better. Kissing him on the cheek in a bold show of affection, Ann sat down again, her face drenched with tears. Lillias, who was significantly more outspoken than Ann, broke out into her Glaswegian tongue and protested the arrest. Edwin was astonished by her language as he had never heard her speak in that way, but the constable was not surprised. Difficult circumstances affected people in different ways.

"If you take him away then you'll be sending us to the workhouse. My man is not long in his grave and we have no one else to take care of us. My daughter can't work right now because of her bad hand. She has three bairns, one just brand-new."

Constable McGlashan knew the veracity of Lillias' statement. He also knew that if the two women and their children ended up in the workhouse they would have life even worse than Edwin in prison. Fear of the workhouse was very real and threatening to the working classes. Once inside, yes, you were fed, but the work was frequently backbreaking and the chance to earn enough to get out was beyond most people. When Ann's children were sick they would be sent to work and might live their whole lives in the workhouse, assuming they did not die of disease at an early age.

Pushing aside his own thoughts, the constable ignored Lillias and stepped past her to reach Edwin. He reached into his jacket and pulled out his Darby cuffs. Her personally hated to use these as they were so ill fitting. One size fits all did not work for handcuffs if the prisoner had slim or fat wrists. The walk back to Leith was long at night though and he did not want to take chances with this prisoner although he did seem a nice sort of fellow. At the sight of the cuffs, Ann cried even louder. Lillias had learned stoicism over the years and she merely put her arm around Ann, looked disapprovingly at the constable and at Edwin who had caused this situation. Secretly she was afraid of the workhouse but she was not about to show her concern to the two men.

Edwin and the constable set off for Leith Police Station and the house settled down for the night, fresh in the knowledge that one of their own had been arrested. For the two women there was little sleep and a lot of discussion about what to do. First they would seek help from Ann's brothers in Dumfries. Lillias would send word to them in the morning. She did not hold out much hope of help from them but perhaps the image of their mother in a workhouse might spur them to help out.

CHAPTER 36

The trip to the police station passed without incident. These days, people were getting used to the sight of policemen and prisoners. The old Edinburgh Guard had been seen rarely but nowadays arrests were becoming commonplace. If anything, there were so many that it was creating a problem with lack of prisons to accommodate them all.

Edwin and the constable walked in silence, Edwin all the time hoping that none of his customers saw him walking, bound in handcuffs. Fortunately they did not meet anyone and after the constable had officially charged him, he took off the handcuffs and put Edwin into a cell which was already holding two drunk seamen, an older rather distinguished looking gentleman, and a young boy barely old enough to have hair on his face. From what Edwin learned, the seamen were accused of a burglary and had been caught red-handed with the stolen goods; the other two had been found in a compromising situation in the public convenience in Princes Street Gardens. Edwin recounted his story to the others who showed little interest and even less sympathy.

The night passed slowly. Edwin was unable to sleep, his mind wandering from his crime and arrest to thoughts of Ann and Lillias and the children. Hopefully he would see the Sheriff in the morning, and that man would be reasonable and understanding like the constable. He thought over how he could retrieve the watches, and wondered again where he might have placed the pawn ticket. That man should be here instead of him - what a robber!

When daylight appeared Edwin had still not slept. No food had arrived either and by now he was getting hungry. The drunken seamen snored loudly in a corner of the cell and the other two occupants studiously ignored each other. Edwin cried out for the constable but he did not appear. Time passed with no sign of life outside of the cell other than a rat that scurried by from time to time. No use looking for food here, thought Edwin about the rat, there's none for you or me!

Edwin wondered how he would be tried. He knew the Scots did things differently from the English in so many ways. He suspected they had their own system of justice. He did not know how long they could keep him without seeing a Sheriff. He had never even heard of a Sheriff in England. Perhaps that was the same as a magistrate. He hoped so as that would make his case go faster and maybe better. Edwin could only hope for a lenient Sheriff. He had been charged last night but the constable had indicated that he would have to see the owners of the other pawned watches to see if they wanted to file claims. That might hold things up. For sure he could not pay off his debt while he sat in prison.

His thoughts were disturbed by the cry of a warden who was delivering food - bread and gruel. The gruel was congealed and cold but he ate it hungrily. The bread was buggy and Edwin could not face eating it. He was just not that hungry. He remembered with a pang Ann's homemade bread and hoped he would get out later today so that he could sample it.

"Hurry up and eat - you are the next one in court," the warden informed him. Edwin did as he was told but left the bread for the young boy who seemed blissfully unaware that he was eating buggy bread. Smoothing his hair down, he wished he had a spot of water to damp it down from its unruly air. He had also been given some skimmed milk but he could not use that on his hair. Instead he gulped it down, wiped his mouth with the back of his hand and sat down again, leaning against the wall.

Two more hours passed but Edwin, without a watch, had no idea of the time. There was no window in the room so he had no idea if it were still daylight although he could assume it was as the days were long at the moment.

Then, with a start, he heard his name being called. "Turner, Edwin!" The man who shouted it came with a large ring of heavy keys attached to a belt around his waist.

Edwin had been standing leaning his head against the bars of the door looking out, demonstrating what some called "polishing one's eyebrows with the Queen's metal". As the warden walked up, Edwin stepped back and allowed him to unlock the door. The warden unfastened Edwin's fetters but put on handcuffs which chafed Edwin although he did not complain. Silently the two went upstairs and through a series of passageways until the hall widened and they walked into a courtroom, the likes of which Edwin had never seen. The bench where the Sheriff was to sit was significantly higher than the stand where Edwin was placed. The wooden bench and the chairs in the room were polished to a high gleam. On the wall behind the Sheriff's bench was a large portrait of the Queen and on the other walls there were oil paintings of dignitaries, presumably former Judges. The windows were high in the room so one could not look out, or look in either.

As Edwin stood at the dock, the Sheriff walked in, wigged and bespectacled. He looked over the top of his glasses at Edwin and asked his name. Edwin responded and the Sheriff checked his desk and verified the case. At the Sheriff's request, Edwin was given a Bible on which to rest one hand as he raised the other and repeated his intent to tell the whole truth.

The Sheriff then asked Edwin if he had counsel which puzzled Edwin who looked back at the Sheriff for help. Rather exasperatedly as he had encountered this before, the Sheriff asked if he had a barrister to represent him. Edwin replied briefly that he did not think he needed one as he was innocent. This caused the Sheriff to raise his eyebrows and in a monotone voice he began the account of Edwin's crimes against society. Across the room Mr. Albert Forrest sat at the prosecution desk. It was clear that he had been very diligent in the last twenty-four hours.

When the Sheriff asked Edwin whether he wished to plead guilty or not guilty, Edwin replied "Not guilty" as loudly as he could, hoping that his firmness of speech would convince the Sheriff of his innocence. He was certainly innocent of intentionally stealing watches.

Mr. Forrest asked to approach the bench and he explained succinctly that not only was his money missing for services not rendered, but that he had evidence that the prisoner had taken the watch of his father-in-law, Sir Charles Mortimer. He also had recently become aware that watches from Mr. Henry Jenner and Dr. Archibald Cockburn were also missing, purloined by the prisoner. The Sheriff leaned back in his chair and looked down at Edwin with some disgust.

"It seems that Mr. Forrest is not the only one from whom property has been stolen. Is it true that you were entrusted with the watches of Dr. Cockburn and Mr. Jenner, and that you no longer have them?"

"Yes, but...", began Edwin.

""No buts, a simple yes or no will suffice. Given the value of the property stolen I must move this case to the High Court of Judiciary. You will be held without bail in Calton Jail pending a trial date set by that Court."

Slamming his hammer down fiercely on the bench, the Sheriff offered no further opportunity for Edwin to speak. The Sheriff adjusted his wig, pushed back his glasses onto the bridge of his nose, and left the courtroom abruptly. Meanwhile Mr. Forrest looked with some delight at Edwin, clearly satisfied with the young man's dismay. Edwin in his naiveté had clearly been expecting to receive sympathy from the Sheriff. He sank into the chair behind him but the bailiff was ready to return him to the cells.

This time when he entered the jail he was taken to another area. The cell was only slightly bigger but already had five occupants. Straw mattresses were laid on the floor with barely any room to walk. In the corner stood a bucket which clearly served for sewage and which also clearly was not emptied frequently. To add to Edwin's discomfort, a rat walked across the only empty mattress.

The occupants looked Edwin up and down, sizing him up to see if there was anything that they could take from him. Fortunately he had already been relieved of his possessions when he was arrested and his fellow prisoners realized that he was just one of them, another poor person who was on the wrong side of the law. Because the prisoners were housed together in close quarters one could be housed alongside a pedophile, a murderer, a forger or a petty thief. Calton Jail knew no class distinction and occasionally a wealthy man might be imprisoned there which always aroused interest from fellow prisoners. Generally though the criminal class was just that, a class apart, lacking even the social distinction of being working or middle class.

As the day progressed Edwin became acquainted with his fellow prisoners even though he would have preferred not to speak. For once his cheerfulness dissipated and he wondered how long he would have to stay there. He had hoped to leave the jail immediately after his court appearance. Now he realized just how foolish he had been to expect that. Living in Old Town had made him wise to the judicial system; the sentences meted out were almost always inappropriate for the crime committed, in his opinion. He had heard tell of victims' family members crying and pleading with the judge to prevent the perpetrator of the crime from being sentenced to transportation or hanging. Now the very real fear that the case might go badly against him pressed on Edwin making his hands shake slightly and his forehead break out in a light film of sweat. A man could be sentenced to transportation for stealing a chicken, or fencing stolen property, or even stealing a dozen cucumber plants. As the day passed into night the other prisoners honed in on Edwin's fear and with black humor recounted the minor infractions which led to terrible punishments. Edwin was gullible; he had already visited the Sheriff's court and realized how quickly he had been despatched to linger in prison for a while, with no hope of bail. Not that there was any money for bail anyway.

He slept fitfully that night, partly aroused by the violent shouts and thrashing around of some of the other prisoners. Edwin realized that there were several other cells on the same floor, each housing an unknown number of prisoners. He learned that at least one of his fellow prisoners had been there for six months awaiting trial. Sometimes bribes could be paid to set the trial date earlier yet not many had interest or money to do that. After all life in Calton Jail could only be better than a hanging or transportation to a far away country on the other side of the world, cut off from friends and family forever. Few returned to Britain from that distant shore. After all, that was the plan.

CHAPTER 37

Meanwhile back at 15 Jamaica Street life seemed to have stopped still. Lillias, still bereft from William's death and the loss of their savings, sat in front of the empty fireplace each day, staring into space. Fortunately it was summer and they had no need of a fire for a few months. One less worry. Ann was breast-feeding Lydia but with little success. The shock of Edwin's imprisonment and the reduced diet had dried up her milk. She had started to buy milk but Lydia cried lustily when it was offered and clearly disliked the change in her diet. Taking on the mood of the women she whinged at the slightest upset to her life.

Ann's hand was healing very slowly and she had not been able to sew. She had made a couple of deliveries for Lillias but it was difficult to manage the sewing and the baby, and Lillias could not take care of the baby well. Ann had tried to see Edwin but had only been able to see him once. She was shocked at his appearance. In just a few days he had turned from being a red-cheeked, cheerful young man to a gaunt and morose one, who was clearly embarrassed to be seen in this way. He had begged her not to return until after his trial but she was determined to ignore him. Admittedly this was not something she had anticipated when she married him a few short years ago!

Ann missed her father too. He had always provided stability to their lives. Always rather dour and perhaps lacking a little of Edwin's charm, he had been steady and conservative. He had never failed to provide for his family and had established a good business. Now with Edwin in jail their customers were going elsewhere for their watchmaking.

Ann looked around the room and wondered what they could sell to help themselves. She had found a pile of bills in the workshop for supplies which Edwin had bought. Perhaps the merchants would accept the goods back and not press for payment. Tiredly she gazed over at her mother who was staring into the fireplace as usual. Now it seemed Ann was responsible for everyone. At least she had inherited her father's resilience. She would need plenty of that until Edwin's trial. She just hoped that he would survive that long in the jail. She had been shocked by his appearance, and even more by his desire not to see her until the trial. That was a side of Edwin which she had not previously seen her and it hurt her immeasurably. Irritated that he was in this mess and had not told her beforehand of his financial problems, they had married "for better or for worse". To this point the marriage had definitely been for the better for both of them. They would just have to deal with "the worse".

Ann had already sold William's armchair. That was heartbreaking; yet it had been hard to see the empty chair where he had sat each evening. It just made the women realize how much they missed him. She had also sold his watchmaking instruments to another watchmaker. She knew that would be difficult for Edwin as he would have prized them just because they were William's. He had however built up his own collection and had no need of them, she reasoned.

Lillias had sent a message to Ann's brothers in Dumfries requesting help but they had heard nothing from them since William's funeral. They had certainly offered nothing towards the funeral costs and had complained that work was slowing in their factory. Hopefully they would come with money soon to help out the little family. Edwin's two young boys were still too young to find work. Once they turned six they would be able to lend a hand and go to work in one of the factories, or perhaps as a chimney sweep. For now though they were just more mouths to feed.

As Ann contemplated for the umpteenth time how to manage their paltry finances, Lillias suddenly stood up, wrapped herself in her shawl and simply said, "I'm going to the poorhouse. It won't be for long, just until Edwin gets out of jail."

Surprised and frightened by the idea, Ann grabbed hold of Lillias and tried to bar the door but Lillias, in a fit of unexpected strength, calmly pushed her aside, hugged her briefly and walked out.

"No, Ma! Don't do that. Please don't! We'll manage!"

"I don't see how. I'm just another mouth to feed. If your brothers send money I could be home within a week."

"But Ma, you can still sew and you could help me with the boys. I need you!"

259

"Maybe I should take the boys with me and then you'd only have to worry about Lydia."

"No, Ma! We need to stick together!"

"Let me be, lass. I want to go there. It won't be forever!"

At this Lillias continued down the stairs and silently Ann watched her, tears rolling down her cheeks. When it was obvious that Lillias was not going to come back, Ann went inside the flat and closed the door. She sat down heavily in her chair and then just allowed the tears to flow.

Meanwhile Lillias turned her steps to the poorhouse. She had walked past it several times but never had expected to need it herself. In fact her own church contributed money on occasion to the poorhouse.

It was located, not surprisingly, in the Old Town, in Canongate on the corner of Tollgate Wynd. A five-story stone building, the Canongate Charity Poorhouse looked surprisingly sturdy and was clearly built to last. It was mainly supported by churches and they obviously expected to have the "poor with them always" as Jesus Himself had suggested.

Lillias had never been inside but she made her way there slowly now, each step seeming slower than the last. She was already beginning to regret her decision but it was done now and she really did not see any other way out. If Ann could manage on her own and not come into the poorhouse herself then Lillias felt she would have achieved something. Lillias could not bear the idea of Ann having to submit to poorhouse life which Lillias had heard was worse than going to prison.

Arriving at the poorhouse door, Lillias told the porter that she needed a place to stay. He sighed but stood up and led her to the administrative office which was in the central part of the poorhouse complex. There Lillias was told to wait as the warden was busy. After a two-hour wait Lillias was given an extensive questionnaire to complete. Already tired and unable to see the questionnaire properly, Lillias sat in despair. Finally the warden realized that Lillias was struggling and with impatience she took Lillias' papers from her and helped her complete the forms. Lillias had never expected such a strict examination. She could read and write well, when she could see the papers, but her eyesight had suffered because of her age and all the years of sewing in poor light.

Finally everything was complete and the warden even knew where Lillias was born and raised, whom she had married, how many children she had and why she needed the help now. Lillias was hungry; it seemed like a lot of work just to get a meal. She hoped that she would be able to eat soon. That was not to happen though just yet. She was led to a bath which she was forced to use and then, while still stripped, she was examined by a nurse who carefully checked her skin and declared her free of disease. She was asked to turn over any medicine she might have, but Lillias had none. The nurse was clearly disappointed at that news.

Lillias' clothes were whisked away and in their place the warden gave her a uniform of a grey coarse material. The skirt was long and rather large for her, the matching grey blouse rather small. By this point Lillias' nerve was beginning to disappear but she had been blessed with fortitude and determination so she did not buckle. Finally the warden led her to the women's wing, for in this place men were separated from the women and children from their parents.

There was a dormitory in one room and Lillias was assigned a small narrow bed in the middle of the room. There was no bedding and silently Lillias wished she had brought her own. Perhaps Ann would check on her. She knew that she herself would not be permitted to come and go. Work had finished for the day and some of the other women were lying on their beds, exhausted from the day's work.

Suddenly a gong sounded and the women all rushed to the door and headed for the dining room. The woman who had the bed next to Lillias introduced herself as Morag. Grateful that it seemed she had someone to help her, Lillias followed Morag to the serving line where she picked up a spoon and metal plate and cup.

Food this evening was one of the better meals, Morag reported. There was a small piece of fatty meat with a piece of cheese and bread. Each inmate, as that was what they were called, was also given frumenty, a slightly sweet wheat dish. The cup was filled with beer. Lillias was surprised and pleased to see that and enquired of Morag if they normally were given beer. Yes, she was told, and it's better than the water. Some people here drink nothing but beer as the water is bad.

"How long have you been here, Morag?" enquired Lillias and was told, "Six months but I am hoping to get out soon. There's folks here who have spent all their lives here and some we see regular as clockwork when they run out of money."

"I am hoping I can leave when my sons send me money," explained Lillias to Morag, who looked as though she had heard that story many times before. At that, the two women lapsed into silence and supped their beer. Bedtime for all was at eight and most people looked bone-weary by that time.

Surprisingly Lillias was able to sleep, exhausted perhaps by the worries of the last weeks. She was able to sleep through the moans and the snores. Most people slept as she did, tired by the day's work and ready to close out the day.

Lillias was awakened by a loud clanging. It was six o'clock. Contrary to what had happened for dinner the women moved slowly in the morning, going into the communal bathroom to use the few washbasins and toilets. Lillias did not see a bathtub there and there were no fresh clothes for the new day. She really had not expected that. After all, she had been one of the lucky ones. Many people never had a change of clothes or water in which to bathe.

Breakfast this morning was gruel, dry, almost cold and not very filling. There was however beer again for the adults although Lillias noticed that the children at the other end of the room were given milk.

This time Lillias took more note of her surroundings. They sat at long tables each with small backless stools which were rather low to the table. The walls were decorated with samplers, each with a spiritual message. There should be no doubt that this was a Christian environment and that the Christians who were helping the inmates would take care of them even though the inmates clearly did not deserve such charity. A respectable person would never find himself in such an unfortunate position as these inmates. Definitely sin had brought on this shameful condition and at least working in the poorhouse the inmates would be exposed to an upright life.

Most ate in silence; some mothers looked over at their children but they were not allowed to mix. The parochial board that managed the poorhouse was of the belief that if a family were in the poorhouse the parents were incompetent to take care of their children and that the children should be managed by the authorities. Yet Lillias could see the tenderness with which some of the mothers looked out for their children and sometimes saved food for them. Poverty had been made a sin; love was pushed aside.

After breakfast was over work began. Most of the women, including Lillias, were assigned to oakum picking. It was a tedious job and to Lillias did not seem to have much purpose. Morag worked in the same area and willingly showed Lillias how to do it.

Fortunately Lillias did not have to complete a quota each day but she was expected to work all day even though she found the job tedious and hard on her hands. She was given a piece of rope from an old sailing ship and she had to pick it or strip it apart. Gradually the cable became yarn, became thread, and then thin filaments of hemp. These were placed in baskets and taken to the docks where they would be used for shipbuilding. The oakum was hammered in as a filler between the planks and when it was in the water it swelled and formed a very effective watertight seal.

Lillias had no idea what the oakum was used for, neither did she particularly care. By the end of the day the ends of her fingers were raw from picking at the rope; she noticed that Morag's fingers were red and bleeding from picking. Yet she did not complain; the men were assigned to breaking rocks or bones, and that sapped their strength.

Lunchtime came and went with more gruel and more beer. At least the beer seemed to make the day pass easier. After a week Lillias no longer really noticed what day it was. She was bone-weary each day and her hands ached from her work. She noticed that her fingers were becoming misshapen and the joints were red and swollen. One of the nurses gave her some medicine for the pain but it made her sick. Later Morag told her that she should not have taken medicine from that particular nurse as she could not read the labels on the bottles.

The week turned into a month and then two months. Ann had stopped by once and left a package of tea for her but Lillias had no way of brewing it and frankly by now she preferred the beer. Lillias knew that she could leave the poorhouse at any time of her own volition yet she hung back. Edwin's trial had been delayed twice and Ann seemed to be coping, but barely. She had sold Edwin's instruments as the children needed food but she was managing to stave off the debt collectors. At least while Lillias was in the poorhouse she had food and a bed, such as it was.

CHAPTER 38

Albert Forrest leaned back with satisfaction in his chair. He had managed to persuade both Dr. Archibald Cockburn and Mr. Henry Jenner to report the loss of their watches and Forrest had no problem in putting together a clear-cut case against Edwin. The trial date was set for tomorrow. It seemed that Forrest had permanently lost his money to Edwin as that young man would never be able to repay him. Sometimes though the loss of money was worth the trade in being able to win a case in court. That happened all too rarely for Forrest who ended up providing background information to his more senior partners and rarely exercised his right to try a case.

Forrest gathered all the papers on his desk into a neat stack and decided to call it a day. Mary would be waiting at home and they were having dinner that evening with his father-in-law. Mortimer was still smarting from the loss of his Longine, not least because Queen Victoria had given it to him. It had been no issue for Forrest to suggest to Mortimer that he bring charges against young Turner.

####

Ann sat in her chair by the fire. The air was chilled now, the summer long past. These last few months waiting for Edwin's trial had been a burden to her. She had visited Lillias in the poorhouse but had found that extremely difficult. Lillias had said little and seemed to have adjusted to poorhouse life but she was stoic and Ann knew she would not complain.

The room was fairly bare now as Ann had sold off their furniture to cover the bills. She was managing to keep her head above water with her sewing. She was frequently hungry but had managed to see that the boys and Lydia had enough to eat even though very often it was merely porridge. She just needed to wait a while longer, a few more hours, and Edwin's trial would be over and he would be home again. She regretted now selling his instruments as he would need them for work. She had not told him and she did not know how he would react to that news. Ann hoped that he would understand. Even after he was freed he would still have to pay back for the watches and the money owed to Mr. Forrest. She silently wondered if they would be free from debt ever again.

Sir Charles Mortimer looked at his watch to see how much longer it would be before Mary and Albert would arrive. Once again he lamented to himself the loss of his Longine. Looking at the new one, which was a beauty to be sure, only served to exacerbate the wound of the lost Longine. He wondered how long it would take before he would forget that watch. As much as anything, the loss of something so sentimental jarred significantly with him.

Albert had asked him to go to the High Court tomorrow to recount the tale of leaving his watch with Mr. Turner to repair and then learning later that it had been pawned and sold. The reticence of the pawnbroker to name who had the watch now galled him mightily. Pushing aside that thought, he remembered that Mary's baby was due any day now. She really should have stayed at home for her confinement but Albert was pushing her to visit her father. That man would do anything for a free meal and a good wine!

Lillias sat opposite Morag who still had not succeeded in leaving the poorhouse. The two had become friends, bound together by dire circumstances. Lillias had heard many hard luck stories in the poorhouse and hers was typical of most. Trying to remain optimistic had taken much of her strength. Her hands were blistered now and calloused. She had always been rather proud of her hands. William had commented many times that he liked to see them fly as she sewed with neat, even stitches. "Tiny little hands," he called them as he caressed them lovingly from time to time.

"Tomorrow's the big day for my son-in-law," she reminded Morag, who really needed no reminding as Lillias talked of little else these days.

"I hope it goes well for him. Have you heard who is the Judge?" Morag had been there long enough to know who were the tough judges and who were more lenient. You still did not get to choose your judge but it certainly improved your mood if you thought you were to be tried by a kinder soul.

"Ann told me that it was Judge Abercrombie. That doesn't mean a thing to us."

It did not to Morag either. She knew the name but nothing of him. She pursued more information though. "Did you tell me that the prosecutor is the man Edwin owes money to? Is he a barrister or a solicitor?"

Ann replied, "I really don't know. He says he is in chambers in Falkirk."

"He's probably a solicitor then. They don't usually spend as much time in court and stay back in the office with the books. It's probably good like that for Edwin - less experience in court," offered Morag sagely. She continued, "Is he having a jury trial?"

"I think not. They said it was his first crime and there would only be a judge. I really don't understand any of it and neither does Edwin. Our minister is going to vouch for him!"

The two women continued their porridge and beer, wishing they could linger instead of going to work but they were summoned shortly to work and the tedium of another day began.

####

Edwin's stomach was in knots and though he was hungry he for once could not eat the gruel in front of him and he passed it to his cellmate. By this time tomorrow he would know the outcome of his "crime". He still felt no sense of guilt over what he had done; sometimes you do what you must to get by. He missed Ann and the children immensely; he would never have thought five years ago that he could be so attached to other people. He was only glad that his parents could not see him now.

Edwin hoped that Judge Abercrombie would be lenient to him and give him time to pay back what he owed. He would do that if it took the rest of his life. There were plenty around who liked to steal but he had not been brought up that way. When the census was done in 1841 he had heard and laughed at the time for some people even said their profession was "thief"! Now who would admit to that!

Of late, Edwin had started to worry about his trial. Being in prison he heard many tales of the possible sentences. He knew that his offense was no longer considered a capital offense but the rumor of transportation roamed large around the prison. Sentences were for life, fourteen or seven years. If he were sentenced to transportation the length of time would be unimportant; after all, Australia was so far away you rarely heard of anyone returning. Money for the return ticket was hard to come by. The potential loss of his family weighed on him even more than the loss of his homeland. Being sent to Australia was like being shipped off the end of the world. He could imagine just arriving at the horizon and dropping off. That would be better than a life without Ann and the children.

He had scorned the idea that he could be transported when a fellow prisoner suggested it. After all, he had no criminal history. This was his first offense. The other prisoner had destroyed that security though by telling him about someone he knew that was transported for stealing two chickens, one dead, one alive. That had been the man's first offense. Edwin gave an involuntary shudder at the thought and tried to think of happier things, like returning to 15 Jamaica Street and seeing Ann and the children.

CHAPTER 39

The High Court of Justiciary was an imposing granite building on the Lawnmarket. Its very style conveyed an idea of stability and strength, of privilege and permanence. Edwin had never paid attention to it when he had previously walked by but today, as he was taken there by carriage, he could not help but find it intimidating. It looked threatening and immoveable. It registered on Edwin's conscious mind for only a few seconds though before he returned to his thoughts about the pending trial. Not surprisingly he wondered if Ann would be there.

He was glad that he did not see her as he arrived with the other prisoners, shackled, with standing room only in the police carriage. The horses moved along unperturbed by the throng of people waiting at the entrance to the Court. He wanted so much to see Ann but he did not want to be seen in chains, surrounded by murderers, thieves and rapists. There were some like he though; he noted the little old grey-haired man who was almost collapsing under the weight of the fourteen-pound fetter attached to his right leg.

Edwin had talked to him. He was a mild mannered man who kept to himself and he seemed to comport himself with dignity but he was clearly out of place in the prison. He was being tried today for stealing a jacket. Edwin had noticed that he never had visitors. The man, George, had told him that he had no family here in Edinburgh. After his wife died, he had moved to the city to find work, having been a farm laborer previously. He wanted to start his life over and look for better paying work.

That had eluded him though and one particularly cold evening in the spring several months ago he had stolen a jacket for warmth. He was homeless and needed the warmth, he explained. He had been to the workhouse but had found that breaking stones was too hard for him at his age even though he had been a farm laborer all his life. Unfortunately he was caught just as he was stealing the jacket and that is how he ended up with Edwin this morning, rolling to his trial. George was going to have the same Judge as Edwin and they both hoped he would be merciful.

Finally the horses stopped in front of the High Court and the prisoners waited to be released from the carriage, which was in effect a mobile cell. George had to be released from his fetter as he was unable to move with the weight on his foot. Edwin managed but it was very slow and painful. The motley group hobbled into the front entrance and the police wardens guided them to their respective courtrooms. Edwin's trial was to be on the second floor and he limped slowly up the stairs, only mildly chivvied by the constable. Over the last few months they had become acquainted and had struck up a friendship of sorts, as well as one could when one man is a prisoner and the other his captor. The constable felt sorry for Edwin and had seen Ann and understood very well why Edwin was so anxious about her.

On the second floor they stopped outside some large oak double doors and waited until Edwin was called. There were already other prisoners waiting for their trials. Most were quiet though, as they prepared mentally for the outcome of the trials.

Finally, after waiting several hours, Edwin was led into the courtroom where he was permitted to sit alone at a bench while he waited for Judge Abercrombie to enter. His fetter was removed, which relieved him as he saw Ann up in the visitors' gallery. Suddenly the door on the left of the Judge's bench opened and in walked a man of medium build wearing a shoulder-length wig, a pair of spectacles, and a white robe trimmed with red crosses. Everyone in the courtroom stood to attention as he settled himself into his large black leather seat, arranging his rather voluminous robe around him. Having settled himself he looked down at Edwin and then at Mr. Albert Forrest, who was dressed in a shorter black robe and a small rather neat wig.

Judge Abercrombie opened the proceedings by asking Mr. Forrest the nature of the prisoner's crimes and Albert gave a very long and detailed summary of Edwin's crimes against society. The Judge looked rather bored, perhaps as he had heard similar tales many times. So many of the criminal classes used pawnshops; it made no sense to an educated man to do such a thing. The Judge leaned forward and looked very carefully at Edwin as if by examining his face he could tell his character and the authenticity of the crimes he was purported to have committed.

Finally it was time for Edwin to stand in the dock, be sworn in and answer questions. He remembered to call Judge Abercrombie "My Lord" and to be polite even though Mr. Forrest pressed him and treated him with disdain.

Much to his surprise and dismay he found that Dr. Cockburn, Mr. Jenner and Sir Charles Mortimer were all in attendance and testified that they had left their watches for repair with Edwin Turner and the watches were now missing. Edwin had hoped that Cockburn and Jenner would still be out of town or at least that both men would be so busy they would have no time to go to court to bear witness against him.

Judge Abercrombie was unusually deferential to Albert Forrest, certainly not because of his skills in prosecution. It was clearly not his forte but he was relishing his "day in court". The Judge was not unaware either of Forrest's parentage and while normally the Judge would have been critical of Forrest's delivery he tolerated it as he had no desire to mock the son of the Lord Provost.

The Judge was not unkind to Edwin but he had heard too many of these cases. What saddened him though was that the young man had chosen to represent himself and clearly he did not know how to do that well. He had certainly taken and pawned the watches with no intention of committing a crime. The Judge sighed as this tale was all too common. For

Edwin the problem was compounded by the value of the watches and who owned them. Sometimes the Judge could confer a prison sentence and a warning but in this instance the crime was too great.

He was surprised though to see that Edwin called as a character witness a minister. It was James Bruce, who had married Edwin and Ann. Ann and Lillias had faithfully continued attending church together for years and therefore were well known to the minister. Ann had called upon the man to speak for her husband, hoping that it would have some bearing on the case. Unfortunately Edwin had not visited the church again since he married and the Judge very quickly extracted that information from the minister, and the minister was summarily dismissed. Regretfully as that man stepped down he looked at Edwin. He was fond of Ann and knew the toll this would be putting on her and her mother.

Finally the Judge spoke having heard all the evidence.

"Young man, I have never heard of such a heinous crime in a very long time." He paused, knowing that the weight of his words flew beyond Edwin's vocabulary. He looked away from Edwin and at the visitors' gallery where one young woman stood out looking wistfully at Edwin. She was clearly Edwin's wife. She had two young boys with her and a baby. They all stood mouths agape, suspecting that it was not going well for Edwin.

Calling it a heinous crime was a slight exaggeration but the criminal classes needed to understand the gravity of their offenses. Laws were there to be upheld. The Judge also needed to justify in his mind the sentence he was to confer.

"Because of this heinous crime against society (the Judge particularly liked the word heinous), this Court sentences you, Edwin Turner, to seven years transportation to Van Diemen's Land. You will be transported immediately to a prison hulk, the HMS *Unite* at Woolwich, pending arrangements to be made for your transportation forthwith."

At that the Judge slammed his gavel on the desk signifying that the case was over and that the constable should escort Edwin out of the Judge's court. He tried not to notice the woman standing in the gallery who had fainted. It happened all the time, he told himself, and he rearranged his robe as he stood.

Everyone stood as the Judge left and, as soon as he had left, noise broke out in the courtroom. Albert Forrest was heartily slapped on the back by his witnesses and he savored his victory. Even his father-in-law whom he suspected rather despised him was pleased. Hopefully that would translate into payment for Albert.

Edwin saw Ann faint and he wanted to rush to her but now he was a convicted criminal and his leg-iron was firmly set on his foot and he was not rushing anywhere. He did not know where Woolwich was but was familiar with the hulks as his roommate Tim had been transferred to one before going to Australia. He only vaguely knew where Van Diemen's

Land was. He believed it to be an island off the coast of Australia which was so far away that it took several months to get there. He had heard that life in Van Diemen's Land was even worse than in New South Wales where criminals routinely went.

Perhaps New South Wales was over-populated, like America. Since its independence from Britain, America had refused to take any more convicts. This had caused a hue and outcry from Britain but nothing was to be done about it and transportation had increased to New South Wales, and later to Van Diemen's Land. It made no significant difference to the justice system as long as they could get rid of the criminal classes so that they would not return.

From a financial viewpoint America had been preferred, as the loss of life was less and the cost to get there cheaper. Each ship would travel with a doctor but the prison ships were contracted and their owners were not always generous with food and clean water for the prisoners. Diseases and death were unfortunately too common.

Edwin knew none of this, save that he was going a long way away and would not see his family again. He had heard of wives who committed crimes so they could be transported too but he did not want that life for Ann. She was too sweet and trusting a girl to be in prison with the hags and whores who spent their lives there. This would probably mean the workhouse for Ann. At least she would have her mother there. Thank goodness William was not around to see it, nor Edwin's own parents.

As he looked at the visitors' gallery the women surrounding Ann were helping her and she was coming to. At a distance he recognized Mary Mortimer Forrest who had come to witness the proceedings as the case was in Edinburgh and her husband was prosecuting. She was looking at Ann with some compassion but made no move to assist her. Mary waited for a moment and then sent her personal maid over to Ann to give her smelling salts.

Pleased at his victory Forrest was putting together his papers and looked up to see if Mary was watching him. He saw the transaction with some displeasure and made a mental note to chide Mary that evening for her behavior.

Edwin was transferred briefly to a small holding cell which had a bench and nothing else. He had been told that they would bring Ann and the children to him and he waited, distraught, unable to sit down so tense was he. Presently Ann was escorted into the room, holding Lydia, the other two children clinging to her skirt. Ann rushed up to Edwin, tears flowing down her face copiously.

For a moment neither could speak, they just clung to each other. Then Ann spoke, "I will find a way to get there. I won't let you go alone!"

"Ann, don't be silly. Please don't do anything stupid!" Edwin implored.

"I won't. I'll manage it somehow. I was talking to some of the other wives while I was waiting for the trial and someone told me that some wives can go."

"Only if they take up whoring or something like that," said Edwin glumly. "I'd rather be dead than see you do that for me."

He turned to the boys and said, "Take care of your Ma, boys. She is going to need you to be the men of the house for a while as I have to go away."

The boys did not really understand but nodded dutifully.

"Little Lydia, how I wish I could see you grow up into a beautiful girl. You'll make some man very happy one day, sweet baby."

At this, Ann's tears became even more profuse and she hugged Edwin so tightly that he thought he might suffocate. Gently he pried her from him and held her at arm's length. The constable in the room shuffled his feet from side to side, indicating to Edwin that it was time to move on.

"I love you so much, Ann. I am so sorry! I never wanted this to happen to you, to us! I'll come back as fast as I can. Perhaps if I work well they will release me sooner."

Then, no longer able to bear the departure, he turned to the constable who led him out of the room, leaving Ann sitting on the bench surrounded by their children.

CHAPTER 40

The HMS *Unite* had a brief wartime career in the French Navy as a fifth rate frigate. It had been commissioned in 1795 to act as a scout. It was a fast ship and was able to outmaneuver larger warships, but not enough to outrun the Royal Navy which captured it eight years later. Originally named *Imperieuse*, the Royal Navy renamed her the *Unite*. Sadly however, she had missed the Battle of Trafalgar in 1805 as she lay with her mast dismantled in Lisbon harbor. She redeemed herself in the next few years as she engaged in battle against her former owners, the French, but after Napoleon was defeated she lay in dock for several years before her conversion to a prison hulk.

The hulks had proven to be an effective way of holding prisoners pending transfer to Australia. Stripped of their masts, rigging and anything which could make them seaworthy, they were still able to float and had become like floating apartments as more decks and rooms were added, giving their appearance a somewhat ghostly quality if you happened to see them on a moonlit night.

The *Unite* was docked with a few other hulks at Woolwich, in the south-east corner of London. Edwin had never been to London. Normally this would have been a great adventure, particularly as part of the trip was to be completed on the new railway from Edinburgh south. He had not even been on a train but knew that it would be far faster and more comfortable than the 17 days which were needed to travel between Edinburgh and London by stagecoach.

The North Bridge terminus had been built a few years previously and Edwin and Ann had gone to see it when the first train arrived into the station. He had never anticipated then that he would be traveling by rail himself, and so far too.

Several other men had also been convicted and sentenced to the HMS *Unite* that day and they were all to travel together in the carriage and by train to Woolwich.

Since Edwin had arrived in Edinburgh, progress on building rail tracks was running at a phenomenally fast rate. The line from Edinburgh to Berwick-upon-Tweed, England's most northerly city, had been open for a few years and just recently the line had been extended to Newcastle although the station had not officially opened. From Newcastle they would have to change trains several times before they arrived in London. That was still considerably more convenient than traveling by prison stagecoach.

Edwin had expected to return to Calton Jail for a while but there was to be a train the next day and so the policemen, including the constable with whom he was most familiar, took the prisoners to the North Bridge station where they were placed in a special cell. It was already late in the day and Edwin had not eaten since his porridge that morning. He said nothing, lost in his thoughts and his grief. His fellow prisoners were more belligerent though and loudly complained about their hunger. After a very long wait the constable returned with one loaf of bread to be divided between them. For once Edwin turned away and chose not to eat.

He could not sleep either. There was no bench on which to sit and his movement was confined by the nearness of the other prisoners. He sat on the floor his knees scrunched up, his arms wrapping his knees. Putting his head on his knees as a pillow he tried to sleep but he could not think of anything else but the length of the sentence and the loss of Ann and his family which it would bring.

Somewhere in the early morning he was aroused by the sound of a truncheon rapped against the cell bars.

"Wake up, boys, time to move! Here's a beer for the trip!"

The warden whom Edwin had never seen before was indifferent to the plight of the prisoners. His main concern was to get rid of them as fast as possible on the steam train which had pulled up to the platform the night before. It sat idly waiting, vast volumes of smoke belching from its guts like a dragon with an upturned head.

Breakfast this morning was cold gruel, along with a cup of beer. Edwin had by necessity developed a liking for beer with his meals and he drank it thirstily. The gruel was hopefully filling as they did not know when they would eat again. Then it was time to leave. Their fetters were checked and they were freed from their wall chains. In their place handcuffs were set and then they were joined to each other for the walk along the platform to the train.

As they walked along, other passengers stood back, reviled by the men's appearance. They were a shabby, dirty bunch. Each had his own clothes again but some wore barely more than rags. The prison clothes had been taken back for the next inmates. They walked past the first class carriages whose drapes were closed to keep out the unwanted; the prison carriage was at the farthest end of the train.

Edwin and several of the others were overwhelmed by the sight of the engine, powerful and majestic as it sat at the platform. He stopped to stare which caused the man behind to trip into him.

"Watch where you're going!" cried out that man, irritated by Edwin's behavior. "Sorry, mate!" replied Edwin, getting back into step again.

One by one they filed into the prison carriage, up one short step and then into an enclosed compartment with a guard at each end of the carriage. Once inside they were assigned places along the wall to which they were chained. It would be a long journey sitting on the floor but it would be easier than lurching along for days in a stagecoach.

Finally the train was ready to depart. Edwin heard a shrill whistle and then the train gradually edged forward slowly. Not having been on a train previously he did not know what to expect and he was surprised by the regular motion, the lurching to and fro which he learned to anticipate, and the occasional sudden stop. Once the train was underway the harsh noises subsided somewhat and gradually several of the prisoners were lulled into sleep with the rocking motion.

Time passed but Edwin did not know how long. As a watchmaker this frustrated him yet he was fast getting used to not knowing the time. Time, which had been his life for a while, was of significance in the prison world only as far as it affected when the food arrived and how long they had worked, both of which were controlled by the warden's sense of time. Edwin remembered how he and William had synchronized watches at the Observatory and how each second seemed important then. As the days blurred together he could not even remember exactly when he had met William.

After several hours of travel the train arrived in Berwick. They were finally in England and Edwin experienced a raw pleasure at being in his homeland once more. Scotland was very close and he loved it very much but he was pleased to be on English soil again, if only for a short time.

They were taken out of the carriage for air for a few minutes and the prisoners were able to take a look at the River Tweed for which the town was named. The station was high on a cliff. They would have to cross the river by viaduct, work upon which was still being completed. Far in the distance they could see the North Sea. From here it looked friendly and attractive but tales of its strength and fierce storms were known to all of them. You could not live on an island and be unaware of the brutish force of the surrounding sea.

Their next stop was in Newcastle, a dirty, loud and thriving city. The station had just opened and the prisoners gazed to the wrought iron rafters and the little tea stands which dotted the platforms near the trains. This was a station built for the future as the train traffic had clearly not yet developed. A youth with flaming red hair came along with a pot of tea and the prisoners were allowed to buy tea from him if they had money. That was their only refreshment. Edwin listened to the young man's lilting accent with some amusement. He had not heard a Geordie speak before, and he enjoyed the sing-song accent and the banter which passed between the Geordie and the other prisoners. The man was friendly and outgoing and it felt good to be treated with friendliness in contrast to the derision the prisoners sometimes received.

York was the next stop. Edwin had passed through here previously on his way to Edinburgh and he remembered now how much he had enjoyed the city. He had walked along the river and wandered through the old town, fascinated by the Roman ruins and Tudor buildings. He had even gone in the Minster and admired the Rose Window. He did not know much about art but he knew he had liked the splendor and elegance of the cathedral.

Entering York this time he was in an enclosed carriage and he could not see the city. As it was only a short stop they were not allowed to exit the carriage.

Suddenly the train started to go backwards and the prisoners momentarily were alarmed; they thought they were going back to Edinburgh. After a few minutes though the train stopped again and this time headed forward in the direction of London.

The hours passed without incident and without much conversation. The lucky ones were able to sleep as the train sped through the English countryside. Occasionally a man would cry out in his sleep and his next-door neighbor would shake him to awaken him and arrest the horrors of the nightmare. For most though it was a light sleep, broken by changes in speed and sound and by increasing hunger.

Ordinarily Edwin would have been fascinated by this feat in technology. He and William had discussed how rapidly the British landscape and industry were changing with the advent of rail travel. Different rail companies were vying for power and even arguing over the gauge that should be used for the tracks.

York to Doncaster and onwards to Peterborough East and finally into Maiden Lane, London. A new station called Kings Cross was to be opened shortly. Londoners were getting ready for the Great Exhibition although there was little talk of it in Edinburgh. What happened in London was of scant concern to the average Scotsman. Only recently had people started to travel more, usually looking for work.

Edwin tried to sleep but found that he could not. His anxiety overwhelmed him. He had loved his life with the Berridges so much, had enjoyed watchmaking and now everything was stripped from him. He just wished that he could have provided better for Ann and the children. It seemed now that she would have been better off without him.

Chapter 41

Mrs. Mary Forrest and her personal maid, who had accompanied her to the trial, returned home in silence. Mary had been moved by Ann's fainting and, although she had never known poverty herself, she recognized the hardship which Ann would have to face. Many women in Ann's situation would turn to prostitution. Ann was a pretty girl and that would be an easy enough field to enter yet it would not be long before that fresh complexion would give way to lines, a hard mouth and a pock-marked skin. There was no shortage of prostitutes in Edinburgh and competition was sometimes fierce.

Even though Mary realized that Ann's husband was guilty of taking Albert's money she felt sorry for the couple. She could understand how Edwin had ended up in this situation and she knew that there were few options available to them. While she herself was not in a happy marriage she could imagine how it would be if she had loved her husband and he were to be shipped away for seven years to a faraway country. The likelihood of them being a couple again was very remote.

As much as anything, she was rather disgusted by her husband's shameless glee at the conviction. She felt his glee came not just from winning a case but a real satisfaction at putting away one of the criminal class. Mary had been moved by the words of the minister who had spoken on Edwin's behalf but Albert had destroyed his testimony in very short order. Instead of being impressed by her husband, she was disappointed and she decided that day that she would have other places to go whenever he was in court.

That evening Albert was home for dinner which surprised her as she had expected him to visit his club with his friends so he could revisit his success in court today. Despite his victory she sensed he was unhappy and she sat quietly waiting to see what was upsetting him. She had learned early in the marriage not to provoke him.

Finally he said, "I do not want you to help every person whom you feel sorry for."

"I don't know what you mean."

"Ma'am, I know you do. You gave your smelling salts to the wife of a convict today. That is very inappropriate for a lady in your position, particularly when she is the wife of the very man whom I had just convicted! Leave it to some of the others in the visitors' gallery to take care of her. It certainly isn't your place or your responsibility."

"I felt rather sorry for her," said Mary, rather boldly.

"Sorry! How can you be sorry for these people when they dig their own circumstances?"

"But she didn't. They were robbed, her father died and they lost everything. She had nothing to do with what her husband did. And even he was in difficult circumstances, wouldn't you say?"

"No, I wouldn't say. He brought it on himself. What he did was stupid. I would say she was better off without him!"

"How can you say that when she now has no one to take care of her? I heard her mother was already in the poorhouse. She may end up there herself."

"That's her problem, not yours. You shouldn't be worrying about such matters. Leave that sort of thing to me to take care of."

Mary pursed her lips and decided it was best to say nothing further on the subject. Presently her husband, having finished almost a whole bottle of burgundy, decided to head to his club and find a poker game. Slightly unsteady on his feet he came to Mary's end of the table and placed a kiss on her forehead before heading for the door. Satisfied that he had explained the circumstances of life to Mary he now considered the matter closed.

It weighed upon Mary though for several days and finally, as her personal maid, Fiona, was brushing her hair one morning, Mary came up with a plan.

####

Ann sat in the now empty living room looking at the small fire. She was burning the last of her wood. Toby sat on her knee, stoic and comforting. At least he was able to get food for himself as he still went out each evening and hunted. He had however started to come home earlier and bring presents of rats to Ann who was still not given to eat them although she knew many who did.

She had been to visit Lillias who was not surprised by the outcome of the trial. Time spent in the poorhouse translated frequently into feelings of dislike against any authority and Lillias had heard her share of sad tales while she was there. She knew that sentences meted out in court were frequently given by over-zealous judges.

"What are you going to do with the boys?" asked Lillias. She loved her grandsons and had found them not being with her to be one of the greatest hardships of life in the poorhouse.

She continued, "Why don't you bring them here for now? They can't stay with me but I would see them every day and can see that they're all right. They will soon be able to work in a factory. When they can, they could stay with you. In fact I might be able to get out of here if they could find work."

Ann did not like the idea but it seemed the most practical for the moment. The boys seemed so young to be working but that was normal. She herself had started dressmaking before she was ten. Ann had hoped that they would go into watchmaking like their father and grandfather but that was clearly not to be.

Ann had thought about it overnight, which gave her a sleepless night, and then the next day she had delivered the boys to the poorhouse. She kept Lydia with her as she felt she was too young a baby to be in the workhouse. She could not stand either the idea of having all her children in the workhouse. Her mother would watch over them. Both boys cried as she left them there and Ann managed to control her tears until she came home. She tried to persuade herself that it was not for long, that if things improved everyone would come home.

As she sat in front of the fire she heard a hesitant tap on the door. For a moment she hesitated in case it was her neighbor Mrs. Brodie. She really did not want to hear Mrs. Brodie's opinion of Edwin and his shortcomings again. However, at the door, dressed in a dark cloak with its hood over her head, stood Fiona, Mrs. Mary Forrest's maid.

CHAPTER 42

Finally the train slowed down, but the steam continued to spew from the engine. Edwin could not see what was happening but he suspected they had arrived in London for, as the noise of the engine decreased, the noise of shouting, banging, clattering and a multitude of conversations broke through into the prison carriage. Presently they were released from their wall chains and their fetters were checked before they were released into the general public standing around the station.

The noise here was almost overwhelming; perhaps some of it echoed back from the high ceilings with their glass panes and ornate wrought iron rafters. A coach was waiting for them and very soon they were making their way through the London streets. Most of the prisoners had never been to London previously and they welcomed the chance to peer through the bars and see something of the city.

Edinburgh had seemed to Edwin to be a busy, bustling place but nothing prepared him for the sights he now saw as he traveled through London.

They passed market barrows with their owners shouting their wares to anyone who would listen; there were smaller shops, more permanent, lining the streets. The crowds surged along in all directions - women pushing perambulators, beggar children scattering through the crowds, men in business suits, some wearing strange round hats, and elegant women in fancy hats and matching dresses.

Edwin could hear languages that he had never heard before and they mingled with the sound of horses, dogs barking and the shouts of the barrow boys, a cacophony which shocked Edwin.

As Edwin looked out he thought he recognized the Houses of Parliament as he had seen a picture of the building when he was a child. Now it appeared to be in the process of being rebuilt and Edwin had read that there had been a fire in it back in the 1830's. Work was clearly underway to restore it to its former grandeur.

The prison carriage passed slowly over the Thames River and then turned left heading east along the river. They went along for several miles without stopping until finally they arrived in Woolwich which appeared just to be a part of London. Edwin noticed that they passed a red brick building which was clearly marked "Royal Arsenal Gatehouse". There were three archways leading back into the Arsenal, each closed with wrought iron gates.

The warden who was in the carriage with them pointed it out with a laugh, "Take a good look at it. Some of you are going to be working there!"

One of the other prisoners asked what it was and he was told that it was where the government stored its ammunition and weaponry. He was not told however what the work would be. Most would be working in the dredging process on the Thames. After that the warden lapsed into silence again until they reached the dockside where a small boat was waiting to carry them the last yards to the hulk. They could smell the hulks before they could see them. The odor of unwashed prisoners, dirty clothes, excrement, and vermin permeated the whole dockside. For a moment Edwin thought he was going to throw up, and indeed at least one prisoner did. Edwin's stomach turned hollowly, as fortunately he had not eaten for several hours.

All the prisoners peered to see the *Unite*. It was getting dark and the old warship looked eerie in the twilight. Several small boats were pulled up alongside the hulk and prisoners were being unloaded into it. Because its mast and rigging had been removed it looked somewhat like a large box at anchor in the river. Yet it was rather lop-sided as various rooms had been added to the sides and even on top of the upper deck. It seemed ungainly and was clearly no longer seaworthy. There were other hulks too in the river but because of the light the prisoners were unable to compare their new home to the other hulks.

Edwin wondered just how long he would be able to stay here before he shipped off to Van Diemen's Land. This time was additional to his seven-year transportation sentence so he had mixed feelings. The fear of going somewhere unknown across the world was worrying him, but he was overtaken more by the loss of his family. At least if he were imprisoned here he would still be in Britain.

Perhaps he would not even need to go if he stayed on the hulk long enough. Talk amongst prisoners was that transportation numbers were declining as new prisons were being built. Maybe he could get his sentence commuted. Yet staying on the hulk did mean that he would have to work longer and for no benefit to him. Indeed he had heard in the prison chatter that the work was killing, and if the work did not get you, then disease would.

The warden handed each man his caption papers. Most of them did not bother to look at them as perhaps they could not read but Edwin read his. It merely documented his crime and sentence. He was told to turn it in as soon as he boarded the hulk. So, papers in hand, Edwin climbed into the small dinghy and headed for his new temporary home. The river was running fast but smoothly and the oarsmen had some difficulty in navigating the current to get to the hulk. There was a rope ladder on the side of the ship and the men scrambled up it, trying not to look down. If they fell they would surely drown as they could not swim.

As they stood on deck Edwin noticed a rather ornate deck with a door leading into a cabin. He learned later that this was the poop deck and it was where the governor and the other staff officers lived. As an officer emerged he carefully padlocked the door behind him and approached the new prisoners, walking slowly and examining his new victims with care. He examined their caption papers and then ordered them below deck to be checked by the ship's doctor before they were assigned a hammock.

The convicts stood in line and were ordered to strip. Leaving their clothes in untidy piles at their feet, they stood in the cold air waiting to be examined. Meanwhile a young sailor scooped up their clothes, telling them that they would get them back when they left the hulk. Gradually they were all cursorily examined by an officer who seemed already to have had more than his share of daily grog. He looked Edwin up and down briefly, examined his skin and teeth without comment, and told Edwin to stand aside in a small group of men who were assembling on the doctor's left.

The doctor appeared to be the one assigning work duties based on the felon's appearance but Edwin did not know if his selection would be good or bad. Most of the men with whom he was assembled looked fairly strong and young.

The inspection over, the young sailor returned with uniforms for the men - standard issue was a linen shirt, a brown jacket and brown breeches. If you had the misfortune to arrive without shoes then you were not issued any. The shirt was coarse and itched Edwin but he did not complain. There were bigger problems for him than shirts which scratched. As he waited for the doctor to finish examining the other prisoners Edwin looked around at what would be his new home for the next several months.

On this floor there appeared to be three compartments. One was clearly a walking corridor, the length of the ship, and was used only by the warden. Each side of the corridor was lined with bars, something like you might see at a zoo. The other two compartments held wall-to-wall hammocks. They were empty at this time as the men were eating supper.

The new prisoners including Edwin were assigned hammocks. He was in compartment D1 and his hammock was the fourth along from the left. He noted its position but had nothing with him to mark his spot. His cap had already been taken from him. He had managed to salvage a letter from Ann from his own clothes and he fingered it in the jacket pocket. He did not want to leave the letter though to mark his spot.

Immediately after seeing the sleeping quarters the men were led to the dining room where over a hundred other prisoners were already eating. They walked along the serving line and were given what turned out to be their daily supper - ox-cheek soup, pease pudding and a biscuit. Along with this came a pint of beer, which Edwin seized with relish. It was strong, warm and filled his stomach more than the thin soup. Still manacled to each other, the men had difficulty reaching their food. Eventually they managed to figure out that they needed to eat in unison, each man reaching for his mouth at the same time.

Supper over and it was time to sleep. The men were tired and had little to say to each other. Survival in this place meant that you could form no alliances or friendships. A man's life could depend upon guarding one's moldy biscuit so trust could not take place even though they seemed united in their common fate.

Edwin's hammock was adjacent to the man to whom he was fettered. They were locked together in chains and it appeared that they were to become well acquainted but although Edwin tried to strike up a conversation, his neighbor revealed nothing except that he was called Silas. During the night Edwin heard Silas whimpering in his sleep. He was a young man, barely needing to shave, with sallow complexion and scabs on his forearms. Edwin hoped that it was not contagious. Typhus, scabies and cholera were all too common on these hulks, he had heard.

"I must stay strong," he thought, over and over again. "Perhaps I can appeal. If I could just see Ann I'd feel better."

He considered how he could stay physically and mentally strong. He knew that the brackish water that was frequently served seemed to make some men sick. He knew too that he needed to eat whatever came his way. As a rat ran along the ropes of the hammocks he hoped that did not include eating uncooked rat.

Edwin thought back to his trips to the Observatory with William. It had only been a few years since he met William on Calton Hill. He decided to challenge himself by imagining the sky and the stars. He could still position the stars in the sky and name the constellations. "That will keep my mind straight," he observed, and made a mental note to do that each night.

He also thought about the workings of watches and in his mind's eye he started to imagine broken watches and how he would go about repairing them. He tried not to think of the ones which he had pawned as that only served to remind him of his current circumstances. Yet there had been many others that he had repaired skillfully and that had challenged him. He wondered if there would be a need for skilled watchmakers in Van Diemen's Land. Since he had been in prison he had not seen men wearing watches or even needing them. His own awareness of time passing seemed to be slipping too as day ran into day. Now day ran into night and finally Edwin fell asleep.

Chapter 43

At daybreak the men were awakened sharply by the warden banging his truncheon on the bars. They aroused slowly which caused the warden to run his truncheon for a second time along the bars, this time louder. Still manacled, they headed for breakfast. There appeared to be no opportunity to wash or use a toilet and the air was rank with the smell of urine and excrement. Some had soiled their clothes and no clean clothes were offered to the offenders.

Breakfast of gruel and cocoa was given and then the men were off to their assigned duties. For Edwin and Silas, still fettered together, it was to be a day of setting piles along the riverbank. They were a couple of the luckier prisoners though as they saw some who also had to carry a large ball attached to their feet. The work was hard, the pilings of wood were long and heavy and it took all of their strength and that of two other men to put them in place.

Edwin was glad to be working outside for a while and at least doing a job which served a purpose, to prevent the riverbank from sliding into the Thames. In the distance he could see some men dredging the river, and that seemed almost an insurmountable task as London was exploding in population and its sewage was dumped into the Thames.

Worse yet, he noticed a group of twelve men turning a cylinder by walking on boards, forced to walk forward, eight inches from the next prisoner, for fifteen minutes at a time. They marched in silence, the futility of the exercise seared across their worn-out faces.

On other days he and Silas were sent to the Arsenal to build security walls. As far as one could enjoy the physical labor, Edwin enjoyed this job. He had a precision-oriented mind and he took pleasure in his bricklaying, in trying to make his wall perfect. Fortunately Silas, whom he had learned was convicted of being a petty thief, had a talent for bricklaying too and the two of them worked companionably together under the ever watchful eye of the guard who brandished his stick regularly but rarely used it.

Silas had been married too, with one young baby daughter. Unlike Edwin though, he seemed to have little concern for what happened to his family. He was a happy-go-lucky type who took whatever life gave him with acceptance and calmness. The two were suited to work together as Silas had been a shoemaker and he took pride in his work too. He had come on board with a fine pair of brown leather shoes but they mysteriously disappeared one night as he slept. They knew that they would earn a little money for their work on the hulk and Silas' first order of business was to arrange to get another pair of shoes.

Yet even though they felt they had better work than most, it was still hard labor, the food did not sustain them well, and the overcrowded conditions on board the hulk made their stay difficult for both, even though they had naturally optimistic dispositions. However, one day Silas found that he could not easily get up; he had a high fever and headache. Then a rash started across his abdomen and gradually spread over his body, fortunately sparing his face. He struggled to continue his work but after two days he collapsed alongside Edwin, pulling Edwin down beside him. The ship's doctor confirmed it was typhus or "jail fever". Like Edwin, Silas had been careful to avoid the brackish water but no one could avoid the ticks and lice which infested the ship.

Edwin was unshackled from Silas and he was fettered to another prisoner. Meanwhile Silas was removed to the forward deck of the ship in the hope that the winds there would blow away his fever so that he could not infect others. A week passed and Edwin heard from the guard that Silas had died. He never found out what happened to him. Some prisoners were buried in unmarked graves in the marshy land on the north side of the Thames. He heard that the doctor sold some of the bodies to the hospital nearby. Rumor had it that the doctor did not try to cure you so he could sell your body later.

Carefully Edwin restricted his fluid intake to beer and cocoa. He was given a clean set of clothes each week and he carefully picked off lice and ticks each morning upon awakening. It was hard not to despair; he had not seen Ann for months. In his heart he knew that she would stand by him, even perhaps wait for him, yet time did not diminish his longing to see her.

He missed watchmaking too. He had enjoyed its precision and was proud of his skill. Word had reached the hulk's captain that he was a watchmaker and he was called upon once to repair that man's watch. Without his own instruments that was difficult, yet whatever he asked for he was given and he was able to repair the watch to the captain's satisfaction. It was an easy repair for Edwin but the captain was unaware of that and because of Edwin's specialist work he merited special treatment from the captain. He was now unshackled most of the time and then moved to a compartment which afforded him a little more space to stretch.

The months passed, and then spring and summer, until suddenly in September 1851 Edwin finally received word that he would be heading for Millbank Prison. This was to be in preparation for his transportation. At least the hard labor would end but he heard he would be in solitary confinement while he was at Millbank, which distressed him greatly.

Edwin had received two letters from Ann and had learned that she was living alone with Lydia and Toby in the apartment but she had let the shop go and had sold most of their furniture. She was making do with what she could sew; Lillias was in the workhouse, along with his boys, but Ann hoped it was temporary. When Edwin read this, tears filled his eyes. He had had such high hopes for his boys, even dreaming sometimes of them getting an education at the University of Edinburgh, or perhaps the School of Arts. William had encouraged him in these dreams.

It was natural, said William, to want more for one's sons than one has oneself. Each generation should better itself. Edwin had heard that from his own father too.

Edwin could not bear the idea of Ann living alone; he did not even think it was safe. She had heard nothing from her brothers in Dumfries even though they knew their mother was in the poorhouse. She commented that Mary Forrest's maid had visited her but she did not say why. That puzzled Edwin. Why would a rich lady's maid visit Ann? The woman's husband was responsible for Edwin's current situation. There was nothing that woman could do to help but interfere. He brushed the thought aside, irritated by Mary Forrest and all her family. He still felt that he could have worked out his situation had he been given time, which Mortimer, Forrest and the others would not allow him.

He wrote to Ann regularly but did not know if she received all his letters. He did pass on to her the valuable information that he had heard from a fellow Scot that outside relief was to be available to the poor so that they did not need to be confined in the workhouse. They could live at home and still work. He hoped that Lillias could find out about this and have the children released as that would give comfort to Ann. He knew Ann would do whatever it took to get back her children. She was a proud woman but not in as far as it worked to the detriment of her offspring; she would fight tooth and nail for them, he knew.

Edwin developed a certain reputation and respect from the guards and the captain of the ship. He was known to not cause trouble and be especially handy at whatever task was presented to him. He had sound mechanical aptitude and was happy to help where needed. There had been rumors that transportation to Australia and Van Diemen's Land was being curtailed, as had been the case many years earlier to America. He had even heard of some sentences being lessened, or mitigated, as they called it. It seemed that good behavior might have a reward for him. He certainly hoped so.

Only a day after Edwin received the news he was to go to Millbank Prison, he was taken there by prison carriage. It was a short ride to the prison which was located near the Vauxhall Bridge within earshot of the Westminster Clock and the Houses of Parliament. One of Edwin's guards darkly suggested to Edwin that he might even get lost inside this prison as it was so large and labyrinth-like. The same guard told tales of even the warders getting lost and being mistaken for prisoners. He winked and laughed and Edwin politely laughed too but he did wonder if there were any truth to the story.

When he arrived at Millbank he was astonished at the size of the prison. Millbank was the largest prison in Britain and it could house several hundred prisoners at a time. Many did not stay long; they were merely there to be assessed upon the feasibility of their being transported. That appeared to be Edwin's situation.

A gigantic building of yellow-brown brick, the center of the prison was a chapel and it was surrounded by the governor's house, laundry and some administrative offices which were arranged in a hexagon around the chapel. From this center sprang six spokes each of which had a pentagonal cellblock which surrounded a courtyard which had a watchtower in the center. These courtyards were known as the airing yards where the prisoners were able to exercise occasionally. To complete the cellblock three of the outer corners of the pentagon had watchtowers, ostensibly to hold water closets and provisions but they functioned as their name implies also.

The first order of business was to strip naked again in a roomful of prisoners, while they waited for examination by a medical surgeon. Millbank had a reputation of carrying even more disease than the hulks but the prisoners who had arrived with Edwin looked at least superficially to be healthy, thought Edwin. As had happened previously, the exam was cursory and in short time Edwin was led with a group of prisoners into the first pentagon and then he was taken upstairs. At each cell door a prisoner was detached from his fetters and admitted to his cell, the door slamming loudly behind him. Edwin's cell was the fifth door on the left as they walked along the passageway. He was glad to be released from his fetters but groped his way into the cell as it was a dark day. Light came into the room from the cell window which he found overlooked a courtyard. He could see a guard standing in the watchtower in the center. It felt good to have a window even though it was barred and impenetrable.

It felt good to have more space too, even though he would be in solitary confinement. He would sleep in a hammock but there was bedding too. In the corner of the cell on a wooden stool Edwin found a hymnbook, a Church of England prayerbook, a Bible, and an arithmetic book. To round out his education and reformation was a handful of pamphlets published by the Society for Promoting Christian Knowledge. Ann would be pleased about that, thought Edwin wryly.

As the months passed by Edwin became glad of the reading materials as the hours alone were so long. One unexpected find was that the walls between each cell were thin and he found he could comfortably talk to the prisoners on either side of him. Both prisoners were younger than he, barely turned twenty. Edwin at 35 felt like an old man but he was able to offer wisdom to the younger men and they took his advice. He suggested that they behave well in hope that their sentence would be mitigated.

One of them, Robert Wilson, a Scot, had been a slater but he had been arrested for assault and battery in Jedburgh. Like Edwin he had been sentenced to seven years transportation. As a single man he seemed to find it an adventure but he had been running in bad company for a while and he had no expectations for a better life for himself.

Wilson had been arrested at the same time as his friend, Simon Kossack, who had the cell on the other side of Edwin. Kossack's conviction for assault and battery was his first and he was also facing seven years transportation. Unlike his collaborator in crime though, Wilson was terrified of being shipped overseas and took Edwin's advice to mind his behavior.

Battling tedium while awaiting transportation was a challenge to Edwin. He found himself listening for the toll of the Westminster Clock and tried to anticipate when exactly it would strike. It served only to remind him though of what he had lost. He had only been watchmaking for a few years but he had loved it. He had a quick alert mind and these last few months of imprisonment had taken a toll on his resolve. He challenged himself by imagining the stars and constellations; he sought work from the guards and fast developed a reputation for being skilled at repairing tools.

Some of the time too was taken up with chapel. This was important to the governor, a minister who had taken it upon himself to ensure that all the prisoners in his care had access to chapel and any Christian literature they wanted. The guards were even encouraged to pray with the prisoners. This made Edwin uncomfortable but if piety offered him a chance of escape from transportation he could become pious. He had learned from some of the other prisoners that pious expressions and devotion to the Scriptures impressed the governor. That gentleman would submit his report on each man to the Secretary of State for final disposition of the prisoners.

Yet time, which had always been so important to Edwin, passed slowly now. His children were growing up without him. Fortunately though, he did learn from Ann that Lillias had left the workhouse and everyone was together again at 15 Jamaica Street. They had applied for outdoor relief and were able to get some money and some food fairly regularly. While life was not good for his family at least they were together. The two women were getting work again and clearly Ann was learning to handle her situation well, although she still clearly missed Edwin very much. Her letter said that she hoped it would not be for much longer. She was still hoping that he would not be transported.

CHAPTER 44

Life at 15 Jamaica Street had settled down. Another watchmaker friend had set up shop where Edwin and William used to work. It grieved Ann to see this but she knew it was a sound business decision for the new watchmaker. When people wanted a watch repaired they went back to the building where it was last repaired. It did not matter if the watchmaker were different. A watchmaker is a watchmaker, thought many. Yet Ann had learned enough from her father and husband to know there was a vast difference in the quality of watches made and repaired. Some, like Sir Charles Mortimer, knew the difference although that gentleman was perhaps more influenced by the name brand than the actual quality of the work.

In her worst times of despair Ann considered committing a crime so that she could join her husband. She had heard of women doing this. It was easy enough. She could not face prostitution; it paid well and fast but the idea of sex with someone other than Edwin was abhorrent. She did consider stealing as that frequently brought down a transportation sentence. It did not take much. A pound of potatoes could do it.

Yet how could she leave the children? Sometimes she voiced her thoughts to her mother, admittedly rather shamefully.

"You know, I'd get myself arrested if I could be in prison with Edwin," she told her mother one evening.

Lillias, who was older and more skilled in the ways of the world, said rather dryly, "It would be just your luck to end up in another prison, with an even longer sentence. It's best to leave well alone. You're being daft!"

She continued, "They don't even put men and women together in prison."

"That's not true! I've heard that there are women in Millbank," rejoined Ann.

"You don't belong there and you still wouldn't be together," persisted Lillias. "Anyway, what would you do with these bairns? You need to take care of them." Clearly Lillias was not ready to assume responsibility for them.

Ann gave up the discussion at this point. She picked up her sewing again and looked around the room. It was still bare but at least they had enough to eat most days. The children all missed their father but they were already beginning to forget him, as children do when they are separated from their parents for a long time. Ann had told them that their father was at sea. They were too young to know he was in prison and, when he had been on a hulk, technically he had been on a ship. That wasn't totally untruthful, thought Ann. Yet the truth was not good either.

Ann continued to go with Lillias to church and had been delighted to find that Edwin was now visiting chapel regularly. He had never had a taste for her church, she knew, but she liked to think it was perhaps just the differences between the Church of England and the Church of Scotland. She did not understand much of that but knew that the Church of England was considerably more ornate than her church. Edwin always thought her church rather austere but she liked it. Fine trappings in a church had no value to her if the people attending the church were poor.

She was heading along the street now to church, her mind still occupied with worries about Edwin. If he could just survive this and not become ill or, worse yet, die. His letters were cheerful though although he obviously missed her. She was grateful that he could read and write. His penmanship was like his watchmaking, precise, neat and beautiful. That had been one of the things which had impressed her about him when they first met.

As she entered the doors of the church she was struck by how cool it was inside. It always felt like a sanctuary to her and she instantly felt more calm as soon as she went in. The service was to begin in a minute. For a moment she let her gaze swing around the church. This is where she and Edwin had married and she thought back on that day with affection. They had both been so happy. He had kissed her and she had thought that she might need smelling salts to recover. How silly - thinking like a rich lady!

The altar was oak, carved simply with a single line of Scottish thistles across the top edge. Behind it on the wall was a large wooden Celtic cross. The pews were also of oak and were unadorned and without cushions or kneelers. They encouraged piety and certainly discouraged somnolence.

Ann always sat towards the rear of the church and this gave her opportunity to look around the others who were gathering. To her surprise she saw the maid of Mary Forrest, sitting behind the Mortimer family pew. They nodded to each other briefly and then the maid looked away. Her employers were walking up the aisle right now and everyone's attention was drawn to them. If the church was austere and encouraged piety by its simple design, the message had not reached Mary Mortimer Forrest who was clearly dressed to impress.

Mary's domed skirt was one of the widest Ann had seen. Mary walked alone as there was no room for anyone else in the aisle as she walked. Her bodice was tight and tapered in the front, probably fastening in the back with hooks and eyes, observed Ann, who obviously kept up with the latest fashion even though she herself could not wear the dresses that she made for others. Ann had not seen this particular dress and she admired the flounces in the skirt which seemed to give the skirt even more body. Ann needed to learn how to make those as they were clearly going to be fashionable. Mary also wore a hooded cape of black velvet. To complete her elegant appearance Mary wore her hair parted and set in sausage curls.

As Mary passed Ann, she gave no immediate hint of recognition even though they had met at

Edwin's trial and Ann had made dresses for her previously. Since Edwin's imprisonment Ann had not been asked to make any more dresses for Mary Forrest. Knowing that Mary was sensitive to Ann's situation, Ann was sure that Albert was controlling what Mary did.

Then, with the slightest of smiles, Mary acknowledged Ann and then quickly turned away as her husband was watching her closely. Taking her cue from Mary, Ann curtsied almost imperceptibly and then looked straight ahead as the service was about to begin.

"The grace of the Lord Jesus Christ be with you all," began the minister. At this, Ann turned her thoughts to the service. Only here could she really find comfort and for a moment push aside the keen sense of loss which had bitten her since Edwin's departure. She had talked to the minister about Edwin and had found him to be sympathetic and comforting. He had known Edwin and knew that Edwin's actions had been caused by poverty and a care for his family.

There were so many sad situations like Ann's in this city. The second son of a wealthy man, the minister had been drawn into the church almost by default. It was expected of him, yet it suited him too. He was a kind man and felt he was entrusted by God to take care of his flock, particularly those less fortunate. It would not advance his career but he had no interest in that. His older brother had all the ambition in the family, and that suited him well enough. He worked quietly and saw his family rarely. Even at Christmastime and Hogmanay he was busy with church services and he frequently missed the fancy parties which were popular within his family. Some might say that he avoided them but that was not true either. There were other things that occupied his mind.

As he surveyed his congregation he recognized the irony in the situation between Ann Turner and the Forrests. Because of what he personally considered a misdemeanor of her husband, Ann was struggling to feed herself and her children. Her future looked bleak. Mary and Albert Forrest were highly respected in the congregation amongst the other parishioners although he had heard sly talk about Forrest's gambling habits. He just wished that Albert Forrest had exhibited more grace and forgiveness towards Edwin Turner, who had just fallen on hard times.

He looked towards Ann who was holding her hymn book and her head high, intent on singing. He resolved to help Ann if he could. He knew that she wanted to go to Van Diemen's Land with her husband. If he could help her hold her marriage together then he would. That was after all one of his duties as a minister.

CHAPTER 45

At the stocking factory in Dumfries, Henry and Hugh Berridge continued to work side by side. It was tedious work, noisy and dirty. Yet at least it was work. There were many people vying for too few positions. They were both glad to have left Edinburgh. Their father William had been too authoritarian for their taste and they enjoyed the freedom of being able to take a drink or a woman without receiving their father's disapproving comments. Now he was gone they did not have to face that but they felt their jobs were secure and they had learned to like Dumfries.

They lived together in a boarding house run by a portly, cheerful widow named Mrs. Rutherford. There were ten others living there and they shared an evening meal together most evenings. Henry and Hugh had become friendly with some of the other boarders and whiled away some of their evenings playing cribbage and whist. Whenever they were paid they went to the local pub and enjoyed the conviviality and warmth they found there.

Their sister Ann had sent word to them of what had happened to her husband and their mother. They had gone to Edinburgh for their father's funeral but had not returned since. They were aware that the family needed help but it was easy to ignore it when they lived far enough away that they did not see each other regularly.

As far as Edwin being sent to Australia, then they considered it good riddance. They had known of their father's affection for Edwin and they considered him a bit of an upstart, too big for his breeks. They had no interest in watchmaking, it demanded a concentration that neither of them possessed. On the other hand they had not been happy to see Edwin so readily accepted into their father's business. Then when he married their sister it became even more undesirable to them. So, good riddance!

Over the supper table one evening they were talking about what they thought of as Edwin's comeuppance. Surprisingly though, Mrs. Rutherford, who was listening as she brought the bread to the table, expressed sympathy for their sister and mother. She sat the platter on the wooden table, wiped her hand on her apron and sat at the remaining empty chair.

"You know, boys," as she called Henry and Hugh, even though they had already reminded her on several occasions that they were men. "You are making good money now, you should be helping your Ma. Being in the poorhouse is no place for a woman of your Ma's age."

This was conversation which both men did not want to hear and they looked in disgust at each other, wishing they had not embarked upon the story. Yet Mrs. Rutherford persisted. She was a businesswoman but she had a kind heart and she could imagine how difficult it must be for Ann

Turner, and even more so for their mother, Lillias Berridge.

"You could stop going to the pub so much," she now said, looking at them with a hard expression on her face. "Sitting here playing cards for money is no way to live either."

Both men liked Mrs. Rutherford very much; she cooked well and took care of the place. A little bit too religious for their liking but she had a good heart. She spent her free time embroidering samplers with religious aphorisms and displayed them in the parlor. Her favorite, from the first chapter of Proverbs admonished, "Hear the instruction of thy Father and forsake not the Law of thy Mother."

Mrs. Rutherford looked at the sampler on the wall behind her and merely pointed to it. It always made Henry and Hugh uncomfortable. They were not happy to hear their mother was in the poorhouse but they were not disposed to help her either. Later that night as the two boys slept in the same bed in their tiny room Henry broached the subject again, "You know, Hugh, perhaps we should go and visit Ma and Ann after we get paid next time."

Hugh did not like to hear this but he knew that once Henry had it in his mind that he would not set it loose. He agreed that it might be all right to see his Ma, at least give her money to get her out of the poorhouse.

Soon the idea slipped from their memories and life continued as usual at the boarding house and the stocking factory. Mrs. Rutherford was nothing if not persistent though and eventually several months later the two men set off for Edinburgh. By this time Lillias had been able to get out of the poorhouse, along with their nephews. They heard that Edwin had been transferred from a hulk at Woolwich to Millbank prison and he was expecting to be shipped to Van Diemen's Land shortly.

Henry asked his sister, "What have you done with Da's instruments? They could fetch some money."

"I had to sell them, and Edwin's too. I've had to sell most of what we owned. As you noticed as you came upstairs, I've had to let the workshop go too. The watchmaker there now, John Samuels, was a friend of Edwin's. He needed a space to work and was glad to get it. He's a pleasant enough fellow, keeps to himself and minds his own business."

Henry and Hugh looked around the room which had been pleasantly comfortable when they had lived there. Now it was almost empty and the fireplace was bare. Finally Henry said, "We have a little money if it would help."

Ann was surprised after so long that they would help her. She could have used the help when their mother was in the poorhouse, yet she refrained from making such a comment. No use antagonizing them. Lillias used to say, "Don't look a gift horse in the mouth." She did not know why, as she had never wanted to look that closely at a horse, but she knew she should be grateful for whatever her brothers gave her.

"It would help, and that's for sure. The boys are growing so fast that I can't keep up with them in clothes. I can barely afford to feed them so they are going to have to wait on new jackets. Ma is having a lot of pain in her hands but we can't afford anything from the apothecary. She can barely work these days because of her hands."

Henry slowly took out his coin purse and looked at Hugh requiring him to do the same. Together they carefully picked out a few coins which they handed over to Ann. She thanked them graciously and put the money away fast into her pocket before they changed their minds.

"There is something I'd like to talk to you about. I'm glad you came to see us." The two brothers waited to hear what she would say, wondering what would make her so serious.

"I have a plan," she began. "I've been talking about it to the minister and he thinks it will work." Intrigued, the brothers listened without comment as she laid out her plan.

CHAPTER 46

Edwin heard that his brothers-in-law had visited Ann and their mother and had given the women money, for which he was grateful. He had never had much time for Henry and Hugh; they had been given a wonderful opportunity by their father and had chosen to turn their backs on it. Fortunately that had worked to Edwin's benefit. He wondered if he would be able to repair watches in Van Diemen's Land where he was headed. Unlikely, he decided.

Edwin knew his case was up for review with the Secretary of State but he held little hope that his sentence would be lessened. His guard had told him that he might get an answer any day now. As he sat flipping through the latest set of Christian pamphlets that had been delivered earlier in the day, he was disturbed by loud noises and some cheering farther along the hallway. He wondered what was happening but did not have to wonder for long as his door was unlocked and it swung back to reveal the sight of his burly, red-faced warden.

The man was not smiling however. "I'm sorry, Edwin, but the news isn't good. You are to be sent to Plymouth."

The warden was disappointed for Edwin; in the time he had been here he had been a model prisoner. The warden had seen men much less deserving than Edwin have their sentence mitigated. He did not understand why this had not happened to Edwin. Sometimes the people in authority seemed to make arbitrary decisions, based on a whim. Of course you never knew who knew whom in this town. Although Edwin had been arrested in Edinburgh it was entirely possible that some bigwig up there had influence in London too.

In his mind Edwin had prepared for that news but he had truly expected to have his sentence changed. His work was exemplary, he had been told. He had tried to behave well, had avoided some of the petty fights in which some of the prisoners engaged and he was polite to his guards.

Casting aside his Christian pamphlets which served only to remind him that he was a sinner and that he was condemned, Edwin climbed into his hammock even though it was only late afternoon. This last bad news served to break his resolve. He was angry and felt betrayed by a system which harmed the poor man and protected the more wealthy. Worse than that though was the realization that he would be leaving Ann and the children permanently.

When suppertime came he could not eat, and again at breakfast he was still unable to muster any interest in food. At this his guard reminded him that there was no use in getting sick over it, he needed to keep up his strength. Uncharacteristically Edwin slammed the table and pushed away his plate. The guard, who was significantly kinder than most, recognized what was happening as he had witnessed it so many times before. He chose to ignore what Edwin had done. In time Edwin would come around.

Early the following morning the guard again opened the door, his large frame obliterating the light from behind. "Time to go, Turner," he cried. "Leave everything here but take these."

The guard handed over the now familiar caption papers to Edwin. Edwin glanced down at them. Added to the original information about his arrest and crime, there were additional comments. They showed his time on the *Unite* and then, written in fresh ink, he now read: December 22, 1851 - Behavior at Millbank good. Prisoner is extremely handy at any labor. Transferred to Plymouth. Transportation to Van Diemen's Land on the *Aboukir.*

Edwin had not slept much the night before. He could not forget the enormity of what was about to happen, the changes to his life that he did not want. Life had been so perfect, it now seemed, as he thought back on his time in Edinburgh. He was glad that William Berridge and his own parents were not alive to see this. He was glad too that his children were young enough that they would not remember. He thought of Lydia and her sweet toothless smile. It was good that she could not see this.

He did not even dare imagine his children with another father although he did not want Ann to live alone. Pushing aside these thoughts he ate breakfast even though he was not hungry. He did not know when he would be able to have another meal. The trip to Plymouth was a long one. He had never been so far south in England. He had heard of

Plymouth - all schoolchildren had - but he could not have placed it on a map. He worried about the voyage too. He could not swim. And even if he arrived in Van Diemen's Land after months at sea, how would he survive?

CHAPTER 47

Ann turned over in the bed carefully so she did not wake the children. She was excited now. In the corner Lillias was still asleep and briefly she worried about her. With the medicine that they had bought with her sons' money, Lillias' hands had improved and she was dressmaking full-time again.

Last night after the children had fallen asleep Ann had told Lillias about her plan. Lillias had been surprised but stalwart. She tried not to express a strong opinion against what Ann planned to do yet she was frightened. She was frightened for all their futures.

Lillias had suspected something was amiss as the minister had spent some time talking to Ann recently after one of the services. She also knew of the visit paid to Ann by Mary Forrest's personal maid and Ann had been unusually secretive about that visit. Lillias felt though that if a man of the cloth were involved with Ann's plan then it would work out well. Briefly she had been worried that the minister was interested in Ann. Ann was a pretty girl and the tragedy in her life had not marred her appearance. She would not have been surprised by the minister's interest although Ann had clearly not encouraged him.

There was no clock to tell the time (how that would have disappointed her father!) but Ann could see that it would be daybreak soon. It was time to get up and prepare for the long day ahead.

Lydia stirred and started to cry. She was hungry yet again. Fortunately she was still young enough that Ann could breast-feed her, and that was one less mouth for which to buy food. Ann sat down in her chair by the unlit fire and offered Lydia her breast, pulling her shawl around her to protect the baby and give her some warmth too. Edinburgh was a cruel, cold place in winter. She had never known anything different though and it was home to her. Even though she had never traveled she was sure she lived in the finest city in Britain, if not the world.

After Lydia had finished eating, Ann placed her on the bed and turned her attention to the small package at the end of the bed. It was light enough for her to carry and still carry Lydia too. The boys would have to manage on their own. She had talked to them last night and they were excited. They clearly did not understand what she was saying. They would find out soon enough.

CHAPTER 48

The waves continued to lap against the dockside as the *Aboukir* was loaded. The men had been standing for hours, some unable to move much because of the balls attached to their feet. Edwin remained shackled to his rather well-dressed neighbor, Jim, who still managed to look dignified despite the hours of waiting in the cold as the ship was loaded.

Edwin wondered what the weather would be like in Van Diemen's Land. He knew from its location that the seasons were different. This would be his last cold Christmas Eve. Next year he would be warm, perhaps even hot. He could not even imagine that. It was rare for it to be warm in Edinburgh even in the height of summer. Again he wondered what Ann would be doing this Christmas Eve. At least Lillias was out of the poorhouse and his family would be all in one place.

Edwin looked up at the *Aboukir* which was to be his home for the next few months. It was a big improvement on the *Unite*, the prison hulk where he was imprisoned earlier in the year. This ship was only a few years old and it was well maintained. It had three masts although at this point all the sails were still furled. Under sail it would be an impressive ship. Edwin did however wonder how it could house so many prisoners. He had heard that it would pick up supplies and fresh water on the way, but it would still be very full of sailors, prisoners and everything it took to feed them. He was getting used to living in close quarters though. He no longer noticed the smells of the other prisoners and he suspected that he smelled as badly. Suddenly there was a stir amongst the prisoners; rumors were rife. Even though the Secretary of State had signed off on their transportation to Van Diemen's Land, Edwin had heard of last-minute reprieves. The stir was caused by a finely dressed officer, sitting on a black horse. The officer wore a navy wool jacket, double-breasted and adorned with fine, shiny gold buttons. His sleeves sported gold braid and each one had three additional buttons. Edwin recognized it as a Navy uniform and was a little surprised to see the officer as he understood that transportation to Australia was the responsibility of a civilian ship's master. The officer dismounted, leaving his horse with one of the sailors and he climbed the gangplank in search of the master. Whispers amongst the men started near the head of the line and continued past Edwin. Perhaps this man would offer the last-minute reprieve they all wanted.

After half an hour though the men became subdued again. The officer was still on board ship and the men's excitement dulled. Only a moment later though it quickened as a group of women and children approached. The *Anna Maria* lay at berth one hundred yards further along the dockside. It was a female convict ship and it was expected to leave about the same time as the *Aboukir.* The two ships were to sail fairly close together as it was the first trip to Van Diemen's Land for the *Anna Maria's* master.

331

Edwin looked towards the approaching women without much interest. Aside from boredom because of the long wait and anxiety at the pending voyage, he had no interest in female convicts. Yet when he looked again he realized that these women were not shackled and they were carrying packages. They were not convicts, so what were they doing here?

Suddenly he looked again as he thought he recognized one woman. She had two small boys with her and she was carrying a baby. One of the boys carried a package. It was Ann! Overwhelmed, he could do nothing but stare as she approached. She caught sight of him in the crowd of prisoners and smiled, almost gaily.

Edwin was not the only prisoner who had a wife in the crowd of women, and the guards watching over them permitted each one a moment to greet his wife. They knew these men were in for a hard time on the voyage. Some would not even survive it. What did it really matter if they stole a few words with their women?

Ann rushed up, followed by the children, who then stood back in awe of their father. It had been several months since they had seen him and they were not even sure it was he.

"What are you doing here?" inquired Edwin as he recovered from the shock of seeing her after so many months apart.

"We are going to Van Diemen's Land with you. Well, not exactly with you. We are on the *Anna*

Maria. It's a women's convict ship heading the same way as you. We have free passage there. They want females to go out there. There's a bunch of us going!" At this, Ann waved her arm generally in the direction of the other women who were also greeting their spouses.

"But how did you get here?"

"More directly than you," laughed Ann. "I told you about Mrs. Forrest's maid visiting me. I don't know if you got my letter about talking to our minister. He helped me set this up. Mrs. Forrest goes to our kirk. She never speaks to me directly, of course, but I know she knows who I am.

"After you were convicted I think she felt sad for me. She was kind after I fainted. You know she's the one with the money in that family. Her father makes the money and her husband spends it. I think she doesn't like him much actually. Well, she said that if I wanted to go to Van Diemen's Land with you she could arrange it. Actually she just came up with the money to get here; the minister knew how to get our passage for free."

Edwin was thunderstruck. He had kept abreast of prison gossip while on the hulks and in Millbank but had never heard of women being shipped to Australia. He looked from Ann to the boys and then to Lydia. He was manacled so he could not hold her even though he wanted to. He could not believe that Ann would go through this for him. The woman never ceased to amaze him.

Their attention was suddenly drawn to the gangplank where the Navy officer was just disembarking. There was a stir again amongst the prisoners as they waited to see if their sentences were to be mitigated. The ship rocked slightly in the water. It would be a calm day for sailing.

About the Author

Christine Morris Campbell was born and raised in England, graduated from the University of London and emigrated four years later to marry her Navy dentist husband, Larry. Christine followed several career paths including being a personnel director of a department store in California and in England; she also worked as an event planner. She and her husband have traveled extensively and are enjoying their retirement in northern Alabama. This is Christine's first novel which was inspired by her genealogical research.